SWAMP SISTER

Black Lizard Books

SWAMP SISTER

by Robert Edmond Alter

A Black Lizard Book
Creative Arts • Berkeley
1986

Copyright © 1966 by Fawcett Publications, Inc.
Black Lizard Books edition published 1986.
For information contact: Larry Sternig
Literary Agency, 742 Robertson Street,
Milwaukee, WI 53213.

Swamp Sister is published by Black Lizard
Books, an imprint of Creative Arts Book
Company, 833 Bancroft Way, Berkeley, CA 94710.

ISBN 0-88739-008-0
Library of Congress Catalog Card No. 85-72782

Printed in the United States of America.

PROLOGUE

The cypresses stood up from the marshy prairies. Straight up from the surface covering of water lettuce and the runty elderberry shrubs, until their tall moss-draped arms flickered silver in the sun against the vast spread of turquoise sky, like the walls and roof of a great greenhouse, covering and protecting in its sullen warm shadows a myriad of dank growth and crawling activity.

But to the pilot sitting behind the puttering motor, it was like a giant spider web awaiting a crippled fly.

The motor of the Piper Cub had been acting like a cranky child ever since the plane had come over the swamp region, and there wasn't a thing the pilot could do about it. He looked at the instrument panel — the glass dials that were the visible nerve ends of the ship, the score pad of her metabolism. Everything was quivering.

And in that instant the motor konked out completely. He looked at the panel again, like a magician searching through his bag of tricks. Then he looked out the window and watched the swamp coming up at him fast. Too fast.

And too close. *Can't jump.* He snapped the switch and the plane went into a glide.

Then he felt a hand on his back and even though he'd been expecting it, he started.

"What is it?" an urgent, already-frightened voice insisted in his ear. "Why has the motor stopped?"

The pilot shook his head, watching the green roof of the swamp.

"Master rod froze, I guess. I dunno. Shut up, huh? I got enough grief."

The hand beat an impatient tattoo on his leather-covered shoulder.

"Well, but what are you going to do about it? I mean, my God, aren't you going to correct the trouble? Is it bad?"

1

The pilot had to grin even though it hurt his cheeks.

"Want me to step out on the nose cone with my wrench?" he asked, then forgot about the frightened man.

He wondered why he hadn't used his head when he was a kid. Why he hadn't become a deep-sea diver, or a mountain dynamiter, or a secret agent. Something soft where I get it fast. But not this.

As his mind leaped along idiotically, trying desperately to shove back the cold fear with tough-boy talk, he was busy with the wheel, trying to correct his glide, grimly looking at the unstable landscape for a clearing.

If you're unlucky you don't die right away. You get to kick around inside the wreck for a while, with your clothes and skin on fire and your hip bones shoved up into your stomach. Why wasn't there a clearing?

He felt very badly, sensed that this was one time he wasn't going to walk away. And the prescience, he knew sprang from the vast rugged swamp. It was endless, stretched as far as the eye could see.

What if they did get down in one piece? How would they get out? Who could find them? But I'll take it! I'll take the goddam alligators and water moccasins and quicksand. I'll take a month of it. No, a year — if that'll make You happy. God, I'll take it!

And it annoyed him too, that he had to die with a louse like Hartog, the payroll agent sitting on the jump seat behind him. He knew it was a silly thing to think about, but couldn't help it. His mind was like that. A man shouldn't have to die with a guy he didn't like or respect. Him and his goddam floozies he's gonna have in Jacksonville — was gonna have, Willy boy. Was.

The Piper was planing steeply now, too steep. But maybe there would be a lake beyond the cypress barrier ahead. Well, maybe beyond the next one. God, let there be something open beyond the next one.

But there wasn't. The cypress, cabbage palm, sycamores reached up, fluttering, nodding in a zephyr, as though in accord with the inevitable, coming to them like a speeding gift from God.

Hartog, leaning forward, the brief case with the small fortune in it clutched tightly in his damp hands, was watching the swamp also. His eyes, bulged and staring, were incongruous with the narrow shape of his head and face. He was feeling what Willy, the pilot, was feeling, perhaps differently, but feeling it. For the first time in his life he was facing something that was totally inexorable.

"How-" The first word gagged in his throat, but he kept at it doggedly. " — How bad will it be if we hit?"

"Like an egg against a brick wall."

Hartog's lids stretched over his swollen eyes. God. He'd been in an auto accident once when the car had been doing fifty. Everyone said it was a miracle he lived through it. Two others hadn't. And that had cost him three painful months in the hospital under morphine and Demerol. Like an egg —

Did that mean he wouldn't be able to meet Milly in Jacksonville? Then a half-conscious stab of contrition touched him. He shouldn't think of Milly at a time like this. There was Doris, his wife, for a moment his irrational brain confused the two. He was saying Doris' name, but seeing Milly's long nyloned legs — the nylons he'd brought her on the last trip, with the black toes and heels and black seam running up to black tops.

No, no! He raged in backwash of helplessness, fear and shame. Doris — oh God, Doris. I do love you. I —

His eyes darted to the window, saw the earth quite close, vague and turtle-green, scampering underneath.

A new, very personal thought struck him and he cried out against it. My God! I'm only thirty-seven! You can't take all that away from me!

Exactly what the "all that" was—whether the fifteen years of complacent domesticity with Doris his wife, or the motel-room orgies with Milly and her long nyloned legs—he never had a chance to explain to God.

The pilot screamed LOOKOUT! and seemed to fly forward. Beyond the pilot's moving black shape was nothing but a whirling green blur. Hartog felt himself rise to meet the pilot, speeding toward the green windshield. It was the longest trip he ever made.

PART I

Chapter One

Shad Hark had left the river early that morning, striking a north-east course along a shadowy, still, cypress-bordered slough. He was standing aft in his small skiff, stobbing the dark stagnant water with the stobpole. Overhead, Spanish moss hung from the branches, long and hairy, fluttering.

"Like a crowd of simple old men, rubbing their beards and a-giggling over a dirty story," he said.

If the coon and otter hunting turned against him, he'd get himself a long pole and go into the moss-collecting business. The harvest he could sell to furniture manufacturers for stuffing sofas and chairs. It wasn't lucrative but would keep body and soul together.

A ball-bodied, stork-legged limpkin, with a white and black neck like a charred log, went limp-hop-limp-hop out on a petrified log and sabered its long bill into the shallows to snap up a hunchbacked snail. With a bob of its head it placed the future meal in a crack along the upper side of the log and looked up to blink at Shad. It let out a loud, false cry.

Shad grinned good-naturedly. "Git on, you old phony. Go at to frighten some coloured mammy. I know you."

The limpkin, sensing no danger from the distant man, turned its attention back to the snail with bright-eyed patience. Slowly the snail relaxed and opened its trap door. Instantly the long bill flashed down and nipped the living meat, shook it loose from its house.

Shad worked the skiff around a low tussock of water grass and cursed when he saw a dense cloud of mosquitoes form in agitation. They came at him persistently, their tinny threads of sound humming in his ears. He did some slapping, damaging his ears and cheeks more than the mosquitoes, then got out of there.

5

He stobbed easily, taking his time, giving everything that his eyes, ears, nose and mouth could fetch his full observation. He could enjoy it more that way, and also it was a safety measure. The swamp was a poor place to become careless and start balling the jack like a young dog first time out. He spotted a long, scut-backed gator sunning itself on the right-hand bank. Grinning, he shouted—"YAH !" He hated them.

Right now the gator was all startled action. Its flat reptile head came up, wide-eyed, and it scrabbled, unwieldy on its unproportioned legs, down the bank like a rough log coming down a chute and lumbered into the water. Shad watched the scutellated humpback sink, and then heard the air around him go mad for a moment as limpkins, bitterns, ibises, jorees and ducks took off screaming and flapping. The silence settled down again like a sick man lowering himself in bed and stayed there.

Shad hauled his pole inboard and set it athwart, letting the skiff drift smoothly into a floating bed of golden-heart. He pulled a bandana from his hip pocket and took a slow, pressured rub at his face with it.

Then he sat down on the thwart and looking up and around at the cypress wall, fished a cigarette from his shirt. He snapped a match with his thumbnail and held the flame to the tailor-made.

The prow of the drifting skiff pared back a cluster of surface bonnets and went *thung* against a cypress root, setting a climbing cat squirrel into a nervous chatter of protest. Shad relaxed, feeling lulled and peaceful, smoking. He thought about the Money Plane.

Four years now since the airplane went highballing overhead, crashed, and was swallowed on the spot by the swamp. Shad had been sixteen then, and his brother Holly had still been alive. They had gone out together, along with all the other swamp folk, to search for the wrecked plane. None of them had any luck, and after two-three days of it they all said "to hell with it," and returned home. But they didn't know then just how important that lost airplane was. It was Mr. Ferris, the insurance investigator from New York, who told them about the money.

He was a tall, rhythm-stepped man, with dark skin

topped by a salt-and-pepper crewcut. His eyes sat far in the shadows under the cleft of his brow, the most penetrating eyes Shad had ever seen. Mr. Ferris looked at something—a man's face, a house, the dress on a girl—and Shad swore he saw right through it.

Over eighty-thousand dollars in a locked brief case had been on the airplane, is what Mr. Ferris told them. A payroll being flown to a factory in Jacksonville.

"Help me find it," he said to the group of booted, denim-clad swamp men as they stood in embarrassed, thoughtful silence, eyeing him with cautious respect.

"Help me find it," he'd said, standing in the wagon grove facing Sutt's Store, the swamp behind him. He had been wearing a charcoal-grey suit with black shoes so new you could still see the polish through the dust and his strange, sad eyes picked out each one of them in slow turn. "My company underwrote that payroll, you understand? And I'm authorized to guarantee ten per cent of the money to the man, or men, who finds it for me. I'll put that in writing."

Then he waited, and they waited—waited for him to ask them again. Not out of bullheadedness, but because they didn't understand the protocol of city manners, and this damn Yankee in the sharp city suit, with the gentle city face and talk, made them uncertain and shy.

"What do you say?" he urged finally, quietly.

They said yes. They said they shore God would find it for him. But they didn't. They tried; they went hungry, without sleep, got lost trying — but they didn't find the money. And after a month, they gave up. After a month Mr. Ferris was ready to give up. He shook hands with those who had helped him, with those he had grown to know and respect, and said, "I'm leaving my telephone number with Sutt, and with the Culvers. If you hear of anything, find anything, let me know. Reverse the charges. Thank you very much." And then he went away and they saw him no more.

Four years. The big search had ended then, but it was only the beginning for the little search parties—the private ones, a threesome, a couple, a one-man search. Where at you going, Link? That's my nevermind, I reckon. Going at the Money Plane, eh? Mebbe. If'n you find her—give me a call. I'll be obliged to help you tote hit out. In a pig's eye you will!

Ten per cent of eighty thousand. That was something to swamp men; some had never held or seen more than ten dollars at a time. But one hundred per cent of eighty thousand, that was something else.

Shad's older brother, Holly, had been one of the first. A taciturn cliff-shouldered youth with wide-apart eyes and a Negroid nose, who as a boy had spent his time wandering around the fringe of the swamp, kicking up rocks, pawing behind bull grass, rooting up dead leaves, looking for something. He had made many tentative passes at the heart of the swamp, but always came out fast—his eyes haunted, bewildered, but enchanted.

"Got me a sack of coin to git!" he'd called to Shad on the morning he had shoved off in his skiff. "Got me a car to buy, and a red silk shirt, and a yaller-haired gal! See you!" He was one of the first to go, and he was the first not to come back.

There were others. The Dawes brothers who had their skiff smashed from under them by a bull gator trying to get at their dog. The brothers made the sandbank. The dog didn't. They were two weeks clawing their way back to civilization. They returned with strange, staring eyes in gaunt sunken faces, and they never went into the swamp again.

There was Ben Smiley, Old Dad Plume. Torry Wegg and Al Howell found Ben spread-eagled on a mudbank, swollen and ghastly, his skin black and blue. "Cottonmouth-bit," the men said. They didn't have the heart to bring him back for his wife and two daughters to see.

And there was George Tusca. He was going to find him that old Money Plane or know the reason why. Yes he was. It was Shad that found him, when he was eighteen and looking for Holly, found him hanging by the neck from a tupelo tree. It hadn't been an accident. George's clothes were mute testimony to the time he'd had for himself alone and lost in the hurrah and titi and hoop bushes. Shad buried him in an old Indian mound. It was another sight no one would ever want to see. The birds had been at the suicide's eyes, and his head was nothing but a soggy maggot bag.

Chapter Two

Shad had tossed his cigarette butt overboard and watched it take a quarter-turn in a sudden surface ripple. It was his last tailor-made. He looked up, suddenly sensing his aloneness. The swamp was still, brooding. It made him feel like an intruder in a rehearsal for eternity.

"The thing not to go and do," he said, as though passing on information to another not-quite-so-intelligent him, "is fer to lose your skiff. Don't lose your skiff and you won't lose your head. Amen."

A gliding shadow came across the water, reached the skiff and made Shad's eyes flicker. He looked high and watched a pure white egret drift against the turquoise sky, heading for its rookery with a bill filled with wiggly things for its young. The bird cleared a stunted, dead cypress and banked for the north.

Shad looked at the cypress, then fell to studying it. The tree actually wasn't stunted; it had been broken, sheared off at the top. A short dead limb stood out from the trunk near the top, and something round was caught in its fork. Shad's interest was alerted. He came to his feet, rocking the skiff slightly.

Something round, with a black stick coming out from the centre — or was it a stick? A strut maybe? A fever of excitement tidal-waved through him. He felt like a coloured boy finding a fat wallet in the woods. "Hi, God," he breathed. "A round something that goes for a wheel, strut and all. Shore as they's little apples, that's a wheel off'n the Money Plane!"

He slapped his hands together pistol-crack sharp, and a flock of wood duck hit the air as though they'd been thrown against it and splattered there. Shad pulled out his pole and shoved off toward the tree.

The broken cypress stood alone on a hummock island, a scaffolding of matted roots and silt, riddled with holes and teeming with life. The small animals Shad didn't care about, but the large was another matter. The long rumbling *baar-oom* of a bull gator came as a thundering warning and the hummock trembled. Shad hesitated, holding back on the pole, smelling the familiar musky odour which is peculiar to the gator's excretory fluid. "Gator ground," he said angrily.

Two — three — four long tapering objects slued through the maiden cane and slid with a surface crash into the water. Those were the young gators, the ones that retreated to the water at the sight or sound of anything new.

Two bumps like the knots on a floating log rose above the surface and gave the man in the skiff a malignant stare. Still stalling, one hand on the pole, the other resting on his carbine, Shad murmured a warning. "You son-o-bitch. Got me a gun here. You come at me and I'll kindly blow a hole through your flat head."

Shad didn't want to get anything started that he couldn't handle. But he wanted to land on the hummock and scale that cypress; maybe get a sight on the direction the Money Plane had taken after it had struck the tree. Other gators, little ones, were nosing around in the water now. But it was the big fellow with the mean eyes that Shad watched with wary suspicion. The gator opened its great jaws, trailing long riffles of silver water, and hissed. Shad stared at the large crooked teeth and the beefy lump of tongue and for a sickening moment vividly saw himself caught in that trap. A tingling sensation of dread needled up the back of his legs and petered out in his buttocks.

The bull gator closed its jaws with a steel-spring snap lowered its head from sight. Shad felt it was just as well. He removed his hand from the carbine, straightened up, and looked up at the ragged cypress.

There couldn't be any doubt that the round something in the fork was a landing wheel from the Money Plane. He could see the hub metal now and the tyre tread. "It shore didn't just roll in here on its own and up that tree," he said. "Money Plane done put it there, and that's a frozen fact."

The cypress trunk was snapped high on the north and low on the south side, so he figured the Money Plane had been heading south in its glide. He looked across the slough, trying to spot further evidence of a crash path. But it was hopeless. A bog land of lush maiden cane and dead stumps covered five acres of slough, and beyond that was a thicket of catclaws, hurrahs and pin-downs; farther on stood the tangled, moss-hung, vine-draped wall of cypress, sycamore and titi. All right, but it couldn't do any harm to explore south. He started stobbing across the slough into a prairie of water grass and log litter.

He skirted the skiff alongside a trampled mudbank, not liking the look of it, watching the skyline. Everywhere was gators.

Shad spotted a broken tupelo along the bank, and though anything might have caused the break, decided to investigate. You don't go to venture nothing and you shore God goan gain just that. He ran the skiff ashore, and taking his carbine, stepped onto the bank.

The ground was semi-solid, quivering under his weight. He scowled, bringing the gun to port-arms, smelling the musk again. More goddam gator ground. He studied the numerous small openings in the tall thicket, knowing them for gator tunnels — escape passages.

"Gator hole right smack behind there, shore's mud's soft," he whispered. He stalled, his mind dragging up shorings of courage to his queasy guts. If he tried to push on through the thicket he might be cutting a gator off from the water, and that was bad. He *tsked* a chipped tooth and started across the peaty earth in a half-crouch. Venture nothing and gain just that. He had to see what was beyond the thicket.

It worked out just as he'd pessimistically thought it might. He went toward the nearest tunnel, nearly bending himself double at the thorny entrance, and paused. The soggy ground trembled again and he heard a gator grunting. Instinctively he threw himself sideways as a swollen she-gator charged down the passage at him. Its paws scrabbled on the leaves and twigs; its jaws were apart. Shad started to level the carbine when he realized that the gator wasn't looking right or left. It slammed past him like a runaway wagon, its short stumpy legs chopping furiously at the muck, and went aflop in the slough, disappearing.

Somewhere beyond the thicket a bull gator uttered a loud roar, which, from its harshness and reverberation, resembled distant thunder. Shad held his breath, listening. Far off, a limpkin wailed its lost-child cry, then stopped.

Shad put his lower lip between his teeth and went into the passage on hands and knees, the gun pointing the way.

"Look out, boys," he warned. "I'm coming at you all. Got me to see what's in your homestead; and if one of you gets it in your brainbox to come at me, I'll purely blow your snout clean through your backside."

He made a fast, frantic crawl of it, catclaw briars snagging at him every inch of the way, and pushed out onto more muck. He was on a shelf so low and boggy that when he stood, the brown water rose over the soles of his boots. It was a water prairie, land-locked with forest, draped with strangler-fig vine as fat as fire hoses, and jungled with thick bamboo-like stalks of cane. The massive trunks of seven-hundred-year-old cypresses thrust skyward, so high their tufted crowns rubbed across patches of blue sky. A few rays of brilliant sunlight lanced through to the watery floor where a shadow-still pool sported jutting cypress knees — "breathers" some folks called them. The grey mossbeard, hanging in streamers, stirred slightly. And then he saw it. Across the prairie and half-hung in the matted jungle wall, nose-down, crumpled tail and rudder up — the Money Plane.

He sucked in breath, bringing a hand to his mouth to rub it absently, staring. Eighty-thousand dollars. One hundred per cent of eight-thousand dollars waiting for him across the pool. "Yah, hay," he breathed.

He had looked for the Money Plane for so long, had dreamed of it in the long tossing nights so often, that now when he'd found it at last it left him momentarily incapable of directing his own will. Like the slough, everything inside of him seemed to have stopped. He knew he should shout, bang off his gun, kick his heels and do himself a cakewalk there in the mud. But he didn't.

The spell broke as the surface of the pond splintered quietly and a bull gator brought its flat head clear of the water. Shad watched the monster spread into a floating prone. And it *was* a monster, far and away the largest he'd ever seen. He judged it would go for fifteen feet, easy. The gator nosed shoreward, propelled by its long laterally-compressed tail.

"Uh-uh," Shad grunted. "Cain't have us none of that."

He glanced across the pond again at the distant Money Plane. It looked like a crumpled grey bird hung in a tree.

How to get there without a skiff? The pond proved to be not a true pond but a swollen place in the waterway. Not so damn good. He moved away from the gator, slogging along the bank.

Unwittingly, he stumbled through a stand of cane and into a gator nest. The reeds had been beaten down for half an acre around, and the curious little obtuse cones of mud and grass that housed the gator eggs looked like a jungle village for Pigmies. Instantly there was a great yelping and whining as hordes of little foot-long gators came swarming from their huts.

Shad kicked off the first batch of four that made a voracious charge at his ankles, and leaped back toward the cane. The little devils, twisting and yapping, scrabbled across the marshy ground after him with a fury that was almost unbelievable. They were nightmarish, appearing to be six inches of jaw and six of tail, supported by crooked little spider legs. Then an outraged roar that drowned all other sound broke over the slough, and Shad saw coming from the water on a run, a mama-gator.

Shad beat a hasty retreat, not stopping until he was back to the shelf fronting the thicket. He was well aware that he had marched himself into a ticklish situation. The gator is generally disposed to retire from man — providing the gator has been frequently disturbed by, and has a standing acquaintance with, man. In situations or locales where they have seldom or never been bothered by men, it was a different story. Then they could show a ferocity and perseverance that was downright alarming.

And now the gator in the prairie was kicking up a storm, rearing its head from the water, bellowing and snapping its jaws as its tail thrashed up great sweepings of white water.

Shad retreated even further along the bank, then squatted in a hurrah-nest to roll a smoke and think it over. The trouble was the law wouldn't allow shooting a gator — unless the gator attacked.

He started grinning. "What law is goan know what I'm about way out here?" he asked, stroking his palm over the oiled butt of the carbine. "Besides, I kin always say he done come at me. I got me eighty-thousand dollars to git at. Ain't no son-o-bitching big-mouth gator goan keep me shed of that."

He went back along the bank, watching the placid water so intently he hooked his right foot in a pin-down hoop and went sprawling into the warm muck.

Shad rolled over, sat up. "By juckies!" he grunted. Then he shut up, thinking — only thing that surprises me about now is why didn't I trip on a cottonmouth, or fall my fool head into a panther's mouth? He grinned savagely, telling himself to take it easy.

He came to his feet and saw the gator skimming through a bed of golden-heart. He levelled the carbine and took a sight along the barrel, panning slowly with the drifting reptile. He fired.

The *Plam!* of the shot caromed off the water and rolled away, and the gator rose clear of the pool, coming straight up as if standing on its tail. Then, with an agonized bellow, tipped over, curving itself into a capital C, and fell back with a splash. The pool gurgled, and a rush of blood bubbles wobbled to the surface.

Shad lowered the gun. "That's done fer you, old eatmouth," he murmured. There was nothing left now but to get into the water and go for the Money Plane.

With his boots, denims, shirt and carbine tucked in the fork of a titi bush, Shad entered the torpid water gingerly. He held his hunting knife shoulder high in his right hand. For a good ways he was able to wade, the pool graduating up his naked goose-fleshed body in slow degrees; knees — hips — armpits. The oozy muck underfoot was ankle-high and cold. He hated it. And snags, sharp and dull, reached for his toes each time he shuffled a cautious step. Once something bumped his lower left leg, wrapped around, then wiggled on. It turned his blood to ice water and the sick knot in his stomach took another half-hitch. Cottonmouths wouldn't strike under water — so he had always heard.

But when he was neck-high and only half across, he knew he'd had enough. He wanted out. He kicked his feet and levelled himself into a slow crawl. There was the heavy suggestion of ominous danger in the shadowy pool and in what he was doing, a sense of not-too-safe adventure. He slacked the crawl to a cautious dog paddle, taking care that his hands and feet never broke the surface to shatter the watching silence.

Ten yards to cover — and the green rosettes of the water lettuce were so thick that for a vivid moment he thought he was tangled and would go under. The panic came at him like a female bobcat guarding her young. It clawed his nerve ends into dripping mush. He opened his mouth to shout as his legs, twisted and captured, sank down—and touched the silty bottom. He was standing on his feet, armpit-high in the water.

His glands discharged relief juice through his body, and for half a minute he just stood there with the nervous giggles. Then he got himself in hand, put his face down among the rosettes and in the water and massaged it. "Cain't lose my head like that again," he said.

He started on, feeling the ground rise until the water lettuce fell to his waist. Then he was before the dark, wet bole of the great cypress that had pared back the left wing of the Money Plane.

The under belly of the wreck was right above him, four or five feet over his head. The tilted nose cone was completely obscured by the hole it had punched in the jungle mat. Shad stayed where he was, studying what he could see of the problem. The heavy nose was probably well supported by the matting, and parts of the body and crumpled wings had been caught in a crazy network of strangler-figs.

He didn't relish the idea of climbing up into the plane and having the whole shebang break loose and dump him into the swamp. But how else could he get the money if he didn't give it a try? He nodded with resolution, put the knife in his teeth and, reaching up, tested the give of a vine. A moment later he was scrambling upwards.

The sorry-looking left wing was in his way. He had to detour — climbing down, around, over its tip. Then he worked his way back along the face of the cypress. Once, about mid-wing, he set a tentative foot on its metallic-like fibre. It punched right through. Shad left the wing alone after that. He worked around the rough bend of the tree and found himself at the canted top of the Money Plane's cabin. Hanging by one hand he cleared away a litter of ivy trumpets, leaves and jasmine with his knife blade, and lowered himself into a warm musty pit of the jungle wall. He was squatting on the hood of the plane, facing the shattered windshield.

The cracked glass was in a star pattern, opaque with scum. He couldn't see a thing. By a spider-like suspension bridge of vines he was able to swing down under the starboard wing to the door. He took the handle and gave it a try. Jammed. He put his right foot against the side of the fuselage, his back into the vines, and reared backwards. He almost upset himself for a header into the swamp. The cabin door was hanging open. Shad pulled himself up and in with a grunt.

The smell was bad. Dead. He had to come right out, bringing with him the vague impression of two dead men— a clutter of old bones in parchment skins and baggy, dusty clothes. He wedged himself in the wing strut, waiting for the cabin to air. And he thought about the two dead men. "At least they went at it together," he said. "And that was nice fer'em — seeing that they had it to do."

But the tragedy was four years old, and it was the death of strangers. He forgot about them and brought his mind back to the money. Suddenly he couldn't wait any longer. To hell with the smell. He wanted that cash. He swung up into the cabin again.

It was there. He knew it when he saw the dusty brief case with the lock. It was clutched in the skeletal hand of one of the dead men. Shad tore the case from the hand. The forefinger came with it by right of adhesion. That bothered him. He made a face and gave the case a quick snap, flicking the bony thing into the musty shadows. Then, for a moment he hesitated with just a touch of superstition. But the tactile feel of the brief case that contained a fortune conquered.

He didn't monkey with the lock. He punctured the case near the clasp with the knife and sawed a six-inch incision. He didn't have the patience for more, dug his hand inside and brought it out with a fistful of damp ten-dollar bills.

He laughed. He couldn't help it, didn't want to. He tipped back his head and roared. Until that moment the slough had brooded with the hush of an empty cathedral. Now the strident cry of a water bird ripped up the silence and was joined by the high lonesome tune of a hermit thrush.

Shad chuckled and began digging more and more bills from the gutted case. All of them were tens. For a while he busied himself counting them, but then gave it up. It would take too long. Eighty-thousand, give or take a ten or two. What did he care?

He still had the pond to cross over. What if some sassy cottonmouth or gator came at him, and him up to his chin in water lettuce? What if he lost the brief case? He looked at it, sorry now that he'd hacked it. Money, money, spilling everywhere —

He could take what he needed for now — say ten of the bills — cashe the rest — where? He looked out at the savagery of unrestrained growth. Yeah, where? Not just any old where in the swamp, not with nosy bears and buttinsky coons poking around. Right here then. Sure. Right here in the Money Plane that no one had been able to find in four years. Then the next time he came back, he'd fetch along some tools. Slap me a log raft together to cross the pond in. He caught a distant glimpse of the sky and saw that the blue was turning pale. He had some rambling to do. He'd have to blaze a trail clear back to Breakneck Lake; after that he knew his way.

But he delayed the departure, looking at his money. He had lots of plans to make, a way had to be found to get the money out of the swamp, out of the county, out of the state if necessary. He'd go to Jacksonville and take up with some young slick-looking girl—hell, he'd take up with three or four of them. He could afford it. He wouldn't have to play around with Iris Culver ever again.

The great gator wasn't dead. The .303 slug had ploughed a hole in one of his horny starboard scuts, passing on to gouge a deep gash in the softer section of his flank. When the bullet first struck, he didn't know what had happened and reared out of the water on reaction alone. Then the burning began. He had sounded hurriedly, trying to evade the thing in his side. Twisting, S-shaping himself in the muck on the bottom, he'd finally fled down the waterway in a paroxysm of fear and pain.

A pair of playful otters met him at the mushy base of a

reed bed and went for him in a mood of frivolity. They made quick fleeting nips at his paws and eyes, keeping clear of the dangerously thrashing tail. The scut-shot gator drove after them in a snapping fury, though it was a hopeless chase.

Mad, tail-whipping, the gator rammed himself into an oozy thicket of water grass and settled. The pain didn't go away. He surfaced and bellowed his anger at the swamp. Then he thrashed ashore and waddle-legged himself down to the gator nest. There he went amok, demolishing cones, snatching up two-three young gators in a scoop, crushing them to baggy pulp.

Then the she-gator charged him with thunderous bellows of rage. But it was a mistake. The bull opened his mouth, emitting a sharp hiss, and went for her with a short, fast lunge. They tangled — paws, mouths and tails — over the smashed nests and little mashed corpses of the pups. The bull's tail swung heavily through the air and landed solidly against the she's flank, spinning her into the cane. He went at her again with hissing mouth, snapping at her throat.

In the end the she-gator lumbered for the water in a blind panic, two of the scuts on her back flapping loose and showing red blood underneath. The bull felt better after the fray. He grunted and snorted and ploughed himself through the thickets until he found a boghole. There he rolled his wound in the plastering swamp mud, and finally settled down to rest, too exhausted to fret.

Chapter Three

Sutt's Landing was a bend in a country road, by land, and the union of a crippled creek with a minor lake, by waters. It was on high land, built on the fringe of the scrub oaks. A nowhere place, lonely, yet it was a corner of the world that drew a measure of enchantment from its own solitude.

It was dark when Shad rowed across the lake and tied up at the landing. Up at Sutt's Store, and in some of the little village shanties in the grove beyond, the lighted windows stood out like square sheets of flame.

Shad left the jetty and started up the path. Somewhere near at hand an owl — self-appointed sentry of the landing hooted the inevitable challenge, and further out in the open pine woods a dog cut across on a deer and loosed his deep night-running bay. For a long tremulous minute after that the night was full of music.

Shad chuckled with warm delight as he neared Sutt's porch. He could have himself a rare time right about now, could waltz into the store and say, casual-like, "If they be any of you fellas thinking on going at that old Money Plane next week, I wouldn't go to git myself in an allfired stew overn it, if'n I was you." And they would look at him all big-eyed and mouths unslung, and Jort Camp would gulp and say, "How's that, Shaddy? How's that agin?" And then, and not a word more from Shad, he'd spread his ten bills out on the bar.

It was tempting, but he knew he wouldn't do it.

I'm goan keep my big mouth shut fer once. And when I clear out, I'll be the richest son-o-bitch that ever did clear out'n here.

It bothered him though that he would have to break one of his bills; but he wanted a drink—needed one. And he was going to buy some tailor-mades, a full carton for the first time in his life! He'd be eternally damned if he ever again had to roll a Duke.

Oh, Sally Brown's a bright mulatto,
Way, hay, roll and go!
She drinks rum and chews tobacco,
Spend my money on Sally Brown!
Oh, Sally Brown's a Creole lady,
Way, hay, roll and go!
She's the mother of a yellow baby,
Spend my money on Sally Brown !

It was Joe Tarn, the guitar-banging man, leaning back on a cracker chest, singing. Shad grinned coming in the door. He always liked to hear of the perversities of Sally Brown. When he was twelve (when he first heard Joe sing the song) the imagery of *Sally Brown* would plague his tossing summer nights. He'd lie on his Spanish moss tick, naked and sweltering, and stare up at the dark cobwebby rafters, not seeing them, seeing Sally Brown. He pictured her a high yaller, the colour of new corn, with long black hair and black wicked eyes. She would start each evening sitting on the edge of a sati bed, herself in a red silk dress—very skimpy. Her right leg cocked on the bedstand, her left on the bedframe, and she wore shiny red highheels. And because her legs were spread that way, and her skirt high in her lap, he could see her red silk panties. On each leg she wore a blue garter.

That's how he and she started the evening. Later, as the night dragged on, it grew worse. Trouble was he never knew what to do about it. It wasn't until he was fourteen and ran into Lily-Mae Duffy that he forgot about Sally Brown. He superannuated her to a dusty corner along with his other childhood toys.

Frequently Shad wondered just how many times he'd been in and out of Sutt's Store in his life. Nothing ever seemed to change, not even the customers. He could picture it looking just as it did now clear back to the day it had first been raised, and that had been during the Civil War. The long dusty rows of canned goods with their fading labels, the cracker chests and flour barrels, the always half-unrolled bolts of cloth, the scummy glass breadbox, and in the front right corner the hardware, shotguns, axes, spades, and the enamel ware.

High up along the south wall was the aging display of heads—a decoration of the birds and beasts of the swamp. Stilled, stiff wings tacked on boards, and the glass eyes of the bears, bucks, and bobcats staring straight ahead at the north wall year after year through a film of dust. The crusty lips and dull teeth showing in the stark open mouths had a dusky unwholesomeness about them, and all of the trophies were dog-eared and moth-riddled. Somehow they always bothered Shad, as though man, in stuffing and hanging them, had made a mockery of death. Shad had seen their descendants in the flesh, and the contrast was too incongruous.

Man stuffs and hangs what he catches from the swamp, he thought absently. Maybe the swamp ort to stuff and hang what it catches: Ben Smiley, George Tusca, the two men in the Money Plane, Holly—

The air in the store was still, hot. Joel Sutt's nightly regulars, some with shot glasses of corn-of-the-hills in their hands, looked up as Shad entered. They knew he'd been out searching for his brother again, and they waited for him to speak, though it was plain to them that he hadn't found Holly's body.

Shad grinned, nodded, and called, "Joe—don't stop Sally Brown on my account. She's an old lady friend a mine."

They laughed, and Shad stepped up to the counter.

"Joel," he ordered, "see kin you git me some of that what you pass off on crazy folk fer corn. Got me a thirst drier'n an owl's nest."

Seven long years I courted Sally,
Way, hay, roll and go!

Joel Sutt fished a jug from under his counter, found a shot glass, gave the inside a wipe with the tail-corner of his apron, and poured Shad a drink. But he held back the glass, tipping a wink to Dad Plume.

"Shad," he said, "I wouldn't want fer you to git yourself in a dather overn this—but in case you ain't ben informed, they's a law agin serving minors hard corn. And when I come to thrash back in my rememory, hit 'pears to me you ain't but a tad."

Shad made out like he was belligerent. "Oh? Well, how in tarnation would you be knowing how old I be? Was you there when my ma breached me?"

Joel Sutt looked appalled by the suggestion. "No, I'm happy to say for the sake of my stomach, I weren't. But I'll tell you what, I was standing right there when Preacher Sims went and baptized you in the creek. And that were only ten-twelve years ago!"

Shad pursed his lips, frowning, as though he'd just butted heads with a poser. "Hmm," he grunted. "I see. I *do* see." Then he brightened up. "Well then, Mr-know-aplenty Sutt, how do you know I weren't already a ten-year-old when I done got baptized?"

Joel Sutt slapped his forehead with his free hand. "Hi,

boys! He's gone and got me on that one. I pure out *don't* know! He was kicking up enough fuss to be *two* ten-yearolds when old preacher came to git aholt of him!"

All of them laughed, and Shad, grinning, used to the horseplay, downed his drink. He dug in his jeans for one of the tens.

"Shad," Dad Plume spoke in a voice proper to the subject, "I don't reckon you saw airy of Holly?"

Shad blinked. He hadn't consciously been thinking of Holly, not since he'd discovered the broken cypress with the landing wheel. A stab of contrition ice-picked him and he shook his head, not looking at Plume. "No. Nary a thing."

Someone else asked, "Where at did you try this time, Shad?"

Shad stalled, wetting his lips, "Oh — off a Breakneck."

"Well, but where off'n?"

"Oh—up Cotton Creek some"

"Cotton Creek!" It was Jort Camp who shouted, and now he chested his way through the men at the counter to confront Shad. He was a huge, bawling, swaggering man with ten-some years on Shad. Not skilled in anything except singing dirty songs and telling dirty yarns, Jort had become a gator-grabber, catching gators alive and barehanded to sell to tourist centres for display. The man was all nerve, it seemed to Shad, and not much sense. And because of this, men knew him as dangerous.

"Why, ain't no sense a-tall a-looking up Cotton Creek," Jort said in Shad's face, and his breath, wild as decay, set the younger man back, "Ever'body done ben up that creek onetime another."

Shad nodded, turning back to the counter. "Had me a trap up there I had to git."

Jort Camp looked interested. "Any luck?"

"No," Shad said shortly. "Not airy."

He still had his hand in his jeans and he wished the big man would move away. He didn't especially want to bring the ten-dollar bill into Jort Camp's sight. But Jort stayed right at his elbow, and Joel Sutt was waiting for his money. Like it meant nothing, Shad pushed the crumpled bill over the counter, saying, "I want me a carton of tailormades out'n that too, Joel."

Jort Camp leaned forward, following the bill from Shad's hand to Sutt's. "Hayday," he said. "Lookit what Shaddy's done got him."

Joel Sutt seemed a bit surprised himself when he flattened the bill and saw the denomination. He looked quizzically at Shad.

"Where at you come by this, Shad?"

"Fella down river owed me that fer some skins. I finally collected." Shad was offhand.

"Oh?" Sutt said. "Thought you was selling me all your skins?" His voice hinted at the touch of hurt he felt.

"No," Shad said stiffly. "Not quite all."

Sutt fetched a carton of tailor-mades and gave Shad his change. He didn't say anything more. But Jort Camp, watching Shad stow the money in his pocket, asked, "What fella be that, Shaddy? What down-river fella?"

"Just a fella I knowed. Joel—I'm saying good night now."

"All right. Good night, Shad."

Jort Camp followed Shad to the door. "Shaddy, you ain't forgit you'n me is going gator-grabbing?"

Shad had agreed to help Jort in a weak moment. The big man wasn't much of a hand at swamp tracking, and it was common knowledge that Shad knew more of the swamp than many of the old-timers. Jort had been pestering him for months to help him locate an easy-git-at gator hole. "No, I ain't forgot."

"Well, me'n Sam is fixing to go at her come Monday."

"Uh-huh. Well, I'll see if'n I'm free then." He went out on the porch and down the steps quickly, wanting to get away from Jort. He didn't really like the man.

"Be by fer you nigh sun-up!" Jort called after him.

Beyond the crooked, picket-missing excuse for a fence the yard was stark sand, spotted with sandspurs; and it went on that way around the east and west corners of the house until the bull-grass picked up again, back where it held the sagging privy captive. There was a jasmine vine entwined over what was left of the porch, but it looked like something old and discarded, like something a previous owner had left behind. And there was the neck of a whisky bottle jutting up from the sand midway between where the gate should have been and the porch. Shad remembered because his pa had thrown it at him. That was the time Shad had first returned from the swamp, having spent three nightmare days and nights looking for Holly.

The old man had been waiting on the porch, drunk. He had raised his troubled, bleary eyes from the empty bottle in his hand to stare at the boy coming through the fence.

"Where at's your brother?" he'd shouted.

The boy had stopped short in the yard, annoyed — hurt even—that the old man hadn't asked first about his trip. Don't give him a damn if'n I near got me cotton-mouth-bit and gator-et he'd thought savagely. No. Just Holly. All the time Holly.

"I didn't cut acrost him," he'd answered sullenly.

The old man had stood silent for a moment staring, sinking the words through the corn. Then—"Nor yet see airy of him?" he'd shouted.

"No."

"Well, why the hell you done come back? Why ain't you still out there a-looking? You done forgit he be your own flesh and blood?"

Shad hadn't moved. He'd learned from bitter childhood experience never to cut across on the old man when he was drinking.

"You done forgit I'm yourn?" Shad had retorted.

And then the old man had thrown the bottle.

"Well," his pa had muttered after a cold moment of embarrassed silence, "pick that up when you come. Don't want nobody to go cut a foot on hit."

"I'll be eternally damned if'n I will!" Shad had shouted "Pick hit up yourself, you want it so bad."

But the old man hadn't and Shad wouldn't; so it stayed there and became a mute reminder of the love that never could have been lost because it never had been.

The house's line had a crippled down-at-the-corner look, low, rambling and one-storied, cracked and grey-boarded from lack of paint, and the shingled room looked like the cuts on a long dead and well-decayed gator's back. The old man was limp in his rocker on the porch.

Shad passed through the fence opening and walked across the yard, glancing at the black neck of the bottle.

The old man raised his grizzled head, and it was an effort. It was almost painful to watch him bring his rheumy eyes into focus. He scraped the phlegm in his throat to a new and higher position.

"You seen airy of your brother?" he asked. It was a question of habit and sounded automatic.

"No." Shad stared at the shadowy shape of the old man, frowning. "Where at did you git it this time?" he asked finally.

The old man decided to circumvent that. He played sly.

"Git what, Shad?" he asked innocently, and his head wavered on its spindly neck. "My cough?" He coughed hopefully. "I dunno. I think mebbe—"

"Stop beating your-fool-self about the bush. Where did you git the money fer the corn?"

Times had changed since the day the old man had thrown the whisky bottle at him, had changed the night he tried it again, with a loaded coffee pot, and Shad had hit him hard in the face, knocked him down and out for five minutes. The old man cowered in on himself, whining. "You ain't a-goan like hit, Shad. You just ain't a-goan to, I kin tell. You—"

Shad covered his smile in the darkness and pretended an impatience that he'd long since given up. "You goan come at it sometime tonight?" he demanded. "Or do I got me to listen to 'I ain't goan to' fer the next hour? What did you go and sell this time"

"I couldn't help it, boy. I was just a-sitting here a-rocking and a-waiting fer you to come home and a-tending my own nevermind, and a-rocking—"

"You done said that."

"—and, Shad—Shad, a thirst done come up at me like I'd ben down on my knees a-licking out a tobacco furrow, a-going at me and—"

"And so you went and sold the house to some passing beggar fer a dollar."

The old man became frantic at the suggestion. "No, I didn't, Shad! On my knees to God, I didn't! It was just that book of yourn I seen in on your bed. That one the Culver woman gave you, is all."

"Loant me," Shad amended.

"Well, anyhow, I gived it to Jaff Paulson because he tolt

25

me his boy was learning to read, and he—and he gived me a dollar fer hit."

Shad had to chuckle. "You old fool. You know what that book were? T'were called *Ulysses*. Hit's a sex book, and Jaff's boy only ten."

"Well—" the old man mumbled in soggy confusion, "well—won't hurt him none, will it?" Abruptly he giggled a low sniggering sound. "Never went to hurt you and me, now did it, Shad?"

Shad went up the steps smiling. "Oh? When did you ever read it? I didn't know you could read, 'cepting fer whisky stickers."

The old man wagged a hand against the dark in protest.

Shad left him and went into the house.

He found a match, scraped his thumb over the head and applied the flame to the lampwick. The expanding saffron glow rammed the corners and angles of the rough room back into brown shadow. There wasn't much to the shanty: a table, two benches, fireplace, two beds, a hutch that was a dismal clutter of pots, pans, cans, and cold garbage. A ragged screen over the open window allowed a steady stream of mosquitoes to make for the oil lamp.

And there was a smell, one that was vaguely familiar. Shad stood still, reaching for the scent with his nose, and finally recognizing it. He shook his head in wondering admiration. That old devil, he said. But he wasn't totally amused. He went back to the rickety screen door.

"Pa." The hunched silhouette trembled, like a man being startled from a doze.

"You done had that girl in here again," Shad accused him. "That Estee."

Sitting there in the dark in his crabbed posture, he reminded Shad of a black beetle caught in a webby corner, not knowing quite where to run for safety.

"Well—well," the old man began. "Well, Shad—" and then the whine came into his voice again, defensive yet with a spark of righteousness, "—got to have me *some* pleasure from life, ain't I?"

"Not in my bed you ain't."

"I didn't never use your bed!" the old man protested idignantly. "Hit's a lie. Got me my own bed."

"Then why's mine all a-rumpled?"

The old man hesitated as if looking desperately for a last avenue of escape; finding none, he broke down.

"I couldn't help it, Shad. I pure-out couldn't help it. That Estee got her a stubborn streak wide as her black butt. When she come here, we done had us a few belts of corn, and then she plumb jumped in your bed. Oh, I told her to git! I sez to her, 'Estee, you black bitch,' I sez. 'You git quick outn there. That bed belongs to my boy Shad, and he don't hold truck with nigras." I never seen me such a fool woman. Couldn't reason with her. Nossir! In your bed ner not a-tall."

Shad said nothing for a while. He thought about the Negro prostitute, Estee. She knew he didn't like her, and he knew that in her helpless little excuse for a brain she was striking back at him by sleeping with his pa in his bed. And what could the old man do about it? If she walked out on him, he'd have nothing. He looked down at the old man, feeling a sort of hopeless compassion, thinking, he's so god-awful weak he'd sell me out fer a whore and a jug of corn; and he'd cry about it and hate hisself while he was doing it—but he'd have it to do.

Then he thought about the money he'd found, and immediately it was like he'd lighted a lamp inside him, the way the warm glow of joy swelled his body. Got me to git outn here, he thought. Cain't stick it no longer. Got to ramble on to better things. He didn't really care, only asked out of curiosity. "What else of mine you sell so's to give that girl a dollar?"

The old man started along his whining trail again. Though his conscience secretly bothered him, he couldn't stand the deep holes Shad had dug in his self-esteem. And now he was hurriedly bringing wheelbarrow after wheelbarrow of excuses to fill them up.

Shad, ironically amused, leaned on the door frame and looked out at the night, letting the old man take his own evasive time to reach the truth; he'd given Estee Shad's Saturday-night shirt, the blue silk one with the yellow buttons.

That's nice, Shad thought. That shore God is nice. The girl sleeps in my bed, and now she'll be twitching her butt around in my best shirt.

Suddenly he knew he couldn't stand the shanty or the old man another minute. He went out through the screen door and down the steps, saying, "I'm leaving, Pa. I'm going to be my own man."

The old man moved in his rocker, trying to come to an upright position. "What?" he called. "What's that you say? Leaving? Leaving here?"

"That's right." And it had to be fast. He was feeling sad and friendless, and it struck Shad as a funny sort of way for a man with eighty thousand dollars to feel.

The old man waited a bit, his mind wildly rooting down among the dead leaves of his active past for some of his old ferocity. Finding some, he started bellowing.

"You as good to go! Well, git on! Don't let me hamper you — just a poor, sick old man. Go on, walk out! Leave me cold! I don't care. I done took care a me afore you come, and I kin do hit after you gone. Walk right on out on your pa! Don't stop to worry none about him—poor sick old man. Just git. You done walked out on your brother—might as well to walk out on your pa."

For a moment Shad thought he'd blow up—grab the old man, shake him. But he didn't, couldn't.

"I didn't never walk out on my brother," he said quietly. "He's dead. Cain't you understand that, Pa? He's dead. I ben looking fer his body, that's all."

"Hit's a pure-out lie!" the old man cried. "You be Cain-'ing your own brother! He's alive—I know he be. I seen him! I done tolt you and tolt you I seen him!"

"You done seen him down the neck of a bottle. Him and pink snakes and fist-size spiders and I don't know whatall trash. You got visitations of the brain from foundering your-fool-self in corn."

"Tain't so! Tain't so! I seen him a-standing one night on the porch, a-looking at me. And I seen him agin one night when I was a-rocking here. Down the road he come likn he always come, and he stopped by the fence to look at me; and when I called, 'Holly, ain't you goan come in?' he turned off and walked back into the swamp. I seen him in the flesh, I tell you! I seen him, and he's a-waiting out there fer you to come git him!"

"And I tell you he ain't alive. Cain't no man live alone in that swamp four years."

The old man shook his head from side to side in dogmatic self-pity. "That's all right, that's all right. Go on, s'git. Leave us both. I kin take care of myself, I reckon—somehow. Go on. Don't think none of us." He gave Shad a sly, covert look; then he shut up and sank himself deep in martyred misery; his silence and posture suggesting that all his life he'd done his best by his family and the world, and that now when he was old and sick the world and his unfeeling son turned against him.

"Sweet Lord," Shad said. It always seemed to end like this, he thought—them shouting at each other. He couldn't reason with the old man; but he couldn't really blame him for the way he felt. Holly had been his first-born.

"Look here," he said quietly, "I didn't mean I was leaving the Landing. Just meant I couldn't stick it here no more. Goan find me a shanty and be my own man. I'll still be looking fer Holly's body. You understand me, Pa?" The old man didn't stir. His head was down.

Shad frowned and tugged one of the bills from his jeans, placed it in the old man's hand. "Here," he said embarrassed. "Don't go to spend it all on corn and that bitch hear? Git you some food fer the shanty."

The old man's fingers worked on the bill, crinkling it, recognizing and liking its tactile quality. He unfolded the bill and held it close to his watery eyes. "What—what be it, Shad?"

"See if it don't go fer a ten dollar."

The old man's heart skipped a beat, flagged, choking him, then continued its laboured rhythm. "A ten dollar?" he echoed incredulously. "Shad," he whispered, "that Culver woman went and gived you more money?"

Shad hesitated, then nodded. "Yes. But you keep your big mouth shut on it, hear? Don't want it to git around and have no shotgun-toting husband chasing me."

The old man's hand closed on the bill and he hugged the fist to his withered chest. He rocked slowly, staring out at the yard where the moon sparkled on the bottle that was in the sand.

"See you," Shad said.

The old man said nothing. He rocked.

Chapter Four

At an angle from the bend in the road was a darkly shadowed sand road that led through hummock and scrub oak and past the east edge of an orange grove down to another shanty. Shad shuffled along through the sand, his thoughts in tune with the shadows and the melancholy stillness of the road.

A low human sound made a ripple in the surface silence, and the night magic broke for him. He stopped and looked off into the dark thicket. It throbbed toward him again like an echo that comes slowly, hollow and mild; but he caught it. It was a husky, sensual giggle. Then he heard a forcible whisper, implying false anger.

"You want to hurt me?"

Shad frowned, testing the girl-voice in his memory. It just might be Dorry Mears. And instantly a swath of absurd jealousy cut through him, not because Dorry had ever meant anything to him, but because she was young and pretty and full of tease. He listened.

"—You're the meanest—" And another giggle.

It *was* Dorry Mears. Shad's lips pulled back from his teeth, slowly. He grinned maliciously and stooping, felt around on the edge of the road until his hand fumbled over a fist-sized rock. He straightened up and pegged the rock into the black shadows.

The immediacy of the silence that followed was something for him to laugh over. He waited, head down, right ear dog-cocked, and picked up Dorry Mears' frantic whisper, " — ones' out there! Git up! *Git up, you fool!* Someone's a-watching us!"

A moment later Shad heard a cautious stirring in the thicket and knew that the boy, or man, was coming to investigate. He waited, deciding on his story.

It was Tom Fort who came through the thicket and stepped into the sand road—stepping, Shad noticed, like it was rotten-egg paved and him barefoot. Shad didn't mind

30

Tom. He was Tom's big, and had proved it many times when they were schoolboys years ago. He knew Tom wouldn't go for him, not even if he'd been mean enough to slip into the bush and kick Tom in the rump.

Tom was startled. He stepped back quickly when he saw Shad standing in the road. "Oh," he said, as though he'd had no idea he didn't have the woods to himself. "That you—Shad?"

"Shore be. Who's that? Tom?"

"Yes. How-do, Shad."

Shad nodded innocently. "Just on my way down to see Bell Mears, is all. How come you out in the bush thataway, Tom?"

"What? Oh well, yes—yes, I just stepped off the road a piece there, Shad, fer—you know."

Shad had a time keeping his face blank. "You know?" he repeated stupidly. "No, I don't. What?"

Tom flapped his hands impatiently at his sides and hurried closer to Shad, lowering his voice. "You know," he insisted. *"To pee."*

"Oh!" Shad said right out. "Well, why you got to whisper it fer?"

Tom gave a nervous tug on Shad's sleeve. "No, no, nairy a thing. Listen, Shad, you just now lob something out in the bush?"

"I shore God did. Lobbed me a great big rock. As I was coming down the road here, a fat old rattler cut acrost on me and took off'n the bush."

An involuntary gasp reached them, and then the rattle and rustle of the thicket. "You heered that?" Shad whispered. "Must—must be that rattler you chased," Tom offered weakly.

Shad nodded and started looking around at the ground.

"Reckon it be. Let's you and me pelt him with some more rocks."

"No, no!" Tom's voice was nearly a wail. "I ain't got me the time to fool with no old rattler.

"Well, all right, Tom, See you."

It had been a mean trick. He knew it, but he couldn't help chuckling over it.

The Mears place was an old grey shebang with oleanders

and dogwood in the big yard. Mrs. Mears kept a row of porch plants along the leaning porchrail—sultana, geranium, aspidistra, all of them in old rusty coffee cans; and Shad always found the colourful display pleasing. At the same time it made him conscious of a sad yearning for the mother he'd never known.

Shad cut across the yard and started up the steps. But he stopped when he saw Dorry Mears' younger sister, Margy, sitting on the porch bench, her long dark head framed in the brilliant window of lamplight. He nodded.

"How-do, Margy. Your pa to home?"

The girl seemed to be studying him. "Reckon. What you want with him?"

Shad smiled. "Be dog if'n I see where that's any of your nevermind."

"If'n you come to borry his money, it's my nevermind."

"I never heered of Bell a-giving his money away afore."

"No—" the girl conceeded thoughtfully. "But there's them that think because he got him some property hereabouts, he's as good to have him some spare dollars."

"Well, you kin stop thrashing your mind to a frazzle, because I'm here to buy, and I got me my own dollars." Then, remembering, he asked, "Where's at's your sis?"

Margy sniffed, significant of nothing, and said, "Inside. Reckon some fool man's ben chasing her agin."

"How's that?"

"Because she come a-tearing by me just a minute ago like a hant had her by the skirt." Margy leaned forward, her long dark hair running over her left shoulder like spilled ink. "Mebbe 'twas you," she suggested.

"Mebbe." He was noncommittal. "But I usually find that when I start fer 'em, they come at me just as quick."

"Oh my! Ain't we biggity and fat-pleased with ourselves? Well, Mr. Shadrack Hark, you don't see *me* a-running at you, do you?"

Shad grinned. "No. And you ain't heered me calling fer you either."

"Well, just don't you bother! Because you'd keep right on a-calling till you were blue and silly in the face!"

"Well," he said, starting for the door again, "we just might try hit sometime er other, just to be certain. Sometime say in about five-six year when you be nearly growed."

"I ben seventeen last Tuesday, Shad Hark! I'll kindly thank you to know!" she called angrily after him.

Shad knocked on the door, ignoring her. Seventeen—didn't seem possible. Last time he'd noticed her she'd been all leg and flat. He'd like to have another look at her now in the light.

It was sticky warm inside the Mears' house though their screens were all intact and hardly any mosquitoes to speak of. Shad said, "How-do, Bell," to Bell Mears and "How-do," again to Mrs. Mears. Both of them were sitting at the table, Bell with the Bible open and his glasses in his hand, Mrs. Mears across from him with her needle-and-stitch. Over by the cold-ash fireplace Dorry Mears was sitting, doing nothing but tuffing up her hair. Shad said, "How-do, Dorry."

The girl was lighter than her sister and two years older. She didn't seem to have it in her to look at a man or boy straight on, but had to do it sort of under-and-around; a provocative type of look that always did something exciting to Shad. Now, after the hair fluffing and the circuitous look, she slowly arched her back, pushing her breasts out a little further. "How-do, Shad," she said, and her voice was pure cat-purr.

Ain't she a something? he thought. Just as pretty and tasty as a new candy box. Red fire! He really had been missing something around the Mears' place. And to think of that no-account Tom Fort with a sweet girl like that. Well, I am damned!

Mrs. Mears' head didn't move at all, but her eyes swung up over the rims of her glasses and she said, "Kindly sit you down, Shad. Warmish tonight, ain't it!"

Shad sat and smiled at Bell Mears. It was just as well to keep his eyes off Dorry, else she'd have him looking like a tongue-tied fool inside of five minutes.

"Shad," Bell said. "I reckon you'll have some corn?"

"Reckon so, thankee."

"Dorry, you fetch me my jug outn the cooler."

The girl stood up and moved across the room without sound. Shad's eyes had to follow her. Panther-walk, he thought. She came to the table bearing the fat-bodied jug,

33

absently tapping its side with a slim finger, making a hollow *tung* of sound. When she came next to Shad she brushed his shoulder. Oh dear my, he thought warmly. There's something tells me a time is a-coming when I'm goan be as busy as a cat.

"Thank you kindly, Dorry," Shad said and raised his glass to Bell. The initial drink over, Shad swung around to business. "I done left home," he announced abruptly.

They looked at hin, each in his way—Dorry doing something with her tongue and her lips, and Mrs. Mears said, "Goan be your own man now, Shad?"

Shad got his eyes off Dorry's scarlet mouth. "Yes'm. But when hit comes to making my own found, I ben my own man since afore I kin remember."

Bell chuckled. "It was that er starving, eh Shad?"

"That's God's truth. So, anyhow, I want to rent me that old houseboat of yourn down to the pond."

Bell nodded sagely, adjusting his features to his business-talk look. "You'd be wanting hit indefinitely, Shad?"

"That's a good word fer it."

Bell tilted back in his chair eyeing the ceiling, his right-hand fingers drumming softly on the table edge. "I reckon I'd have to ask fer thirty-five a month on her," he ventured at last, still not looking at Shad.

Shad nodded. "I reckon I kin take a joke well's the next fella. Now what do you want fer her?"

Bell pulled his eyes down to Shad's. He looked serious. "I ain't jokin you"

"Must be," Shad insisted. "I ast you about that old wreck that's a-laying in the slough mud—didn't mean to try and buy your house er one of your daughters."

Bell smiled and reached for the jug. "Let's have another here. Whatall you think of thirty?"

"Same's I thought of thirty-five. How's fifteen strike you?"

So they had some more corn and some more talk, and before long they arrived at twenty dollars. When Shad left the house he paused to speak to Margy on the porch.

"I wouldn't worry none about nobody trying to beat money outn your pa."

"You worry about your money, Shad Hark, and I'll worry

about my pa's," the girl snapped.

Just what I'm aiming to do, Shad thought as he went down the steps into the yard.

Chapter Five

Joel Sutt was a sit-around man. Walk into his store any time and you'd likely catch him sitting around anywhere. Just where didn't much matter to Sutt because he was rump-sprung and the saggy flesh of his rear seemed to adjust itself to the contours of anything that had an edge to it. Folks like to remember the time Jort Camp came into the store and found Sutt sitting in a corner on a stack of M. Ward catalogues, just sitting there staring at his dead pipe. "Like a mechanical man with a stripped gear," is what Jort had said.

But he wasn't lazy. No. The truth was he was rather obese, and obesity is enough to steer any man away from activity. And if he was sometimes prone to a certain statue look (especially about the eyes), it was because he was a thinking man.

He'd lived his entire life on the fringe of the swamp, made his living off its green edge; and he'd been satisfied. "Let the fools rush in," was a maxim of his. And the natural conclusion to this aphorism (in his mind) was that he was a wise man who kept his feet where they belonged. Oh, long ago, when he was a boy he'd wondered as other swamp boys had—well now, just what is in that blame old place? But he'd never gone to look. It took a certain amount of courage (addleheadedness, Sutt called it) to track the swamp, and he was a man who needed those wise feet of his on security. So he'd grown up on the fringe and had inherited the store from old Rice Sutt, who had inherited it from old Hunk Sutt—the Confederate veteran who had built the little money-maker in the first place. So he grew up with his feet (and the sprung rump) on the security of cracker boxes, flour barrels, enamel ware, bolts of cretonne, and shotgun shells, and never once had to call a Fire Sale or any kind of sale, and made money—not a lot, but enough to afford Jort Camp's observant comment about the mechanical man with the stripped gear.

And so he married a placid-faced girl from down-river and never had to worry about relatives mooching off him because her mother had run off with a punchboard drummer and her father had been killed in a fight with the revenue agents. And he called the blank look she held for him in her eyes Love, because he wasn't the man to admit (even to himself) that he'd married a stupid girl. And he called the quiet attention she offered whenever he spoke Adoring Respect, because he never did realize that every word he spoke entered one ear, wandered willy-nilly through the empty chamber without finding any sort of barricade, and meandered out the other, leaving less markings than a snail leaves on uneven sand. And so they'd bred (an act that didn't require intelligence, or even focal attention) two boys, and one had died early and the other was now hanging about the Landing, growing fat on the thought that he would someday inherit all the wonderful boxes and barrels and benches to break down his own rump on.

Then Mr. Ferris had come out of the north and had told about the Money Plane. Like most of the men in that region Sutt had done his share of night-tossing in his damp bed, thinking of the payroll money. But that was all he did about it. The rest could at least go out and look, but Sutt could only dream.

"I cain't go tom-fooling off into the swamp," he'd sometimes say into the long restless night, apropos of nothing. "Got me my store to tend."

And the placid-faced woman that lay at his side would know then that he was coming to a climax of frustration, and would understand instinctively that he was going to do the next best thing to assuage that frustration. She was like a test dog, in that respect, in which a certain reaction pattern had been instilled. Minutes later the placid-faced woman would stare up past the hump of his shoulder at the dark rafters and think of the pie she would bake the following morning. You take a cinnamon stick and you—

But Mr. Ferris, the man with the penetrating eyes, had looked at Sutt and had listened to him, and finally had said, "Someday, someone around here is going to find that plane. When they do they're going to find that they've discovered more than just money. They're going to find themselves in a soul-shattering battle with their conscience. *And*, Mr. Sutt, eighty thousand dollars is a mean opponent for anyone's conscience. I have a feeling that the man who finds that money will not be overly garrulous about it—" (Excuse me, Mr. Ferris. I didn't quite catch that word of yourn). "I say the man who finds the money will want to keep it to himself. He won't talk about it. *But*—Mr. Sutt: but you are in an ideal position to discover that hypothetical man's secret—if and when he does find it." (How's that, Mr. Ferris?) "Men come to you to trade and buy. Someday one of them will be coming with a ten-dollar bill, and it will be bearing one of these numbers—"

Sutt couldn't wait for the last of his nightly regulars to clear out. And towards the end he was nearly rude to old Dad Plume. He couldn't help it. Shad's ten-dollar bill was burning a hole in his pocket.

Finally, after Dad Plume had quit the store in a huff, Sutt locked up, pulled his blinds, put out the light, and made a beeline to the rear room he called his home. There in his old worm-eaten rolltop he rooted and cursed through an aged litter of receipts, invoices, and lading bills until he found what he was looking for: thirty-two type-numbered pages, bearing the serial numbers of eight thousand ten-dollar bills.

The numbers were numerical, so the job was really quite simple. He placed Shad's bill alongside one of the sheets and started down the list.

L54427135B. That was the number on Shad's bill, and that was also one of the eight thousand numbers Mr. Ferris had given him. Sutt sat back in his chair and reached for his pipe, his eyes bright with speculation and the thought of remuneration. "By juckies," he mumbled. "I be bitched!"

After a while Sutt went out into the front of the store and dialed the long-distance operator on his phone.

Chapter Six

Leaving the main road, Shad passed along a shadow-barred path and approached what at first sight seemed to be a small landlocked lake. Black turf sloped down on either edge, and black snaky tree-roots gleamed in the moon below the black-glass surface of the water. Out in the centre of the pool the moon had thrown a great smear of silver, and it rocked there gently like mercury in a cup. A soothing murmur, endless and smothery, came from the silver shoulder of a small weir at the foot of the pond. On the east bank, snug inshore, sat the squat dark houseboat.

Shad found the short gangplank between bank and boat and stepped onto it, grinning. He was remembering the night he brought Elly Towne out here and they'd tried to break into the houseboat. Elly had been too scared of snakes to lie in the bull grass in the woods, and Shad had suggested Bell Mears' old floating shanty. But it hadn't worked out. The houseboat had been locked drum-tight. Finally they'd settled down on the aft porch, amid a litter of old papers, cans and whatnot.

"Wasn't much of a gal at that," he reminisced. "Then she went to being scared of spiders. Never-seen such a girl fer spookiness."

The forward porch had been an open-air workshop. He could see the black shape of the cutting table, and hanging on the forward wall, a tangle of racks and frames for drying the pelts, square racks for coon, narrow frames for mink. He went aft along the skinny gangway.

He reckoned that Elly had been the most inexperienced girl he'd ever cut across. There had been nothing new, nothing different, nothing exciting about the girl. But thought of her brought Dorry Mears back to mind, and then Iris Culver. Iris he knew about—perhaps knew too much, to the point where it was getting a little old. But Dorry—

His mind, perverse with desire, tricked him into listening again to the giggles and hot whispers of Dorry Mears as she thrashed about unseen in the thicket with Tom Fort. Instantly he was infected with the remembered sound. He wanted to see her again, to mix with her kind, to have himself accepted as one of kindred sensuality.

He leaned against the frame corner, staring hard at the motionless night. "Got to find me a somebody," he muttered. "Somebody soon."

A coon had found itself a frog, had captured it, and now brought its prize down to a moony patch on the bank. Shad watched the minor spectacle absently. The coon held the frog in its forepaws and commenced peeling it, freeing the corrugated skin with a short, jerky, tearing movement. Then it washed the limp blob of flesh in the water, and straightened up to begin its meal.

Shad shuffled his foot, making a scraping sound. The coon froze, its body seemingly all sharp little points of listening attention. Abruptly it shoved the frog in its mouth, showed its tail and became a part of the night.

Life and death, Shad said, thinking now of something he'd read about the survival of the fittest in one of the books Iris Culver had given him. Well, I got mine because I was the fittinest of all of 'em.

And now he was going to buy a piece of the world with it. A big granddaddy piece. But as he unlocked the padlock with the key Bell had given him, he knew at that moment the only thing he really wanted was Dorry Mears.

It was musty inside. It smelled of decay, of mice and old newspapers. He fished up a match and struck the head with the edge of his thumb, exploding a small blare of saffron light. He walked the yellow ball over to the hingetable on the starboard wall and lighted the lamp he found there and looked around at his home.

The cook-stove stood against the forward wall with the dish cabinets on each side of the stovepipe and the iron ventilators above the heating shelf. The windows were shattered. Under the right window was the deal table, and under the left a bunk bed. Over the bunk on a shelf stood an old rust ball-dialled clock, its stiff hands insisting that the time was 5:32—any day, any year. A woman must have lived in the shanty at one time or another, because two or three potted tomato cans with grotesquely twisted dead geraniums stood on another shelf alongside the door. Shad grunted.

He went over the bunk and inspected his bed. The blankets were dustbags with a few nameless little crawling things, and the sheets were filthy. He gingerly gathered up the whole mess, took it out to the aft porch and heaved it overboard. Tomorrow he'd have to invest in some new bed-clothes. He went back inside and surveyed the bumpy mattress. It seemed fairly sound, but the springs underneath screamed like a girl stepping on a cottonmouth when he pressed them.

"Old Bell should'a ast couldn't *he* pay me to live in here," Shad complained.

He went back to the table, sat down, opened his carton of tailor-mades and lighted up. The smoke hung about his head like swamp mist around a cypress knee. He stirred its sagging coils when he moved, pulled out his roll of bills and spread the six remaining tens on the table.

He'd only been back in the village maybe three hours, and already nearly forty dollars was gone. Funny thing, he thought, how short-lived money was.

It was damp hot in the little room where Dorry and her sister Margy shared a bed. And because they were girls, and because this was their room, and because of the summer-thick night there was a heady female odour.

But the not too subtle emanation that compounded the room's atmosphere was merely a nuisance to the sisters. Their warm, supple bodies, naked and only sheet-covered, stuck wherever they touched and formed glowing bubbles of perspiration. When they sighed with exasperation and pulled apart, the sweat-beads would plop and run down their smooth thighs and hips.

Margy was listening to the night music — the male crick-ets fiddling their leathery forewings, the bullfrogs grunting their deep bass notes as they hop-flopped about the garden searching for slugs, and somewhere the ethereal trombone bay of a night-running hound. She listened, trying to forget the heat and her own sleeplessness.

Dorry was listening to her parents' bedsprings, listening for the last squeaking cry as they moved fitfully in their own aura of middle-aged connubiality, settling down into moist sleep.

Five minutes passed without a squeak. And then five more minutes. She smiled in the dark. She'd give them half an hour. That would make it about eleven. Nearly everyone should be asleep by then — except maybe Sam Parks. She frowned, thinking of the skinny little man who was always prowling the night like a moon-feeding wildcat. He'd almost caught her two weeks ago—one of the nights she'd slipped out to meet Tom in the bush. But she'd seen him slouching through the woods before he had seen her and had hidden behind a tupelo. She wasn't afraid of meeting him, not physically; but Sam told everything to Jort Camp, and everyone knew that Jort Camp had the biggest mouth in the county.

If her pa ever found out about her nocturnal activities, he'd switch her. Her smile came again, soft, and she felt an inner warmth of sensuousness wash through her, thinking of Shad, remembering how he'd reacted when she'd rubbed against his shoulder. She had felt that reaction. Twenty dollars he give Pa. Like it was pages from the Sears' book.

When she judged the half-hour gone, she listened a moment to her sister's breathing. She couldn't pick it up, and frowned. But she couldn't wait any longer. My goodness, she had to get some sleep that night. She raised the sheet, easy—and slipped from the bed, holding her breath. Then she suspended herself, standing full-bodied, naked, in the dark, listening. Nothing happened to Margy's shadow.

Dorry went to the battered highboy and eased the bottom drawer open, extracting from it her cheap bottle of Sin's Dream perfume. It had been the suggestive name —along with the symbolic jet, the transparent, twisted cone shape of the bottle—that had prompted her to possess the magical liquid. It had called to mind wicked adventure and shameful but ecstatic caresses. She had received it from a cologne drummer who had stopped in at Sutt's two or three months ago. She had received it in trade, in the hot night under the titi shrubs. The drummer (who could lie as well as any married man on the road) had told her it was listed at ten dollars a bottle, and that had made her doubly happy. And the drummer had been happy, too. After deducting the kickback on his commission he'd put 89 cents in the till from his own pocket and written Sin's Dream off as a sale.

41

Dorry turned the bottle toward the square of moonbright window suspiciously, checking to see if Margy had been "borrowing" again.

She'd bathed earlier that evening down at the creek. But that had been before she'd gone into the woods with Tom. Well, the perfume would have to do for now — it simply couldn't be helped. She spilled a generous puddle of Sin's Dream into her palm and began working it over her body. It felt cool, gave her skin a tang.

"What you at now?" The worded question hit the dark room like a mallet hitting glass. Dorry started, almost dropping her bottle. She looked at Margy sitting up in shadow.

"You hush!" she hissed. "Git yourself to sleep."

There was a pause, then—"You fixing to slip out agin."

"I reckon it don't take no wizard to figure that."

"Where at you going?"

"That's my nevermind. Go to sleep."

Margy sighed disdainfully and settled back in bed on one elbow."You goan find yourself trouble."

Dorry was shocked. "Margy! Ain't you got no shame about you?"

Dorry put Sin's Dream away and came over to the bed.

"Cain't you hush? Do you got to lay there and beller like Jort Camp when he's drunked-up? I'm not going to see no boy. It's too hot and sweaty to sleep. I'm goan take a walk is all."

Margy smiled in the dark. "Want me to go with you?"

"I want you to go asleep and mind your own business."

"You fixing to go out in the woods with Tom Fort again," accused her sister.

Dorry sniffed contemptuously, tossing back her hair.

"Tom Fort!" she said, applying scorn to the name and suggestion. "That boy! No, I ain't going to see Tom Fort. I told you I was—"

"Who then?"

Dorry hesitated, trying to see her sister's darkened features. "Margy, honey," — dulcetly this time — "I kin see a boy now and then if'n I want. You got no call to pester me about it. I wouldn't do hit to you."

"You wouldn't catch me doing the things you do."

"Oh, hush. Leave me be. The only trouble I'll git in is if

you go to opening your big mouth around." She found her dress and slipped it over her head, smoothing it down on her hips. "Be sweet, honey. If Pa er Ma should git up, you tell 'em I went out to the privy."

Dorry went to the window and looked out at the moonflooded yard and distant pasture. "You'll see when the boys begin to hanker after you," she whispered.

Margy raised her head like a bass coming at the bait "Oh? Well, mebbe I know a something about that and you don't. Mebbe I know some boys that do hanker after me."

Dorry was interested. She looked back at her sister.

"Who? Who you know, Margy?"

"That's my nevermind."

"You just saying it. Hit don't really go fer truth."

"It do so!"

"Hush, cain't you? Well, who then?"

Margy hesitated, looking away from the window and her sisters silhouette. She put her lower lip between her teeth thinking of Shad and what he'd said to her earlier in the night, seeing again the cock of his felt hat on his dark head, the slow smile on his thin lips.

"Oh," she said finally, "mebbe a somebody like Shad Hark."

Dorry waited a moment, then came back from the window. Again she tried to see Margy's face but couldn't.

"You're a-lying. Shad don't even know you're alive."

"That ain't what he said on the porch tonight!"

"What did he say? What, Margy?"

Margy was pleased with herself. She could tell from Dorry's tone that she was bothered by the thought that any good-looking boy would look at Dorry's little sister instead of her. But her sense of euphoria stalled. Well —

"He said he was thinking on trying me sometime soon," she said, carefully cutting the part where Shad had added in five or six years.

"Trying you on what?" Dorry said. "What's that mean?"

"I shorely don't know," Margy said with feigned indifference. "Ask him next time you see him. It don't mean corn kernels to me."

Dorry straightened up, satisfied at last that Margy had overplayed her hand. She was a dirty little liar, and she was merely trying to show off. Dorry almost laughed when she said, "Mebbe I will — *when* I see him."

Chapter Seven

Sam Parkes was sitting in the weed near the whispering river. He'd been out rambling that night, as was his habit, but now he just sat in the dark and felt sorry for himself. Nervous, restless, foot-itchy, he was a little, wiry man with bright snapping ferret eyes. A compulsive little man who had to keep busy, had to be doing something, anything—as long as it wasn't work.

There wasn't anything attractive about Sam, scrawny, weightless, head-hunkered—a bucktooth man; so bad that Jort Camp—his best friend, the one who made more fun of him than the rest, and they made enough—once said that Sam looked like a man who tried to swallow a piano and the keyboard got stuck.

But it wasn't only his looks the girls objected to — there was also a woodsy quality about Sam. Smell, is how they put it, and none too faint. But Sam couldn't help that. He was a woods colt conceived in the woods, gestated in the woods, and born in the woods three axe handles from a turpentine still, and no one, not even his mother, could say who his father was. And Jort Camp said that the reason Sam had remained in the woods all his life was because he was looking for that mysterious father. But what made it hard was that Sam didn't know if the old man would turn out to be a bull-snake with buckteeth or a polecat with dandruff.

Sam sat by the river and put his right fist into his left palm and worked it there, making a thick grime out of the dirt, grease, and sweat. He was used to the jibes and the jeers. He could take that. But the girls now, the juicy round little—he jerked his hands apart and put the left one to the back of his neck, the right one to his upper lip. He massaged his neck for a moment while he pulled at his lip, then he gave that up with a start and put the hands together again. Tucked them in his lap.

The aimless, expressive, can't-keep-'em-still fingers started a quiet little knuckle-snapping war, twisting and turning and pulling—and then the right hand retreated, flashing down to the left ankle to pursue an elusive itch that zig-zagged along a nerve end under his rolled sock and into his shoe.

Sam was miserable. If he'd had a dollar—just one dollar—he'd be all right. But he didn't. Didn't even have a dime.

"Aw hell," Sam said.

What made it so imperative was he'd stopped by Bell Mears' place in his ramble that night. Not to visit. No one had known of his presence. He'd taken a post (one he'd used numerous times before) by the edge of the spring house, where he could look smack into old Mears' daughters' room.

He'd only caught Margy twice. She hadn't been much to look at then—though he had—but she was hard to catch now she was getting older. She undressed in the dark. Now Dorry—now that was something else again. She always brought a lamp into the room with her, and she never pulled the blind. "That bitch!" he whispered almost hysterically. "That dirty little she-bitch!"

He looked up then and froze, seeing a shadow flitting through the thicket. Who would be coming down that way so late at night? And off the main road too. Nothing to go at but the backwater and Mears' old shantyboat.

Sam forgot about his troubles. He crouched and darted low and fast through the weed, heading for the trail. He might look grotesque when sitting or standing with his nervous agitation, but when he prowled he was as quick and silent as a snake slipping across sand. And now he had him a something to look into. There wasn't anything happened in the woods and Sam didn't know about. A cross fox made itself a new lair and Sam was sitting up in a tree marking the crossback's escape holes. An oldtimer set up a moonshine still so far out, so remote and hidden, that he was prompted to chortle and remark, "By juckies, they ain't *nobody* on God's hind legs kin find this still, now I tell yer!" and Sam was crouching behind a dead stump taking in the words. The silhouettes of a boy and girl blended into one in the darkness under the titis and Sam was squatting there in

45

the bush, watching, licking his lips. You just never know when somebody's secret might come handy.

It took him fifteen seconds to come within ten feet of where Dorry Mears passed a thicket-break.

Trouble was Sam wasn't a fighter of any sort. Any suggestion of physical violence instantly threw him into a trembling state of hesitant confusion. The fear was so deep-seated that even the thought of tangling with a husky girl like Dorry Mears (he guessed she outweighed him by twenty pounds) left him hanging balanced in self-doubt and indecision.

But he knew that for once in his life he was going to have to make a traumatic decision, and make it on the spot.

Take her from behind—but with what?

He wildly looked around in the shadow. Saw a lightwood stick. Snatched it up. Came to a crouch as the girl unwittingly passed him.

One quick tap on the head — stun her. All right, damn you!

But he stalled, looking beyond her. A light was showing in the shantyboat. Someone was in there with a lantern. The stick lowered in his hand. The suggested presence of a third party brought back the timidity he concealed under his ferocious crouch. The moral fibre of Sam's backbone turned to shreds, leaving him a ragbag of a man. The girl passed through the tupelos and down to the bank and gangplank. Sam dropped the stick.

"All right," he whispered. "All right, you bitch. Git after your fun. Whoop it up. But don't you think fer a minute, missy, you goan git off scot-free. Sam here is goan have him a look at who you misbehaving with."

But as he slipped down the shelving bank he forgot his most important woods-prowling rule. He made a soft little noise in his throat, whimpered like a hurt puppy dragging itself for home.

Shad was sitting with his tailor-mades and his money, feeling fat and drowsy in a warm mood of euphoria. In his mind he was plotting out his future — not too realistically; but it was fun just the same. He thought about the girls he would buy, and the expensive booze, and the cars and snappy suits, and maybe even a boat, some sort of cabin cruiser, say, but mostly about the girls. Then he heard a *thunk* of sound on the gangway and the houseboat stirred slightly.

He swept up his bills, shoving them furiously inside his shirt, letting them drop to where the shirt bloused at his belt. Thank God he'd left the windows shuttered. He started to get up, to go to the door, but changed his mind and sat again, reached for a new cigarette.

The door opened tentatively and four pale fingers curved around the edge and stayed there, holding four red beetles at their tips. At first he didn't understand, then he saw the long lamp-gold spill of hair near the hand and knew it was Dorry Mears. An excitement that was akin to a violent sickness came highballing through his body, tensing him, robbing him of breath. He gripped the table-edge, watching, the tailor-made smouldering in his mouth. He didn't get up—wasn't sure he could ; he sat there, thinking—Oh yes. Oh, indeed yes! Now we are goan have us a something here. I knowed it all the time.

The door inched further into the room and Dorry Mears peeked in at him, coquettishly. "It's just me, Shad. Just Dorry," she said. Cat's purr again.

"Nice of you to knock," he said. "I might ben gitting ready fer bed, and me in my shorts."

She came further into the room showing almost all of her, leaned against the door, arching herself as she'd done earlier for him. "I thought of that," she said softly, and then laughed, low.

"Bet you did. That why you here?" He didn't see any reason to play around. He wanted her, God yes, and at another time he might have gone along with the game just to assure himself of final victory. But today he was a new man — a rich man, and he didn't have to mess with anyone.

Dorry pretended to be shocked. "Why, Shadrack Hark! I'm purely convinced you got you an evil mind." She gave a toss of her hair. "Hit was too hot fer sleeping," she said, not looking at him, speaking in staccato. "So I took me a little stroll. No harm in that, is they?"

Shad shook his head. "And ended up way down here," he suggested. "Coincidence, I guess."

She blinked at him. "Well," she said defensively, "I like it

47

down here. I often come thisaway at night—when I cain't sleep."

"Uh-huh," Shad said.

She hitched her right leg around in a half-circle, tracing a faint dust path on the floor with her toes.

"I seen your light on and guessed you was still up. Thought we might talk. I couldn't sleep—" Her voice went off into the open night at her back and got lost there.

Even at that distance, even in the poor light, it was easy to see that she wasn't wearing anything under her dress. That did something to him, something extra. He approved of a dress that looked like that one did. Nothing for shoulders, and not too much to cover those things she was so eternal proud of. And all the rest of it tight. Her ma made Dorry's dresses, but Dorry always remade them —took them in in places, in all the right places.

"Why don't you fetch the rest of you on in?"

Dorry looked at him and smiled. She closed the door.

"They's a hook right handy to hit," he said.

She looked down at the hook but didn't touch it. She looked at him again, an over-the-shoulder look. And that got him started.

"Why should I lock myself in a room with a boy I hardly know?"

"Hardly know? I had me the idea we was old friends— from the way you were slamming your hip into me tonight."

Her eyes were bright like broken chips of glass in the lamplight. "If you goan talk dirty, I'm going to leave! I don't like that kind of talk at all."

And that was the funny thing about her, he reflected. She really didn't. And yet the things that girl had been known to do for pleasure—or was it pleasure?

"Dorry," he said seriously, "why you come here tonight?"

"I done told you. I couldn't sleep and—"

"All right, all right. I'm sorry I brung hit up."

He walked over to her. She watched him come, but not straight on, which made the look something more than just a look. Shad leaned his left arm against the door, barring her in. He tilted her chin up.

"Dorry, you'n me is goan become good friends."

She said nothing. Her mouth was open, partially. Her eyes were closed. When he kissed her, her mouth was like burning liquid.

He reached behind her as they clung together, body and mouth, and fumbled for the hook on the door.

He awakened once in the time of night that is vast, endless, and everything is dead. No man's time. Not belonging to the intricate mechanism of clocks that control worldly minutes. Universe night. Then he remembered the Money Plane and Dorry, and he smiled and rolled over in the dark, reaching for her.

She wasn't there.

Shad sat up, looking. Dorry was sitting in the square shaft of moonlight from the open window, sitting on the edge of the bunk, spreading his ten-dollar bills neatly on her bare leg. The shirt! The damn bills must have fallen out of his shirt.

Her head moved, her hair shimmering silver in the moonlight. She was looking at him, but he couldn't see her face. He was suddenly aware of the weir spilling, a feathery profound drone.

"Where at you git the money, Shad?" Her voice was low, husky, urgent.

He snapped his fingers. "Fetch it back. That's my nevermind."

But she didn't. She clumped it in a small fist and held it to her bare breast. "Pa says you must a sold a heap of skins to afford twenty dollars outright."

"Mebbe I did."

"Mebbe—but ever'body else ben saying how porely the trapping is."

"Mebbe they don't know where to look at"

"Mebbe they ain't looking fer the right thing."

Shad stalled for a moment, then said, "What you mean by that?"

"Shad," she whispered, "you find that old Money Plane? Did you, Shad?"

"You hush up! Hear? Give me that money." He snatched it from her hand. In that split second he was ready to belt her one, hard. "I don't know about no Money Plane. Ain't nobody kin find that old wreck."

She came for him, hip-sliding across the bunk. He decided not to belt her one. Instead he cupped her left breast in his hand. Red fire! That threw a man all out of whack.

"Shad," she breathed, "they's the most pure-out beautiful dress I seen down to Torkville the other day with my ma. Shad, you'd like me in it. Ain't homemade. I'd wear it just fer you. I could git it mebbe fer ten dollars. Shad?"

He grurgled a little in his throat, and finally shoved her one of the bills. "But you keep shet about this here money, you hear? This is fer you'n me. I God shore don't want ever' Tom, Dick an' Harry pestering me after it. Dorry, you hear me?"

She looked up from the money in her hand and kissed him wetly. "Shad—it ain's pelt-sold money, is it? It was the Money Plane, wasn't it?"

"I ain't got a God-made word to say about that money."

"But it was, wasn't it, Shad? *Shad?*"

Chapter Eight

He was alone in the morning. It didn't surprise him. He grunted and got up, found his pants and counted his money. He wouldn't put it past Dorry to — but no, he had fifty-some dollars left.

He fetched a bucket of water and gave himself a stand up bath on the porch, then dressed, lighted a cigarette, and left the shanty.

He followed the path to the road and started east. He'd rustle up a meal first, then do some shopping. He'd have to see Iris Culver, and that was going to be like cutting a wounded bear off from the bush. He could expect trouble from that quarter.

He came upon silly Edgar Toll, sitting in the dirt smack in the middle of the road before his ma's shanty. A hulking youth with a face like a pan of greasy dough, ornamented with big angry purple pimples and long shiny hairs that grew out of his nose almost touching his lip. Mouth always swinging open, sometimes drooling, witless and with little to say for himself, he'd stand around in nooks and corners like a guilty secret and try to lick his nostrils, cow-like.

Folks were used to Edgar, used to seeing him hulking about in a sort of bewildered waiting. But Shad could never cotton to the moron. He felt an instant loathing, as though he were about to be dumped into a putrid swamp whenever he approached the fool.

But it was more than just a moronic ailment with Edgar. Something was twisted inside —his right and wrong guidepost. He was forever hunting up helpless little creatures, anything, bugs to non-pit vipers, to torture them. Today it was a frog.

The moron had the frog, back flat on the road, holding it with one hand. He was disembowelling it with a sharp stick.

"Sweet Lord!" Shad cried. Then he cuffed Edgar hard alongside the ear, spinning him into the dirt. "You goddam idjut! I ort to God rip *your* stupid guts out!"

He looked at the frog, scrabbling helplessly in its own mire, and winced. Not because a living thing had been despoiled, but because this living thing had been helpless, and because the despoiling had been done by a human being. He couldn't understand that.

Something had to be done. The thing was in agony. But what? "Oh Lord." he said. He raised his boot and brought it down with a slam. Edgar came to his feet awkwardly, dripping dirt and tears. He was clutching the sharp stick, inexpertly, like a woman with a dagger.

"You — you damn — you damn Sh-sh-shad!" he cried.

"I'll kill'n you!" He came at Shad in a shuffling duck-footed run.

Shad stepped aside adroitly and left-jabbed the moron hard in the mouth. Edgar went down like a bag of nails, sprawling out in the dirt. He beat at the road with his hands, opened his red mouth like a fire bucket and bawled, "Ma! Mama!"

Mrs. Toll clumped out onto the porch glaring fiercely right and left. A slovenly old creature, a widow woman who grubbed a living for herself and her idiot son out of the wood somehow. No one was certain just how. She hitched at her ragbag skirt, drape-hanging it on her shapeless frame, and started screaming at Shad.

"I seen you! I seen you! You dirty swamp critter. You hitted my pore boy! You hitted my baby, you—" She went insane with her insults.

And Shad, hating the scene, hating the old lady and her idiot son, and the frog the idiot had made him stamp to death, shouted back.

"Shet up! You stupid old cow! Why don't you lock that goddam fool son of yourn up. Why don't you —"

Old Mrs. Toll caught up a wood-chopping axe and came down from the porch at a wobble-legged run.

"I'll fix yer! I'll chop yer! Beat my pore baby! I'll —"

Shad Hark was no fool. He turned and made tracks, his ears ringing with Mrs. Toll's cackle, "Lookit him! Lookit him, Edgee! Lookit him go! The big brave swampman arunning from an old woman! Hi! There he goes, the dirty, cowardly, spineless, gator-lovin' pig!"

Shad high-tailed down to the next shanty — Rival Taylor's — and came to a panting halt. "Goddam idjuts!" he gasped. "Ort a lock 'em both up." Then his mind slipped back to reactivate the scene, and he started laughing and couldn't help it. "What a God handsome sight I must have made coming fox-fast down the road with the crazy old witch axe-swinging after me!"

He shook his head and looked up. Mrs. Taylor came out on her porch carrying a pan of water.

"Shad," she called. "What's ben going on up the road there? Somebody run over Edgar agin?"

Shad grinned. "I run him over with my fist, Mrs. Taylor. And old Mrs. Toll took after me with a hatchet."

Mrs. Taylor pursed her lips and *tisked* disagreeably.

"You shouldn't ort a done a thing like that, Shad. Pore Edgar."

She swished the pan of greasy water outward like a fisherman casting a net. The water plopped on the ground, fanned into a silver shield and fell again.

"Well, now that you're here, you want a cup of morning coffee?"

Shad smiled, nodding. Mrs. Taylor was offering him the coffee so she could get the full story of why he'd hit pore Edgar; he knew that swamp women had to get their entertainment from some source. At least gossip wasn't a cardinal sin.

He followed her into the house, saying, "Got me a fifty-cent piece here that I'd purely like to see go fer a breakfast. Grits is fine, if they're handy."

Mrs. Taylor looked at him, the empty pan still in her hand. "Why ain't you et to home, Shad ?"

"Ain't living to home, is why. I cleared out last night."

Mrs. Taylor said *tsk* again, shook her head and said, "My!" Then —"Well, sit, Shad, while I redd up the table."

She was getting more than she'd bargained for and she tried to be offhand about it, as if someone had brought her a gift she'd been expecting and didn't much care about. "Want to tell me about hit, son?"

Shad ducked his smile. "No'm. I'll tell you about Edgar, though."

He ate and she had a cup of coffee with him. And then when he brought out his pack of tailor-mades he didn't know what else to do but offer her one. The way Mr. Culver always did to Iris Culver.

Mrs. Taylor cried. "Shad! *Me* take a devil stick? Don't you come trotting in any of your hanky-panky tricks on me. What would Rival say?" Then she laughed and flapped her apron. "And me a fat old woman!"

Shad grinned. "Go on," he said. "I was thinking if mebbe you were to tell me what night Rival stays out with the hounds, I'd just come sneak-footing by this way—"

"Whaah!" Mrs. Taylor let out a shout of laughter and put her pudgy hands up to her apple cheeks. "Shad Hark, you are the one! Now you just stop that air teasing. And me old enough to be your ma!"

Shad liked her. He sort of wished she was his ma. She was real, she was a part of the Purpose. Not artificial, useless like Iris Culver — at least useless for practical living. And Dorry? Would she be like Mrs. Taylor some-day? He kind of doubted it. Mrs. Taylor would have been a pioneer wife—had there been anything left to pioneer. He looked at her, seeing her unconsciously as the embodiment of old-fashioned home life.

"Why'd you say poor Edgar?" he asked suddenly, sensing that she had answers to things he couldn't understand.

"You know he tortures frogs and mice and things."

Mrs. Taylor looked serious. "You cain't really say hit's his fault, Shad. I know cutting up frogs ain't a nice thing to do, but Edgar got a lot of good in him."

"Must have," Shad agreed. "He don't never let none of it out."

"You hush and listen to me. I knowed that pore boy since he was borned. And when he was a little fella he warn't mean. He warn't smart, but not mean. Wasn't till after you other lil' boys come at him all the time he started to change. A-throwing sticks and rocks at him, a-chasing him home and calling him idjut all the time —"

"Not me. I never done those things to him when we was little."

"I know you never, Shad. You always hung away from him, likn you were feered of him. But them othern did. I remember one day—pore lil' fella couldn't ben but eight—they tied cans to his lil' tail and chased him home to his ma. Like a dog, Shad.

"So you see? One day he found out he could catch him little crawly things, things that couldn't fight back, and he started taking some of his hate out on'em. Hate got to come out someways, Shad. It shore God do."

Shad stared at the table, thinking about hate. Then he grunted and stood up. "Mebbe," he said, not wholly convinced. "But I just think he's dangerous as a walleyed bull." From his jeans he dug some of the dollar bills Joel Sutt had given him for change.

"You put that money away, Shad Hark. I ain't setting up no coffee shop here, you know," Mrs. Taylor said crossly.

"What give you the idea hit's fer you?" Shad wanted to know.

He put five of the dollars down on the table, letting them stack crisscross one on the other. "Here. Give 'em to that old fool Toll woman. You don't have to tell her I give 'em to you."

Mrs. Taylor looked at the money. Her eyes turned damp when she smiled, and he thought it was funny the way you could catch some people that way.

"Why, Shad," she said. "You got a soft spot in you wide as a boat-bottom."

"Go on," he snapped. "You gitting foolish along with

your other aliments. Bet in another year Rival won't be able to tell the difference 'tween you'n Edgar — if'n Edgar goes to not wearing his pants."

Mrs. Taylor let out another holler of laughter, and her voice followed Shad out the door and onto the porch. "Shad, don't you go to showing all that money of yourn to those girls you always chasing after. They'll take it off you in one night. You hear me, Shad?"

He felt pretty good when he went into the yard.

Chapter Nine

In the great square frame house with the high-peaked roof, in the house that was incongruous to the ratty peppering of shanties and the vivid wilderness, like a little girl's new doll standing alone in the weeded backyard of an abandoned property, Iris Culver moved distractedly across her living room. She passed the long wall of books—her books—Larry read trash — and went to the front window. Her highheels left the rug and the house-stillness seemed to shudder and recoil from the hollow sound of the heels tapping the wooden floor. The soft purr of the air conditioner followed her. It was a faulty old relic that Larry had picked up somewhere on sale.

Outside the air was sun-warmed, flower-scented. It was the day which last night had presaged — early summer, cool in the shadows, glass-clear. The cabbage palms stood tall and separate. The sky, ragged on the horizon, showed itself detached and whole, going on around.

She turned from the window in an abrupt, deliberate pivot, a movement that would have looked awkward, afflicted, from any other but a woman of her kind. Nerves. She went to a fiddletop table—one made by a local swamp billy and Larry had purchased it for five dollars. Iris hated it. From a jade box she took a cigarette. She stood for a moment looking back at the window, through the screened porch, across the saw-grass lawn and road to the lake, seeing the swamp beyond. She tapped the cigarette on her thumb. Where was Shad?

The three-word sentence stood in her mind like a wall, or like the swamp water out there that was just as much a barrier between them. She hated it, hated the tupelo and titi and gator-thunder; hated the sticky heat and mosquitoes, the free wandering hens and pigs, the dirty abysmally ignorant children and the distorted speech of their elders. Hated Shad; herself for needing him.

She crossed the big living room again, passed through a swinging door, pausing to hold it in her hand. Shad had made it for them. Shad had come to the house a year ago to make the swinging door. Larry had hired him because he was young and smart and because his work was cheap. Later she'd laughed at that, later, when Larry was out in his barn typing—and Shad was in her bed.

The view from the kitchen window was partially blocked by a hillside meadow. She opened the door and looked out. From the back porch she could see the meadow ending in a line of trees against the sky. The barn—Larry's Ivory Tower — was midway in the line of trees, like a white ship drifting to its moorings.

He was still up there, she thought. He wouldn't be bothering her for a while. Perhaps this was her lucky day. She might not have to hear his latest deathless chapter until night. The latest trials and good-natured adventures of Tab and Reb, those one hundred per cent red-blooded all-American boy rovers.

She slammed the door and click-clacked back through the kitchen, returned to the living room and went to the tall gilt mirror over a maple table holding a vase and flowers. The flowers were wilted.

She studied the image of Iris Culver, the surface Iris.

It wasn't a woman she saw so much as a creation of ego. Every minute detail contributed a little to the whole—the meticulous scarlet lips, the lacquered nails, the closely cropped raven hair deliberately messy at the foretop where it blossomed, the svelte dress with the single pin, and much more. All of it done for effect, a part of the purpose, like her speech, her mannerisms, gestures. She was acutely aware of her perfection, her breeding and poise. She was a product of the ruling class, whose birthright stretched back to before the coming of Christ. Only now the thing to which she belonged was dead, finished, outmoded and useless, superannuated by philistines, men like Larry and Shad. *Shad.*

The image of her porcelain face barely changed when she smiled coldly. "You perverse bitch," she said quietly.

A thirty-eight-year-old dilettante in love with an ignorant swamp boy. *Fool. Silly fool.*

And suddenly the mirror showed her something she didn't want to see, something that was like death, only to her—worse. She saw a woman who was no longer a glittering show piece, no longer a fragile glass gift to the world. Only a weary female who was slowly being prodded into her forties by time's wrinkled shoulder. She turned from the mirror without sense of direction, feeling a kind of horror.

It grew. It was the swamp. It was the endlessness, the mystery of the swamp. It was the heat and the violence, violence that spun on always around her and that no one except herself seemed concerned with. It was the people and the animals and the hostility, hostility that was in a league with the swamp billies and the alligators, the coons, the cottonmouths, the Negroes, the climate, the stinking mud and rotting swamp flowers.

What if I can never escape? What if I must go on spending my life in this Confederate madhouse? Stay here until it is too late?

For a vivid moment it seemed that her nerves were going. She wanted to tear a scream from her body, leap wildly through the window, run away from the swamp, to a city, any city, to lights, movement, music, and gaiety.

She took a few aimless steps to nowhere and stopped, realizing the unlit cigarette was in her hand. She found a match, then went to the bar (Shad had built it after the door, when she needed a reason to keep him around the house) and hurriedly mixed a martini.

She felt better after the drink. And mixed a second.

The money was the problem. There was never any escape for her class without money. Even then escape was a word covering a certain deadness that could lead to suicide, if you thought about it. A symbol-word that led to more boredom, more small talk—a particular apathy of reaction to the world and everyone in it. But at least they were all a shaving from the same whittled stick (as Shad put it), and there was comfort in that, a miserably disenchanted comfort.

Larry wrote three "boys' books" each year, under three separate *nom de plummes* (the *Adventures of Tab and Red* being the most popular), one detective paperback, and numerous action short stories for men's magazines. It was a living — here in the swamp, a comfortable living. But it wasn't escape. It wasn't even worth divorcing over. *Money.*

She went back to the long bay window and looked at the swamp across the lake. Eighty thousand dollars was out there somewhere. And now there was a rumour that Shad had found it—

Larry had come back from the country store at noon with a mildly excited look in his eyes. Iris had been sitting before the window with her first martini for the day, sitting with her cigarettes and glass, staring at the swamp, wondering when Shad was coming back.

"Darling," Larry had said, "there's quite a fascinating little story going in the village."

She hadn't looked at him. "Someone's cow give birth to a two-headed calf?" she inquired with cold politeness.

He came over and stooped to peck her forehead.

"No, no," he chuckled. "You remember Ferris' airplane? The one these people call the Money Plane? They say Shad Hark has found it. I got that from Joel Sutt himself. They're all a-whisper with the story in the village."

Outwardly she hadn't shown any emotion. Inwardly a certain excitement had begun to snowball.

"Whisper? Why are they whispering about it?"

"Because they say the Hark boy hasn't admitted it. But he's been passing out ten-dollar bills like a New Yorker on a spree. 'Course it may not be true — you know how these swamp villages thrive on gossip. Still, it's rather interesting, don't you think? Might even be a story there, somewhere."

"Yes," she said absently. "Tab and Reb, the latter-day rover boys find the Money Plane."

He'd blinked at her, pausing in a reflective turn before the window. "Eh? Oh, why no; I was thinking more of an adult paperback. You know, using the gimmick—"

But she wasn't listening. She seldom did. It was a trick

she'd learned to save her sanity. Practice made perfect. She would stare at something as though considering his words, nod at practically the correct time, say *hmm* at the pauses, and raise her brows from time to time as if saying, "Oh. I see." But she seldom listened. Shad had found the money. The eighty thousand. He was being stupid, of course. That was to be expected. Passing the money around like an idiot. But he wasn't admitting it.

She sank easily under a deeper surface of thought, remembering all the long afternoons and short nights when they'd been together in her shadowy room, and she'd prompted him with, "Shad, when you're out there looking for your brother — you look for that airplane too, don't you?"

"Shore. Ever' man and boy that goes into that old slough keeps one eye and half a mind on the Money Plane. But ain't nobody going to find her. Know why?"

"Why?"

"Because she ain't nowhere where a-body *kin* find her. Else one of us would've done it by now."

"But you'll keep looking, won't you, Shad? You'll keep it in your mind (if we may call it that) when you're out there. Eighty thousand dollars, Shad. We could go away with that money. Just you and I."

She didn't need or love Shad as a person. Shad was only a simple boy, unworldly. She controlled him. She could work him around, work the money from him and leave. Perhaps it wasn't pretty, but it was escape—

She came back to the sullen afternoon, back to the big lonely living room. She was standing at the window, looking across the lake. She waited for Shad.

He hadn't consciously noticed he was being followed that morning. It hadn't meant anything special to him when Sam Parks fell into his wake after he left Mrs. Taylor's. He didn't like Sam, so he'd pretended to ignore him. Sam had tailed him down to the store.

Joel Sutt had acted standoffish when he took Shad's order for sheets, food, and miscellaneous whatnot. So had the two or three others hanging around in there. They'd watched Shad, not speaking to him nor to each other; and when he looked at them, they shifted their gaze and tried to look like men killing time with nothing on their minds. With them it was a convincing trick.

Shad hadn't cared. His head was full of plans, full of Dorry and the money. He nodded to them, said, "Thanks, Joel," and walked out. He couldn't remember Joel saying anything.

Hert Reade, a fifteen-year-old, had moseyed along after him all the way back to the shantyboat. It was only when he reached the gangplank that he realized Hert was hanging around near the pond.

"Y'all want something, Hert?" he called.

But the boy shook his head, not looking at him, pawing at the bank-ooze with his bare toes. "Naw. Just fooling around some."

For a while Shad fussed with the idea of hiding his remaining thirty-some dollars somewhere in the shanty, but let the scheme go when he recalled the way Jort Camp had eyed his money the night before. Then, too, there was always the worry of Sam Parks tooling around in the bush. Sam could sift himself through a keyhole like a skinny beam of sunlight, and would too, if he thought there was anything worth picking up on the other side of the door.

So he'd keep his money in his pocket, and there wasn't nobody at the Landing and a damn bit further than that who could take it away from him — Except maybe Jort Camp, the gator-grabber. It bothered him somewhat that there was a man he knew he couldn't whip. Not that Jort had ever tried, but the gator-grabber had whipped every man and boy that ever came his way so far. My turn just ain't come yet, he thought. Then he said, "Well, if he's coming at me, he best come like the wrath of God, because I'll cold go to scratch like hell on feet."

Hert was gone when Shad left the shanty in the early afternoon. But Mel Warren, a nondescript trapper, was there piddling around in the bush, carrying a fishing pole.

If he's going fishing he's mighty God slow a-gitting at it, Shad thought. And if he's already ben — he's had mighty poor luck.

He struck up the path, giving Warren a wave. "Catching anything out there in the bush, Mel?" he called. He thought that was a pretty good one. But Warren didn't laugh. He reacted like Hert had, with embarrassed bewilderment.

"No. Just lost something. Hit don't matter much."

Up on the road Shad saw Jort Camp slowly coming his way. That wasn't so good. He didn't hanker to have anyone see him going to Iris Culver's house. Least of all bigmouth Camp. When he reached the creek bridge he slid down the soft embankment hurriedly and slipped into the blue shadows under the bridge. He waited three or four minutes for the sound of Jort's boots to clump overhead, but nothing happened. He frowned and waited.

The creek was slow, warm, sluggish; knee-deep in most places but rump-high awful sudden if a man wasn't careful where he stepped. A combination elderberry and similar thicket went north with the water. Shad eased from under the bridge and dodged into the bush. By the time he reached the Culver grove he was fairly cat-claw-scratched, but he didn't mind.

He circled around the grove, coming close to the white barn that nestled ship-snug in the trees. Close enough to hear the faint tac-tac-tac of Culver's typewriter clacking away somewhere up in the reconverted loft. He nodded and swung around in the other direction. With the house between himself and the barn he hurried across the lawn and up onto the side porch. "Iris?" he whispered.

She let him in through the dining-room entrance, and she was all over him before he could even get the screen door closed properly. She was a little crazy; he'd known that for some time. She was something like that English lady in one of that Hemingway fella's books she'd loaned him. Shad didn't have a name for it, but he could recognize a danger when he saw it. The trouble was he should have seen it a long time ago. It wasn't going to be easy to tell her. She wasn't going to like it. He disengaged his mouth, saying huskily, "Whoa! Let's git us a breath in here."

She was looking at him from five inches away, her mouth open and the wet pink of her tongue showing. It reminded him of Dorry Mears.

He got all of him untangled at once and stepped clear, avoiding her eyes, a little frightened by the look in them. He removed his hat, as she had taught him to do, and placed it on the table; then wiped the sweat and some of the lipstick from his face. Funny the way sweat never bothered her. Yeah. And a sudden hollow sensation vacuum-packed his stomach.

"I got to talk to you," he began.

She nodded urgently, coming at him again. "I know — in the bedroom. We'll lock the door. Larry'll think I'm napping."

"Couldn't we just talk here?"

She had his hand, looked at him peculiarly. "Are you insane? Do you want Larry to come in and find us here? *Come on!*" She led him. He went helplessly.

The cool-air unit was growling quietly in a corner of the shadowy room. The windows were closed, the curtains drawn. The bed was made. Iris locked the door. Shad watched her like a broken-wing turnstone watching a shore-prowling puma.

"You were so long coming, I thought something had happened to you."

"I went and got me in a bind of gators. Had to spend me a night in the skiff."

She looked at him, a look that he used to admire — cold superiority.

"Shad, don't talk like a Civil War throwback. You know better. I taught you better."

She *had* taught him, and he did know better. But he frequently spoke his own dialect just to show her that he was still independent of her. He knew it railed her. "All right," he said. "I forgot."

She went to the bed, sat on the edge of it, removed her heels, crossing one nyloned leg over the other. "Undress me, Shad" she said simply.

He stalled, keeping in the centre of the quiet room, sensing the trap closing in on him.

"Listen at — to me, Iris. I got something that needs to be said."

"Later, Shad. Undress me."

She held a long slim arm up to him, the pale hand halfhanging.

He could always handle girls — young ones, girls of his own breed, the all-giggles-and-no-brains ones. But this woman with her poise, her intelligence and worldliness was too much for him. He felt stupid and cloddish around her, putty-like. He went to the bed and took her hand, but nothing else.

"It's like this here," he began.

Her right arm circled his neck, tugging his lips down to hers. Her mouth mumbled into his. "I know. I know about it. We'll discuss it after a bit —"

She knew about it? How? About Dorry? No, she couldn't, or she wouldn't be acting this way. What then?

He thought about last night, of Dorry who was young, nineteen young. He thought about now, of this woman in his arms who was old enough to be his mother. He started to struggle, to push her away. Everything was sickening, the clammy sweat, the moist hot mouth, her hands.

"Iris —"

But she threw a hand flat against his chest. A warning, frightened gesture. He saw fear in her eyes.

"Listen!" she hissed.

He did — and heard it. A soft, almost cautious tread in the hallway. They froze like a pair of hound dogs butting their wet noses into a belt of scent. Everything beyond the closed door seemed to be frozen, too. They watched the door, waiting. Then they watched the brass doorknob take a slow clockwise turn. Nothing happened.

Shad wet his lips and eased his head around.

Who? he asked with his eyes.

Larry, she said with her lips.

She was clutching his arm tightly, and it came to him that her nerves were a lot worse than he'd suspected. He could see in her eyes that she might fly apart at any moment. And that made him more frightened.

Her hand gave an imperative jerk on his arm. He looked at the door. The knob was moving counter-clockwise. Shad let out his breath. He thought he heard something moving, but couldn't be sure.

"Thought you said it was safe," he accused her.

"It always has been, hasn't it? I don't know why the fool has stopped writing."

"Well, how do I git out of here? I ain't fixing to git myself husband-shot, you know."

"Hush, won't you!"

Their heads panned together, following the curtained sweep of the windows. Someone' a shadow, was moving silently along the screened porch. They stared at the bedroom porch door in a quiet kind of horror. The knob turned slyly. Shad couldn't face it any longer. He felt like an animal at bay. He started to get up, clenching his fists. Culver was a city man, a soft, not-so-tall man. He'd bust him a quick one in the mouth and be long gone.

"*Don't!*" she whispered frantically. "For God's sake, *don't!*" The shadow was flitting across the windows again, going away.

"Your hat!" she said suddenly.

"What?"

"You left your hat in the dining room!"

"Oh my God! What'll we do?"

"I don't — I'll say you came to check the generator. Yes, it's been acting strangely. I'll say you must have forgotten your hat."

"What was the goddam generator doing in the dining room?"

"Don't be stupid! You fixed the generator and came into the house for your money. You forgot and left your hat on the table."

"All right," he said. "It'll have to do."

He wanted out of there bad. He could see nothing but trouble coming from the Culvers; coming like Jort Camp on a bender. As a rule he played honest with girls, but this one he was going to have to skip. He'd decided against telling Iris that they were through. It was too risky. He had other problems. He was running out of money fast. That meant he'd have to get back to the Money Plane. Well, this time he wasn't going to play around. He'd arrange to get all the money; arrange to meet Dorry somewhere handy, and they'd clear out.

"Shad, you can't go yet. It's safe now. He's gone away. He thinks I'm napping."

Shad scowled. "We ain't got us the time now. Besides, I'm all hop-toady inside after him sniffing around."

"But we were going to talk about the money from that airplane."

They were just words at first. In his eagerness to get free of the woman and her house, which had suddenly become as dangerous as a cocked shotgun, he let the words slip into the back of his brain — but he snatched them out fast and looked at them again.

"What?"

"The eighty thousand dollars. Everyone says you found it." He stared at her, tasting his lips, her lipstick.

"What are you saying?"

She was impatient with him. "The whole village is talking about the money you found. It's true, isn't it?"

He started shaking his head before he could find the words to deny it. "No—no, I don't know what they're talking about. I didn't find no Money Plane."

In his mind was a morass of desperation, filled with skull-crushing deadfalls of self-reproach at his own stupidity. That was why everyone was acting so peculiar, why they were tagging around after him, watching every move he made. *I shouldn't have left home,* he thought. *Shouldn't have gone to pass out all those tens.*

"You're lying, Shad," she said quietly.

He shook his head again.

"You did find that money. And you promised that if you ever did you'd bring it here to me. Why are you treating me like this?"

"You crazy as the rest of 'em! I tell you I didn't find nothing!"

"Don't lie to me, Shad. You said you wanted to tell me about it when you first came. You said you wanted to talk to me. You meant the money, didn't you? What else could you mean?"

He clutched at it. "I was trying to tell you that we was through. That's the something I had to say."

She gave a cry like an animal being hurt. "Shad! You don't mean that! You *can't* mean it."

He stuck to it doggedly, nodding his head.

"Yes, I do. I — I found me another girl — a younger girl."

He'd wanted to hurt— he knew her vanity was the only thing that would get the Money Plane from her mind —and he couldn't have done a better job if he'd gone to the pasture and brought in a handful of dung to throw in her face.

"Younger—" she said it as though it was the one valid word out of all the thousands, making something solid and tangible of it. *"Younger than I."*

"Well, my God," he cried. "I'm only twenty! And you—you—"

Fury blazed up like cornstalk on a hot day.

"You filthy little hillbilly! You contemptible little moron!" She stood up, looking wildly about the room for a weapon, anything. She saw her nail file on the dressing table and started for it.

Shad didn't know what she was going for, but he had an idea. He sprinted for the door, the outside door, and wrestled with the key. It opened and he stepped onto the porch. "I'm sorry, Iris," he called back. "I'm —"

Something smashed against the half-closed door. He ducked and slammed it shut. Then he ran for the woods. He could still smell the sweet stench of the shattered perfume bottle tagging after him.

Chapter Ten

It was twilight when the bus let Mr. Ferris out at the forks. The sun was already below the cabbage palms and now they looked stark, stooped like tired people caught in the suspension of their weary thoughts. Mr. Ferris, holding a small travelling bag, stepped carefully down into the dust and paused a moment, looking up and away with the look of a man who has returned to a remembered place.

A woman was coming from a shanty down in a grove of shaggy trees, coming with the brisk, bright determination of a duty that was almost a pleasure. Mr. Ferris remembered her, a Mrs. Ty Waldridge, and he recalled that she had an idiosyncrasy. She took a daily newspaper. Each day at sunset she came up to her gate near the fork and was handed her paper by the bus driver. The thing that Mr. Ferris had found so charming was that neither Mrs. Waldridge or her husband knew how to read. The newspaper was a red herring. Mrs. Waldridge liked to see who got on and off the bus, liked the moments of gossip with the driver and any of the female passengers she happened to know.

The bus was an ancient three-ton affair with a roaring old monster for an engine. The only time the passengers could communicate verbally was during the stops. When the bus was in motion you had to settle for face and hand signals—unless you wanted to strain your lungs shouting.

One man, sitting on the right, had the dress and manner-isms that marked him for a northerner. He looked out the window and up at the cabbage palms. His expression was cryptic. He and Mr. Ferris had become friendly on the way from the airport. He was travelling to Three Creek to visit relatives for the first time. He looked down at Mr. Ferris standing below him and smiled wryly. "So this is what you thought you'd missed?" he wondered.

Mr. Ferris' dry features moved almost imperceptibly, coming to a slow, considered smile. He turned his head right-shoulder, then left-shoulder and nodded. "It takes some getting used to. But you see what I mean about the primitive?"

"Oh yes, yes, that's plain enough."

Both men smiled, understanding each other, as separate as two European adventurers set down in the center of Inner Mongolia. And the man in the bus emphasized their agreement by canting his eyes meaningfully toward his travelling companions, all of them natives of the district.

"I'm going to miss your company, Mr. Ferris, I can assure you."

Mr. Ferris' laugh was soundless but obvious. "Get to know them," he suggested. "It's worth while. They'll make you feel right at home. Just don't bring up the Civil War."

The man in the bus grinned. "Never heard of it."

Mrs. Waldridge came through her gate and stopped short at the edge of the road, blinking at Mr. Ferris.

"Why —" she began. "Why, it's Mr. Ferris! Well, lan'sake, it *is* Mr. Ferris!"

Mr. Ferris turned, smiling his slow smile and lifted his grey Borsalino hat to her, hearing the man in the bus mur-mur, "Well, I'll be damned!"

"Mrs. — Waldridge, isn't it?" Mr. Ferris said. "So good to see you again. How have you been? And your husband?"

He turned smoothly and held his hand out to the emerging driver. "I'll take the newspaper, thank you. Here you are, Mrs. Waldridge."

The poor fat lady was flustered, at a loss for words. Some of the women in the bus were acquaintances of hers. They gawked at her, saying nothing. Mrs. Waldridge started to take the paper in her left hand, became confused and also started to reach for it with her right, suffered a hand collision in mid-air, and stood for a brief embarrassed moment simply waving both hands helplessly saying, "Why — why, Mr. Ferris — why —"

Mr. Ferris said, "Quite all right." Then, as the worn-out engine burst into a clattering roar, he stepped clear of the road — taking Mrs. Waldridge's meaty elbow and assisting her as though she were made of Dresden — and turned back to wave at the man in the bus.

The old ruin leaped forward as the driver released the clutch, and again Mr. Ferris laughed soundlessly when he heard his new friend shout back at him, "No wonder they make you feel at home! You should run on the Democrat ticket! Bye!"

Alone together by the road, Mrs. Waldridge seemed bent on continuing the stilted conversation that consisted primarily of unfollowed "why's" and "well's." But Mr. Ferris' gallantry had its limitations. He lifted his hat to her again.

"Nice to have seen you again — and remember me to your husband."

"Well — well, yes, I'll shore do hit, Mr. — Mr. Ferris. I'll — Did you come back on 'count a the Money Plane?"

Mr. Ferris looked back, nodding.

"Yes, that's right, Mrs. Waldridge."

"Well! Well, I never! Shad Hark — they say Shad Hark found hit, Mr. Ferris. Did you hear that already? Mr. Ferris?"

He was safely on his way by now. He smiled and waved, "Yes. Thank you, Mrs. Waldridge."

He remembered the way. The trail he was on was used by half-wild cattle and gaunt pigs. It led him down to a deep-rutted turpentine road that was used by Negroes with mule wagons who came to scrape resin from the clay cups on the tapped turpentine trees.

And he remembered the next place very well, remembered the smell. It was a turpentine still. Negroes lived there in ratty cabins and abject poverty. It was a part of the swamp that Mr. Ferris didn't find at all picturesque. The little pickaninnies scattered to the weeds when they saw him coming, their eyes like small snowballs, each dotted with a single raisin. He nodded to a heavy Mammy, saying "Good evening," in passing, and heard her chanted "Yus suh, yus suh," follow him beyond the quarters.

He paused reflectively when suddenly confronted with a shallow dirt path running out of the bush to become a tributary to the road. That was his path, wasn't it? The path leading to the Culvers? Yes, he was certain of it.

A man passing through the shrub stopped a moment to look at Mr. Ferris. Then he put his hands akimbo and cocked his head off centre, as though the unbalance would help his power of observation. Suddenly he called. "Hey! Hi there, Mr. Ferris!" and waved.

Mr. Ferris smiled and waved back without stopping. Mr. Ferris frequently forgot other people, but other people never forgot Mr. Ferris.

The path led one mile from the road, around the head of a horseshoe lake and down to the Culver place. Mr. Ferris stopped and looked at the remembered wilderness. The lake lay like a chunk of blue shadow, lustrous and empty, while beyond the cypress barrier the swamp squatted green under the opaque sky. It recalled to his mind Heyst's abrupt declaration in *Victory*, "I am enchanted with these islands."

He climbed a shaky stile — remembering with amusement that four years ago Larry Culver was promising Iris he would do something about it — and traversed the meadow, coming at last to the grassy yard and the house. He paused on the bottom step, glancing at his shoes. No shine left; they looked like two small loaves of powdered bread. He looked right and left, didn't see what he wanted, and drew a handkerchief from his pocket. He swatted, not rubbed, at the shoes; then shook out the handkerchief, folded it neatly and returned it to his pocket. He picked up his bag and went up the steps to the screen door.

"Larry?" he called across the veranda. "Iris?"

He could hear the mechanical whirr of the air conditioner

pulsating through the open living-room doors, and heard the drone punctuated by a liquid click of sound, like ice in a drink. Then he heard Iris Culver's voice. "Who is it?"

And a moment later he listened to her heels clicking toward him. She was but vaguely visible through the veranda screen, and the shadow from the porch overhang only showed her feet, legs, and bottom of her dress clearly. The rest of her was suggested dimly like a wraith.

"Why, *Tarleton!*" she said. "Why, it is you, Tarl!"

He smiled fleetingly and said yes and tried the screen door. It was open and he stepped inside, set down his bag and looked at Iris Culver.

Even with him, he noted, she smiled her practiced smile, the porcelain pose that belonged to the tall, thin, aloof girls of *Harper's Bazaar*, who give you cold scarlet smiles out of white faces as they stare at you fixedly with green eyeshadow eyes.

She came to him with a slender, pale hand, and that amused him because it was such a contrast to the manner in which she had said goodbye to him four years ago. But no, he amended, that wasn't quite correct. They *had* shaken hands four years ago. She and Larry had seen him off at the bus, and so of course they had had to shake hands. It was the night before he left that he was thinking about — the last night, when Larry was in his loft playing slave to that mechanical monster that typed out one inked letter after another, endlessly. In the bedroom with the Venetian blinds, in the rumpled double bed with the warm, moist sheets —

No. Later may be too late. Listen to me. Find some young man, a stupid one preferably — but of course that means any of them around here. Listen to me. Find some young man and get him interested in you: keep him interested in the Money Plane. Do you understand? Keep him looking for it. But make certain — if and when he finds it— that he tells you and no one else. You can do that, can't you? You can handle a situation like that, can't —

Oh, for Godsake, of course I can. But I don't want to discuss it now.

The rest didn't matter because Mr. Ferris was not ruled by Freudian passion, but he was an accommodating man and he firmly believed in living by the set standards of his hostess, whoever she might be at the time.

And now this same pale, icy woman with the hot Tarquin eyes was holding his hand again, was saying. "I don't understand, Tarl. I only just sent you a wire, only a few hours ago."

He nodded, taking back his hand. "Joel Sutt telephoned me long distance last night. Where's Larry?"

"Where would you expect him to be? He is far off in paradise writing deathless prose. Come in. Let me fix you a drink. Isn't this climate God awful?"

She tapped away from him and he followed slowly in the faint perfume of her wake. She had always been a nervous woman, but as a rule — especially when meeting people — her cover up had been superb. So she worried him, because now her cover was slipshod.

"I'm glad that Sutt person phoned you. I only found out about it this morning. Larry heard in the village." She was at the bar, bruising pale silver and ice in a shaker. Mr. Ferris said nothing. He watched her. His sense of perception was as delicate as radar and he was in tune with her agitation.

She came back to him with a martini glass in either hand. She came all the way with her eyes on his, came up close to him, the glasses now held out from their bodies and giving them the look of a grotesque candelabrum.

"Tarl —" a whisper. "I'm so very glad you've come."

There had always been something about him that stirred her. He had the gift of individuality which sparks excitement by its intangibility. "Kiss me, Tarl."

He did, but stiffly, and she tried to melt him and he stepped back suddenly, precisely, and said, "Watch the drinks."

She stared at him, her mouth open a fleck of red showing in both pupils, still standing with the glasses out like branches. He reached and relieved her of one. "Later," he said flatly. "Let's talk of the money."

She turned abruptly and put the glass to her mouth, drank half the martini in one swallow. He watched her, remembering the time when she wouldn't be caught dead

"How do you know?"

"Everyone knows. It's all over the village." Her voice had an insistent edge. "He found it, but he won't admit it. Not to anyone."

"How do you know that?"

She looked around at him and her eyes were like shards of glass.

"How do you think I know?"

He did something slight with his face, a noncommittal shifting of his features. "Shad Hark?" he tested the name. "I don't know him, do I? Oh wait — no, that was Holly. Yes, I remember a Holly Hark. He went out with me in the skiffs a few times."

"He's dead," she said. "Lost in the swamp right after you left. Shad is his brother."

"Oh yes. He was just a boy. But of course by now he's a man."

She looked away from him. "That's right — a man."

"Is he the one you took under your wing, as I advised you to?"

"Yes, he's the one."

She walked away from him, going back to the bar. "Would you care for another drink?"

He looked down at his hand, remembering that it held an untouched martini. "No thanks. One is enough."

So it had happened as he thought it might. She'd found a stupid boy and made him her slave; had sent him boggle-eyed into the swamp to find that airplane, and lo—he had. But then something went wrong. Very wrong. She'd scared him somehow. And now he wouldn't admit it. Now he was trying to get away from her. And it wasn't the money so much that was killing her, as the fact that she had been rejected.

"What happened?" he asked.

" He's a stupid little swamp creature." Iris didn't look at him. She set down the shaker and put her hand around the stem of the glass. "He found the money, and now he thinks he can keep it all for himself."

"But what went wrong? Why do you think he didn't come and tell you he'd found it? That was the plan, wasn't it?"

"I don't know! How can I be expected to know what goes on in his abysmal little mind! He — he's —"

For a moment he thought she was going to smash her glass, and he felt a touch of superior disgust. She had always been a fool. And he had been a fool as well. He'd trusted her too much, but there hadn't been any help for it. You either trust a woman completely or not at all. There can be no half measures between females and trust.

"I don't want to discuss him," she said.

A silence tumbled between them as if they were afraid to speak, as if conscious, in an obscure sense, of an impending crisis. He knew that for a woman, passing the age of thirty-five created a compulsion of recklessness, a kind of helpless wild defiance against the approaching horrors of middle-old age. After thirty-five everything was down hill — a roller coaster hill going faster, faster, screaming into broken-down skin tissues, unmanageable bulges, greyness and decay. It was something a woman couldn't be expected to take graciously.

"That's rather absurd, isn't it?" he said finally. "I mean this Hark boy is the point of my being here. I feel it's imperative that we discuss him." She looked at him, a long, studied across-the-room look.

"You've never really loved anyone, have you, Tarl?" she said. "Never wanted anyone. Things, yes. But never a person." She paused, searching down inside herself for meanings, finding a clutter of old truths that she usually managed to keep swept back in a corner, but also finding herself in the corner with them.

"It makes our situation rather awkward, doesn't it?" she said quietly, absently amazed at her own new strength and reserve. "You see, I'm not sub-human."

He said nothing. He watched her. She came part way into the centre of the room, stopped.

Mr. Ferris realized that he was surrounded by the mysterious aura of femininity, and felt like a man lost in a fog and afraid to move because of unseen deadfalls.

Because they were playing a game over eighty thousand dollars, and because they were partners on the same team and partners must make concessions, he went to her with an odd little smile and let her swarm all over him, and put his arms around her.

"Tell me you love me," her mouth whispered. And her brain cried — Lie to me! Lie to me! He heard the stem of her glass snap behind his neck and heard the glass shatter on the floor near his feet.

Chapter Eleven

She didn't come to him that night, and he paced the cabin of the shantyboat like a hound dog on a chain in the spring. Each time as he went by the lamp his shadow would leap in front of him and run on to smear its exaggerated self on the bulkhead, then when he wheeled about the shadow was left helpless on the wall and it would have to slide down to the deck and slither after him, hurrying to bypass him and sweep on in the lead again, to beat him to the other wall.

God — was this why he'd given her the ten dollars? So she could go running off sassy and have herself a time? And him hanging around here useless and like an old paint rag hanging on a nail?

Maybe she went to show off to that Tom Fort in her new dress — maybe Tom was button-popping the back of that new dress right now. Maybe she was saying, "I got that money right outn him and it weren't no trouble a-tall, and I bet I kin git more any time I hanker to." And that Tom was saying' "Yeah, yeah. Shet up about him now, cain't you? I don't want we should talk about him now. Hold still there." And she'd giggle like she does and Tom would be —

Shad put his right fist into his left palm with a *splat!*

"I'm cold going at that Tom. I'm goan —"

But then he relaxed, dropped his hands, and grinned shaking his head, walked on chasing the shadow.

"What is it I'm going to do? Tom is probably long gone to his own bed — by hisself. Here I'm fixing to rugbeat him for nothing. Dorry's got hung up to home, that's all. Shore."

That Tom. He was all right. He'd just lost out, that was all. You had to pity a poor fella like that. It didn't do to go and beat him. No. But why didn't she come?

Overhead the moon was fat and gold-dollar proud, drifting high and handsome in the clear vastness of its night kingdom. It shed down a soft thin layer of silent grey snow, and the dark things of the nearby woods and the further-off swamp stood black and stark against the navy blue sky, and some of them were straight but more of them crooked, and none of them moved until a zephyr puffed at them, and then the larger ones merely nodded as though going to sleep, but the little things fluttered and trembled and some of the holly leaves winked dull silver.

The scut-shot gator was drifting bulge-eyed across the water, all but a few bumps of him submerged, going shopping. But a drifting flock of night-feeding ducks were suddenly and acutely aware of his sly approach, and they went streaming off into the star-night honking fear, leaving a good piece of the pond's surface broken.

The gator ruffled a grumble through his throat and big glassy black bubbles formed at his nostrils and popped on the surface.

Suddenly his flat head lifted, trickling water, and he merged his receptive senses with the night. Something was coming toward the pond — coming like fear, quick and brush-smashing. The gator slewed around in the water and looked at the pale ribbon of bank and the black wall of jungle.

A doe came crashing through the wall, skittering to a gawky-legged halt on the bank. It looked big-eyed in every direction, ears fluttering. Right out of nowhere a good-God panther came after the doe.

The doe reared sideways and made three sharp leaps, right-left-forward and gone. The panther scooted helplessly on its powerful hindquarters, head swinging, looking confused, snarling, and the doe went *spang* in the pond and started kicking toward the Money Plane, all neck and ears in the water and the little wet tuft of tail showing in the rear.

The scut-shot gator hurriedly made his preparations for the windfall. He closed his earflaps, dropped the transparent films over his eyes, and wadded up his tongue to close his throat. Then he submerged, waited.

The doe came plodding toward him, four stalky legs

moving rhythmically like pistons in the dark water. The gator froze still in the pond, watching the doe step weightlessly over his head, then his jaw hinged open and with a shove of his tail he shot forward and snapped.

The doe fought with its sharp hoofs all the way down to the mushy bottom of the black slough, but it didn't do any good. The gator's jaws were firmly clamped about the doe's middle. He waited until the doe went limp and then he knew it was drowned.

"You see, Mr. Ferris? You see it's right there in print. That air's the first ten dollar Shad gave me, and here's the number of hit on this paper you gived me. And look a-here, Mr. Ferris, here's the next two he brung into me this morning. And here be the one that Estee brung last night — which was sort of a set back to me, because Shad ain't never ben one to fool with no nigra, but —"

"Yes, yes, I see. They all correspond, don't they?"

"They shore God do. You think now that mebbe Shad went and give this here ten to his daddy? Old Hark he always is playing around with that Estee, but Shad is —"

"I don't see that it really matters, Mr. Sutt. The point is that the bills are showing up, but they weren't until Shad started passing them out. Well — is that all?"

"All? Well yes, I reckon so — no, now wait; Bell Mears has got him a couple. I ain't seen 'em, but I have heered that Shad give him twenty dollars to rent that old shanty-boat of his."

"Bell Mears? Yes, I believe I remember him. Well, all right, Mr. Sutt, I'll go and see Mr. Mears. I'd better take these papers with me to check the serial numbers."

"Well I'll tell you, Mr. Ferris; if you want to git a line on Shad, you best git in touch with Sam Parkes or Jort Camp. You remember Jort, don't you? Well, they ben keeping tab on Shad. Sam'd be the best bet. (He chuckled.) That Sam, he's shore hell fer snoopy."

"All right, and thank you. I'll check back with you later."

"Uh — well, uh — you fixing to take that air forty dollars along with you, Mr. Ferris?"

"Yes (smiling at the crestfallen face). They're evidence now, Mr. Sutt, and rightfully belong to the insurance company, you understand. But don't worry. As I told you four years ago — you'll be amply rewarded for your assistance."

"Yeah, yeah — but — uh —just how much you think that air reward will be worth, Mr. Ferris? In round figures say?"

Chapter Twelve

Jort Camp was sitting in a sumac bush just upwind of the Mears' privy. From his position he could watch the rear of the house, could see most of the clearing in the moonlight, and could follow the road coming and going. So why in God's name didn't something come?

He started to chuckle, reminded of the time the Doaks and Finneys were having their feud. Couldn't anybody remember now, was started the fuss, or how many had been killed, or what ramifications it had caused, or why or how it ever died out. The incident of the Doaks' privy laughed everything else concerning the feud out of the limelight.

The Finneys had attacked the Doaks' place one morning, and long about noon old Jim Finney had gotten all pepped up over some wild hair or another and had slipped up behind the house to burn the Doaks out. But Tully Doaks had seen him coming and Tully had a high-powered rifle and he'd cut loose on old Jim.

First off he'd put a slug through old Jim's right leg, and that had slowed Jim down a mite. Old Jim had went hobble-legged all over the yard looking for cover, and Tully whacking away at him like a kicked-over hornets' nest, and the only cover Jim could find was the Doaks' privy. In he went a'clump-leggin along like a schoolboy who's just had an accident in his pants and sees the teacher coming, and slammed the door. But the walls of that privy were only cardboard thick and wouldn't stop a windblown straw, and Tully Doaks knew it.

"Hi, boys!" he'd called to his kinfolk. "I got me old Jim bottled up in the privy. Let's pepper him some."

So the whole family had opened up on the privy, and they said that old Granny Doaks had laughed till she went into a stroke, and didn't anybody notice it till it was nearly too late, and Old Jim had laid in there on the floor among the corncobs and catalogues, cursin' and duckin' and nursin' his hurt leg, and pretty soon it got so bad there wasn't nothing for it but to rip up the two-seater board and climb down into the pit. And those Doaks' kept him there until nightfall, when he was finally able to slip out and crawl off into the bush. And even then old Jim's kin hadn't wanted to have any part of him for a couple of days, and Tim Finney had even suggested that they dig a hole and bury Jim neck-high like you do when a man gets skunk-squirted.

Jort laughed, his belly shaking around his belt until it hurt, and then he wiped his eyes and shook his head as if to say, don't it beat all? Don't it just? That Jim.

He settled down to business again, watching the house. The light in the girls' room was still on and the shade up, but there wasn't anything of interest to see now. Just Dorry in some kind of new dress, primping herself before the mirror. She'd been going at it for half an hour. It had been better a little while ago when she first came in and turned on the light — when she'd removed her old dress to try on the new one. Oh my yes, that had been much livelier. And wasn't it a caution the way that girl never wore her undies?

Old Sam had been corked off when Jort made him stay down at the backwater to watch after Shad. But it had to be that way because Jort knew Sam. The no-good woods colt would lose track of everything watching Dorry's window, and, too, there wasn't anyone who could trail a swamp man like that Sam. Shad was a tricky devil, but not tricky enough. Every time he made a move Sam would be riding in his hip pocket just as soft and unnoticeable as a bandana. That Shad.

It didn't seem too long ago, Jort reflected, when he used to meander by the schoolhouse and pause to watch all the young hellions scrapping in the yard during recess or lunch. One thing he always noticed — that little Shad Hark never lost a fight. And he had his share of them.

Jort used to lean on the schoolyard splitrail and watch the feisty little devils kick up a storm. He'd grin and chuckle and sometimes call encouragement to one or another of them, but never advice — that would be giving one kid an edge over another and Jort believed that each boy and man had to discover his own edge.

Aside one day, he'd said to Shad, "You ort a start learning you something about eye-gouging. You gitting along to fourteen now, and someday soon some big brawler is goan take after you fer keeps and not fer play."

But the overly tall, scrawny boy had shaken his head and said flatly, "I'm not fixing to damage nobody perm'nent. I make 'em say uncle and that's a-plenty fer me."

"Tough's an old boot, ain't you?"

And the boy, wiping at his mouth with the back of his wrist, staring blankly at the big man, had said, "Enough so's when you fix to come at me you best bring help."

And Jort had bellowed laughter and thigh-slapped himself, and said, "Bet I might at that." And the funny part of it was it had given him a premonition. Something out of the nameless future had told him he was going to mix with that boy someday and it was going to be hell on earth. So he'd gone on watching Shad fight his way out of puberty, and he'd waited, and he'd put it off. He didn't really know why because he knew he could beat him, and yet couldn't seem to bring himself around to proving it. And so Shad bothered him and always had.

Down under the birch and paw-paws and maple Sam Parks sat in cross-ankled restlessness. He was watching the squat black hulk of the shantyboat that never went anywhere in the weir-gurgling backwater. He'd been lurking there for three hours now, waiting for Shad to make a move, and though he was so fidgety he was fit to be tied and placed in a basket, his faculties were always greedy for signs, and there was an alertness about him so tense that at times he thought he could hear the weeds growing. And so, though there were only the thin lines of light where the shanty's shutters clamped to the frames, he detected just the sporadic flickering, and knew that Shad was having himself a pacing time in there.

Plain mad, Sam thought.

And that got him to thinking of Dorry, which made him mad all over again because Jort had put him down here in the slough to watch Shad, while he, Jort, sat up there at the Mears' place.

He fussed around and fretted and mumbled. "That Jort's always bossing me about like I didn't have motherwit of my own. And me that has to tell him what Shad's doing and ever'thing. And what do I git outn hit? That's what I'd kindly like to know? Nothing."

Well, things were going to be different. When he got his share of the money he'd be his own man. He wouldn't have anything more to do with Jort, not ever. He was tired of playing slave to the big bully. He was sick to death of the craven feeling that the big man's physical presence evoked in him. He wanted to stand on his own two feet for a change and answer to no man.

That was what he wanted and that was how it was going to be. But right now the air was humid and buggy and there was a colony of night-rambling ants on the prowl and they were pestering him to distraction.

"Gol durn antses!" he hissed furiously.

The door of the shantyboat opened, throwing a big block of white light on the afterdeck, and Shad stepped through it like someone magically coming out of the mouth of a furnace and went to the edge of the porch.

Sam forgot about the ants and the weight of the cross life had given him to bear. He rose to a crouch and became a statue-man, waiting. Maybe now he'd get some action. Maybe this was what he and Jort had been waiting for. But Shad just stood there a while; then he walked on back inside slamming the door behind him.

Sam sank back on his haunches and the ants with a groan. "Tain't fair," he muttered. "Tain't fair a-tall."

It was getting late. It was getting on to bedtime. Shortly, now she would have to take off the new dress and get into bed with Margy. And she dreaded it because she just knew that Margy was going to be an endless question box. She was going to want to know about the new dress, about the ten dollars. She wasn't going to settle for the story Dorry had given their parents about saving up her allowance. Margy knew better than that, much better. And she would keep at it and keep at it, there in the hot, muggy dark, and she wouldn't go to sleep until she learned, and that meant she would still be awake when Dorry slipped off to go see Shad, and she would want to know all about that too.

"Bother," she said, but then she looked at her reflection in the tarnished mirror again and saw how pretty she was and how beautiful the dress was and how well it fit, and she was pleased that it wouldn't have to be taken in at all, because, my goodness, a dress just couldn't be any tighter than this one — not and be decent — and she forgot about Margy and her nosy questions.

She pushed her hair all away from the left of her neck, bunching it along the right, and gave herself a side look, making her eyes soft and smoky, opening her overpainted lips and putting her front teeth together so that just the tops and bottoms touched — the way those pin-up girls in magazines did.

A muted knocking vibrated through the wooden walls of the house, and she looked at her own closed door, wondering, and heard the rasp of her pa's chair in the other room and a moment later the speak of the door opening, and then a murmur of voices minus words and meaning.

Dorry went to the door and put her ear against the panel. The result was unsatisfactory. She still couldn't pick out the words, but the tone of one of the speakers was definitely foreign. She raised her eyebrows and paused to adjust the dangerously low line of the dress about the burst at her breasts, and then opened the door.

Bell Mears had just given Mr. Ferris a split-bottomed chair, and as he'd been making his first preparations for bed, he suddenly discovered he was in his stocking feet, and it embarrassed him because he didn't want to give Mr. Ferris the idea that they were poor whites. Now he was blinking around confusedly for his shoes while Mrs. Mears was covering up very nicely, asking Mr. Ferris if he wouldn't have some coffee. And Mr. Ferris was smiling, saying politely, "Thank you. That's very kind of you." And so Margy was on her way to the stove to reheat the coffee, and her expression was blank except for that little suspicious frown she always made when anyone she didn't know well approached her.

But Dorry remembered Mr. Ferris — though she'd only been fourteen at the time — remembered him very well. She had never seen a man like him. He was something that had just stepped out of a magazine — one of those *Esquire's* they sold in the drugstore in Torkville that her ma would never let her buy, but that she looked at anyhow while her ma was browsing around the notions counter. There couldn't be another man in the world like Mr. Ferris. He was the type of man she dreamed of having for herself.

Mr. Ferris had just looked at Dorry — a quick, penetrating look, too quick for her parents to take offence —and was trying to place her in his memory, but without success. Good Lord — he'd thought they only bred ignorance, apathy and filth in the deep south. That girl was positively a Freudian study. And then, because he was a man who had full control over all the tributaries of his mind, he switched Dorry onto a siding.

"I shan't beat about the bush with you. Mr. Mears. I'm here to discuss one of your neighbours — Shad Hark."

Bell nodded wisely, said, "Thought so."

Mr. Ferris nodded also. "You've heard the rumours about Shad and the Money Plane then?"

"Couldn't help but hear'em, less I was stone deaf."

"And I understand Shad gave you two of those bills?"

"Yeah, last night he did. You want I should show'em to you, Mr. Ferris? I got'em still, right in my iron box in t'other room."

Mrs. Mears suspended her knitting needles to look over the rims of her glasses at Mr. Ferris. "You really think that Shad went and found him that Money Plane, Mr. Ferris?"

"It looks that way, yes."

She shook her head, looking down as the needles began hopping one over the other again. "Just don't seem possible. Such a nice boy and all. Always so polite and friendly. Just don't seem like the kind that would find other people's money and not give hit back."

"Well," Mr. Ferris said kindly, "he's young, and eighty thousand dollars is a lot of money. I rather imagine his thinking is temporarily confused."

Dorry was biting her lower lip. It wasn't until this moment that she realized what a wrench Mr. Ferris could throw in the wheel of her brightly spinning future. Mr. Ferris suddenly was no longer the suave, educated, middleaged gentleman of her dreams. He was a cold, methodical brain-machine — invulnerable to any attack.

"Will you put Shad to jail if'n you catch him with that money?" she asked abruptly.

"Dorry!" Mrs. Mears said in a fierce undertone.

But Mr. Ferris smiled. "Not if he's willing to turn it over to me. I'm going to talk to him tonight." He looked at Mrs. Mears. "I understand he's living on your husband's house-boat?"

Bell came back with the two tens in his hand and gave them to Mr. Ferris. "If them bills be off'n the Money Plane, do I got to give'em up, Mr. Ferris?"

"Temporarily, I'm afraid. But I'll see to it that you receive a worthwhile remuneration."

Bell said "Oh," and then "Yeah," and looked at his wife to see if she had the hang of the word.

Mr. Ferris brought out his sheaf of papers, spread them on the table and began checking the two bills against the list. Mrs. Mears tried to keep her business to herself and her needles, but Bell couldn't. He leaned over the table and asked Mr. Ferris "what that there was?"

"This is a list of the serial numbers of the money that was on the airplane when it disappeared four years ago. I've already found four bills that Shad passed out, and they tal-lied with this list — Yes, see here? Here's another."

Dorry felt very cold. Who would ever think that city folk had such sneaky ways to catch you out? Serial numbers! Then a new thought whacked her, shattering the brittle veneer of her respectability. That ten dollar Shad give me was marked. I went and bought this dress with hit, and now they goan trace it back to me.

She caught Margy's attention and imperatively gestured toward their bedroom. Margy let out a sigh of exasperation and stood up, frowning. She left the room. A moment later — her parents and Mr. Ferris studying the list —Dorry slipped after her.

She closed the door behind her and grabbed Margy's slender wrists. "Margy, you got to help me, honey. You got to do something fer me right now, hear ?"

"Let go'n me! You took leave of what little sense Pa'n Ma g
gave you?"

"You got to slip out and scamper down to the shanty-boat and warn Shad fer me. Margy — please. You just got to do it!"

"Dorry Mears, you lost your mother-wit? I cain't go do no such thing. Why should you want me to —" She lost the argument abruptly, staring at her sister, then at the new dress, and remembered the night before. The monitor of her mind began sorting facts into the proper slots. Shad had come to the house the night before and had given her pa two ten-dollar bills; later that night Dorry had slipped off to meet a boy; the next day she had bought a new dress in Torkville with a ten-dollar bill.

"Dorry," she said, "you knew last night that Shad had went and found that Money Plane, didn't you? He gived you that money fer the dress — stolen money."

"Of course, you little fool. Margy, please honey, I ain't got time to fuss overn hit now. I got to git back in there and find out all there is to find about what Mr. Ferris is goan do."

"But why? Why do you —"

"My goodness, Margy, cain't you understand nothing? Shad has that money hid out. When he gits it, him and me are going to run away with it. I want you should warn him that Mr. Ferris is here, that Mr. Ferris kin prove he's got his money outn that old plane, and that Mr. Ferris is coming at him tonight. Tell Shad to clear out a the shantyboat right now. Tell him to hide in the woods and to meet me by the old Colt place tomorry night at nine sharp. Margy — do you understand all that?"

"I don't want to understand it. You plain crazy to talk thisaway. Run off with Shad Hark. You fool, don't you know Mr. Ferris will git the law on you? Why, Dorry, you could end yourself in jail."

"Cain't you never do nothing fer me 'cept argue me to death? You the only one kin help me, and you got to! Mebbe I ben mighty and foolish in my time, but what I'm telling you now is purely honest; Shad'n me is running off with that money. I ain't goan let nobody stop me from that. Now you go on, and you go quick. I'm going back in there and pester that Mr. Ferris with questions 'til Pa whales me. Margy — I'll go on my knees to you if'n you'll do hit."

But she didn't. She opened the door and started through before her sister could get after her again. "Go on!" she hissed furiously. She closed the door, leaned against it.

Please, Lord: let Margy do hit. Let Shad git off'n the woods. Don't let Mr. Ferris take that money from him. I'll cold die without that money, I just will. I'll never git me outn this old slough-hole without hit. I'll just grow old here and fat and hank-haired, and git married to some fool like Tom Fort and breech litters and never have no fun ner pretty things — and Lord, I just beg you from the bottom of my heart to let Shad git off with that money.

"Yes," Mr. Ferris said, "that makes six of them. Rather conclusive, I'd say."

Chapter Thirteen

When the knock sounded on his door, Shad already had his boots and pants off. Hayday, he thought, she timed that right close, and excitement poured through him as he started for the door. This was what he'd been waiting for all day. This would wash away the bad taste of Iris Culver.

"Let me in, Shad. It's Margy."

He blinked. Margy? Why in hell's name was it Margy? Where was Dorry? Something's gone wrong. Something's cold gone wrong. He said "Hold on," and went back for his jeans. He was getting as jittery as a man with sow bugs in his shorts.

He went to the door and opened it, didn't say anything, just looked at Margy and then stepped aside. She came in barefooted and quick, and not looking at him after the first time. She stopped just inside the door and stared at the cabin as though expecting great changes.

"Dorry sent me," she said.

She appeared subdued to him, and as he pushed the door shut he sensed that his temper was growing unhandy.

"I didn't reckon it was your ma. Has anything happened to Dorry?"

She shook her head. "No. But Mr. Ferris is up to our place."

Now Mr. Ferris was here to plague him. Iris — Iris must

have phoned that damn Yankee after he ran out on her. No — couldn't be. Wouldn't be enough time for the insurance man to come that far. Who then?

"What's he doing at your place?"

"Come to check the money you give Pa. Got him a list of all the serial numbers of the bills that come from the Money Plane, and he's ben gathering up all of 'em that you've passed out like a drunk fool, and he knows thataway that you've gone and found hit."

"He's coo-coo!" Shad snapped automatically.

Serial numbers. That was something he hadn't counted on. The fat was surely in the fire now.

"Why's he coo-coo?" Margy asked. "Ever'body knows you found the Money Plane."

"Ever'body's got him a big mouth."

She looked at him challengingly. "Shad Hark — you goan stand there and tell me you *ain't* found it?"

"I ain't fixing to stand here and tell you nothing about it. You ner nobody else."

"But you did find it, didn't you, Shad?"

"Shut up on it." He turned away slowly, rubbing the back of his neck. "Where's Dorry?"

"She stayed up to home to keep Mr. Ferris busy while I come down here."

"Busy how?"

Her eyes sparked at that, and he liked the way she looked.

"I'll kindly thank you to know my folks is to home, Shad Hark," she said coldly. Shad grinned.

"Why you always flying off at me thataway? Did I ever pull your pigtails er something when you was little?" he wanted to know.

Margy looked down at her bare feet, then she looked at his beltline. "Dorry says you'n her fixing to run away. Says you got that money hid, and when you git it you'n her goan be long gone."

"She did, huh?"

That Dorry. Had everything figured out as nice as a dress pattern. Well, she was right, but was it safe to trust Margy? He supposed so, anyway, it looked as though he'd have to trust someone.

"Is that what you got against me?"

She looked at his eyes. "You're a thief. And now you're fixing to steal my sister."

He caught her wrist, not to hurt, but to give emphasis to his denial.

"You got no call to brand me thief 'less you know fer certain I got that money out a the Money Plane. And if your sis has it in mind to tag after me, that's her idee."

"Shad -" her voice was low, "you love Dorry?"

Love? Well, did he? He hadn't really thought about that, ever, about anyone. You always say "I love you" to the girls you get in the bull-grass and the hay, but they expect that, whether they believe it or not, because it's part of the game. You accept a brother like Holly just because he is your brother; and it was impossible to love the old man; and he'd never really known his mother. So who had he ever loved? He knew the driving something he felt for Dorry was a far cry from love, from the true meaning of the word. He'd learned that from the books Iris Culver had given him. It had baffled him at first, but later he'd begun to understand.

"Shore," he said. "Shore I love her." It didn't hurt to lie a little, did it? There wasn't any sense in getting Margy mad again, was there? And anyway, this something that made him hunger after Dorry — you might as well call it love.

"And you goan marry with her?"

Was he? He hadn't thought of that either, no more he bet than Dorry had. "Yeah. If'n she wants me."

Margy nodded, looking away, looking at the cabin again.

"Well," she murmured, "she's her own woman. I got no call to try and cut acrost on her. Got her an idee she wants out a this swamp, wants big things out a life."

"Well, you cain't blame her none fer that. So do I."

Margy said nothing to that. She said, "She wants you to meet her at the old Colt place tomorry night at nine. She says you to git out of here now because Mr. Ferris is fixing to come at you tonight. I guess that's all."

Shad looked around at the cabin. Funny, now that he had to leave he realized he was going to miss the old scow. It wasn't such-a-much, but it had its comfort.

"Look a-here, Margy, you see anyone tail you down

here? You see Jort Camp er Sam Parks about in the woods."

"No. Why should I? Why should they want to come after me?"

He shrugged. "Lots of them damn fools ben moseying after me all day. I kin shake'em when I want, but I just got a notion that Sam is tagging me like a man's shadow at high noon."

"Well, if he be, you'll never shake him. You know Sam."

Shad grinned. "You don't know Shad."

"Well —" she said, looking at the deck again. "Well —"

"Well —" Shad said, helping her look.

Now that it was time to say goodbye and there was nothing else to be said, they were embarrassed. He looked across at her without raising his head. She was a cute little thing. He reckoned that was the word for her. Cute. Perky nose, big-eyed, shy-lipped. Not a sex box like her sister, like most. And suddenly he had the absurd compulsion to put his arms around her; not to get fresh or gay with her, just hold her protectively; wrap her in cellophane and put her away for himself.

"Well —" she said, and she started edging toward the door. Shad put out his hand. "Friends?"

She looked up at him, her eyes enormous and very brown but not coquettish or shy. "Yes." And she took his hand.

"Thanks fer helping me — us, Margy."

She nodded. "You'll take care of her, Shad? You won't hurt her ner run out'n her? She — she's kind of flighty someways, needs have people help her."

"I'll be good to her, Margy. I promise it."

She opened the door but didn't go all the way out. She looked up at him. "Good luck, Shad," she said.

He watched her go in the dark, then stepped back and closed the door, stared at it for a moment.

"I'm shore God going to need it," he said.

There was no sense in hanging around waiting for trouble, because trouble waited for no one. He got out his carbine and wrapped it as well as he could in his denim jacket running the barrel up one sleeve, folding the rest right about the stock, trigger-guard and bolt action. Then he tied the lace of the right boot to the lace of the left and looped the clodhoppers about his neck. He cocked his felt hat on his head and looked at the cabin again. The old ball-dialled clock over the bunk was still holding its own, still proclaiming the time to be 5:32.

He shrugged, blew out the lamp and made for the door.

The lamplight still bright in his eyes, he found himself standing night-blinded on the porch. He closed his eyes, waited, and then opened them and looked at the backwater. Moonlight. That was going to give Sam a big edge.

He looked at the dark line of underbrush, backed up by the reaching black woods, and sensed the presence of Sam Parks, felt the woods colt's eyes boring out of the night. But the only way he could be certain was to trick him. You just didn't catch Sam off base unless you could surprise him, and that took some doing because Sam wasn't human in the woods.

Shad moved abruptly. He wheeled around the corner of the cabin, went quickly along the gangplank and out onto the bank, heading upslough. Git your walking legs out, Sam, he said. We got us some rambling to do.

Jort Camp saw Shad come off the shantyboat and knew he didn't stand a waddle-bottomed bear's chance of tailing him without Shad knowing about it within five-six minutes.

"Kin you holt to him?" he whispered to Sam.

The corners of Sam's lips punched into his cheeks like a cat's grin. "Shore's water's wet," he said.

"Then git. I'll double back on that air Ferris fella and see what he's up to. We got to keep him shed of Shad. I ain't about to have *him* walk off with that eighty thousand."

"See you back to your place," Sam said. He glided into his familiar crouch, feeling wildly elated now that there was action he could handle. The fidgets, the self-torture of his abject morality, all were left behind in the bush. Sam was all business. Quicker than a wolf could sneeze and recover he was gone.

Jort grinned. "Damn old fox," he muttered.

He'd been thunderstruck an hour ago when he'd seen Mr. Ferris arrive at Mears' place. He hadn't counted on that happening quite so soon. Now that Mr. Ferris was in the picture, he and Sam would have to look spry. That Ferris fella had come along to get the eighty thousand out of Shad.

And later when Margy had slipped out of the rear of the house and ran for the woods, Jort had understood that too, Sam had told him that Dorry had shacked up with Shad the night before, and that first thing the next morning she had run off for Torkville and had returned that afternoon in a new dress. Yeah, that took a lot of guesswork, he reckoned not. Now she'd sent her little sister down to the backwater to warn Shad about that Ferris fella. So Jort had tagged after her just to be sure.

And he had another idea going, maybe he ought to have a quiet little chat with Dorry Mears. It was just possible that hot little piece had already found out from Shad where he had the money hid. Yeah, and she could do it, too. It was shore God's laughter the way some fellas let a little bit of fluff drag 'em around on a leash.

Shad went along the bank for a while, then abruptly darted left into the bush, going at it in a running crouch. He went ploughing through the brambles with catclaws picking after him vindictively, disputing his passage; held to his course for nearly one hundred yards, then cut left again, dodging among the paw-paws, and crossed back on his own trail, coming to light under a tupelo bush where he could see the glimmer of the backwater through the shrubbery.

He held his breath, listened. Something was rustling the dead leaves off to his right but there was the sweet, pungent scent of mink along with it, so that was nothing. He gave Sam another minute and then shook his head. Nope. If Sam's out here, then he's already swung around in back of me again. Son-o-bitch is harder to lose than a tick on a doe's butt.

Far off a night-running hound cut loose and filled the woods with round-note blues. Then a pack joined him, and in a moment all the hounds were wailing as if they were going to be paid for it. Shad decided to put the baying to good advantage, to cover his own noise. He shoved up and went humpbacked through the bush again.

He came out on the bank and approached the weir. The leading-off silver shoulder of falling water was spilling in monotonous, uniform splashing. Shad stepped onto the ankle-deep rocks and started picking his way across, not too carefully. Gaining the far shore he went at the bush as though he meant business, as though he meant to be long gone. But he wasn't. He went twenty-some feet into the leafy darkness and then cut back to the screened fringe of the bank.

But three-four minutes passed and there was no sign of Sam or anyone else. Don't it just beat all? The little bastard's skipped up-slough and crossed where she shallows. Bet my money he's sitting five yards off laughing at me right now. He stood up and started north.

He broke into a fast run, skimming through chokeberry, catclaw and smilax, cutting up his trail, first right, then left and straight on, and then left again, and brought up panting and stumbling just where he wanted to be, in a boulder-deep glen lorded over by an old lichen-skinned oak. The oak had a hollow hide-hole and Shad had known about it since boyhood. It was just possible that this was one hollow tree in the woods that Sam wasn't acquainted with. He doubted it though, but it didn't really matter. He dropped to his knees and shoved the denim-wrapped carbine and his boots inside the black opening. Then he pushed up and got out of there fast.

He made a wide swing back to the weir, recrossed it and ran down the line of woods past the shantyboat. He approached the lake carelessly, hoping now that Sam would spot him; trotted out onto the beach and entered the water; walked in up to his chest and then submerged himself and started swimming blind.

The first shock of it on his shoulderblades and the back of his neck seemed as cold to him as a well-digger in the Klondike, but he held at it, swimming fast and froglike underwater, aiming in the general direction of a distant hummock he'd spotted.

He swung around under water and surfaced on the far side of the mound. It was a stick and silt-built affair rising a yard high. He pulled himself along in the water touching the prongy, sticky heap gingerly, and eased his head over the tapering hump at the north end. Beyond his back — two hundred feet on — was a projecting tongue of woodland. If Sam was in the bush somewhere, he'd expect Shad to make for that tongue. Shad stayed where he was, scanning the shore.

Suddenly he saw what he wanted — a slow, searching glimmer-pale object poked above the bushes and panned left to right and slowly back to left again. Hayday! He knew it all the time. There was old Sam, wondering where he'd got off to.

The object he took for Sam's head pulled down and was swallowed in the dark shrubbery. And there was nothing else. Shad grinned. The old fox. And him hating water the way he does, he thinks to cut around on me like he done afore in the backwater, and try to pick me up again on the tongue.

Shad pulled himself along to the south end of the hummock, filled his lungs with air and submerged. He set out in the black murk for shore, hitch-kicking soundlessly.

He touched down in a maiden cane bed and crawled into the shadowy pool sink that was the mouth of the bridge-creek. After that he had no trouble getting away under the cover of night.

But his rambles were far from over. He slipped down to Sutt's Landing and found that his skiff was still where he'd left it. And that was a load off his mind. Moving the skiff to a hiding place was the only reason he'd gone through all that business with Sam. He had to have the skiff in a spot where he could get at it quick.

He stepped into the skiff, cast it loose and pushed the end of the stub pole down into the muck and shoved off. He followed along the shore where he could use the pole, where he had the protection of the shadows, and worked his way on down to Horseshoe Lake, just beyond the Culver place. There he rammed the boat into a reed thicket, secured it to a breather with the painter, and slogged off into the woods again.

He had to go all the way down to the backwater and across the weir to get his gear and then return to the skiff before he could call it a night. He was really beginning to miss the shabby comfort of the shantyboat.

He was careful in the woods as he approached the old oak. He circled the glen twice before he deemed it safe to go on in. The glen waited cool, shadow-still. He squatted between two grotesque, moon-grey roots and rummaged around in the hide-hole for his gear. He pulled out boots and denim jacket.

For a moment he couldn't believe it. He clutched the jacket, twisting it, expecting to come up short against the ramrod feel of the carbine. Then he shook it, and then he felt along the left sleeve, and still not believing it, along the right. Nothing. He rooted in the hide-hole up to his shoulder and neck but all he could find were old mice skulls and bird feathers.

Shad squatted back on his haunches and shook his head. That Sam.

The new sun hung low over the swamp when Mrs. Taylor opened the door and stepped out on the porch. A saffron glare lay on the weed patch in front of the shanty and slanted on the road between the skinny trees. She could see Shad coming up from the landing, and heard Rival's insistent hiss right behind her, "You git him on in here. Go on now, hear?" And a moment later she heard the other door close, but she didn't look back. She watched Shad coming and hated it.

"Hi, Shad!" she called suddenly. "Where you going at this morning?"

The boy stopped short, startled, looking like he was ready to take off for the bush, and she wished he would. Then he grinned and came some into the yard.

"Just gitting up to Pa's place fer a spell. Got to see him about something."

She nodded, fussing nervously with the hem of her apron. "Bet you won't find much that goes fer a breakfast up there."

"Bet I won't at that — less hit's some corn Pa had left in the jug when he drunked hisself blind last night."

Well go on then, the top layer of her thoughts said, go to drink the blame corn. Don't make me bring you in here. She hesitated, a little trembly smile nearly lost in her beefy face and said, "Well, I just got some fixings left from last night. You're kindly welcome to that."

Shad said all right and thankee and came up the steps followed her into the shanty. Outside the morning had a touch of the chills and Shad, having slept the night in the

93

skiff in his damp clothes, felt as brittle as glass. The room was rosy bright and glowing warm from the fire in the limestone fireplace, and something was perking in the big black pot hooked to the end of the long swivel bar.

Mrs. Taylor put a plate down and said, "Set, Shad."

She didn't look at him and knew she should, but couldn't. She started mixing corn pone in the skillet watching what she was doing, wondering how to come at it, what to say exactly, and wishing Rival wasn't standing just ten feet away listening behind the door.

"When you going at that swamp again, Shad?" she asked suddenly.

Shad had just tilted back in his chair, giving himself a good stretch and yawn, and her question suspended him.

"Oh, I don't know. I ain't in no great hurry, I reckon."

"No," she said."I reckon not."

And then they said nothing, and they both sensed that there was a great deal to be said, and neither of them wanted to come at it. Mrs. Taylor put the hot pone on his plate and said, "I got some wild salat and sowbelly here."

"Don't go to no bother."

"Tain't no bother."

She dished up the mustard greens and passed him the vinegar, and then she sat down across the table from him. Shad ate, keeping his eyes on the food. He knew something was wrong — different somehow. There was a mouse in the meal, somewhere.

"Where do you usually go at in that swamp, Shad?" she asked.

"Up Breakneck way."

"Tain't much up thataway. Rival says Breakneck's all played out fer skins."

Shad talked around a mouthful of pone. "I try some other creeks too."

"Oh. Which ones?"

"I disremember."

He knows I'm fishing him, she thought desperately. And he's going mean overn hit. But she had to take the plunge for Rival's sake, her's too, because what belonged to Rival belonged to her — problems, pain, security, and a cussed little of that they'd ever had to share.

"I was wondering, Shad, if'n you wouldn't want some-body to go along with you in there next time; it so big and lonely and dangerous-some and all fer one man."

Shad looked at her.

"What I was thinking was that now Rival's got the manure started out in the south ploughing and has got him all the pullets weeded and is nearly done ditching that waste piece—" She couldn't seem to control her volubility now that she had started, and was aware that she wasn't really saying anything, but was only racing word after word in a frantic effort to screen her purpose, and was aware too that Shad realized it, and so she finished with a rush, " — he thought he'd go at that swamp fer a spell, too." Shad said nothing.

"And git him some skins," she added lamely.

Shad went *tsk* at his chipped tooth and looked at his plate again.

Why don't he say something? she asked. Why do he just sit there statue-dumb? "Rival's powerful good with traps, you know, Shad. Kin build him a deadfall like nobody — and he's handysome in the swamp too. A man like Rival would be a big help to you, Shad, and company as well, and — and we thought on him going with you because Rival says they ain't nobody knows the hide-holes of mink and otter an coon like you, and — and we could shore use that money, Shad — the pelt money, I mean."

Why cain't I shet up? Why cain't I just sit here and keep my big mouth shet and stop a-hammerin him with words? And why do Rival got to stand in there like a shaky hant just a-pantin over ever word I say, and me knowin hit, and Shad gittin all mean, and me feelin like a ma to him and wantin to mama him, but got to be a wife to Rival and stand by him and do what he says because he's the man of the family and hit's his job to do to support us, and the pore old fella all saddled with debt at Sutt's, and the land all fallow and not fit for raisin nothin except rocks?

Shad put down his fork and stood up.

"Yeah," he said stiffly. "I know what you mean." He looked at her. "But I ain't fixing to take me no partner."

She watched her fat fingers work along the apron hem.

"Well, I just thought it — being so lonely and all —Rival

needing some work and —" Her voice went off somewhere by itself and she abjectly let it go. The sowbelly and mustard green water went *ploop!* in the pot and she looked at it because it was something to do.

Shad dug into his jeans and brought out a fifty-cent piece and put it on the table by his unfinished plate. She looked at the money as though it were a slap in the face.

"I tolt you yesterday I didn't want no money fer breakfast."

Everything about him was still ramrod-stiff. "That was yesterday," he said. "Today I'm paying. See you."

But she couldn't let him go like that. She stood up quickly, letting the apron unravel out of her pudgy hand "Shad —"

He looked back at her, his eyes as friendly as two knot-holes in a planed board.

"Take care, Shad," she murmured.

"I aim to." And then he was gone and all she heard was his boots clumping down the steps, and then nothing.

She touched the table with the tips of three fingers, holding them there, as if her equilibrium demanded the tactile awareness of material things.

Rival Taylor opened the far door and came into the room. He was a rawboned man with a kinked up back from too many years of stooping; his hands were wide, brown and like scuffed-leather, made for holding tools, for gripping plough shafts, and they were too big and spare for his wrists. He scowled at his wife. "Why you done let him git away like that?" he wanted to know.

"I done said just as much as I could," she said, but not defensively. She was staring at the fifty-cent piece.

Rival put his oversized hands together and worked the palms one against the other. "Thought he was a friend of yourn?"

"I reckon he thought so too," she said softly. "But not now."

And then he went on the defensive.

"Well, damn-hit-all, hit seemed like a good idee, didn't it? Him having all that money out there, and us down to beans, and him being a good friend of yourn. Seems to me like if you'd *tried*, he'd a took me along and let me help him and give me a share. I ain't greedy. I don't want much. Just a little piece of her would a done. If mebbe you'd just gone about hit a little diff —"

"You goan plough that south field today?" she cut in.

He blinked, then did something with his head and face as though saying "Aw, what the hell." He nodded. "Yeah."

"Best git at it then."

He said "Yeah" again and turned away. He knew it wouldn't do any good to pick at her now. She'd freeze up and he might just as well go out and address himself to the privy door. He tramped on out with his back in a stoop, his big tool-holding hands open and hanging at his sides like an old pair of stiff working gloves waiting to be fitted to the next job.

Mrs. Taylor roused herself and went over to the south window, stood looking out at the fields. He'll make it yield, she thought, something, somehow, because it's a part of him. And it's a part of me, too, because he's my man. Mebbe that's wrong, mebbe we're a part of it; mebbe we're its property. And I reckon that ain't saying much — to belong to the land instead of the land belonging to you. Because, God, it's such pore, pore land.

Chapter Fourteen

S had left the road and cut off through the shrub. He started walking faster and faster, not really watching too much at what might be ahead but at his boots swinging out rhythmically one beyond the other.

A root in the ground came at him fast, and he snagged his foot on it, went lurching ahead for two-three yards trying to get his balance and finally gave his ankle a good twist. The pain shot into his stomach like sickness, and he looked back, shouting, "You goddam son-o-bitch!" and felt like going over and giving the root a kick, only his ankle hurt too much.

He gingerly put down his foot and tested it on the ground, pressed hard and grunted. It held.

"What surprises me is I didn't tear hit clean off, and it standing over there in the root and me standing here one-footed."

He went on, favouring the twisted foot some, and he thought about Mrs. Taylor, and the thinking left a bitter, ash taste in his mouth. Didn't think she'd go to do like that at me. Thought she liked me fer what I am and not fer what I might have hid away. Yes, oh my yes; he could see himself lugging old Rival around the swamp like a third leg with a clubfoot. He needed him like nothing. He didn't need anyone — except maybe Dorry.

He went along a split-rail fence, so old and tired it was trying its unlevel best to tumble down, and near to doing it, and beyond the fence and through the willows was the old, empty Colt place. A shell of a shanty, bow-sided and weathered and not enough roof left to nest an owl, squatting immobile and gape-windowed with sassafras sprouting all around.

He approached the old man's place in a circuitous manner, taking time and care in his investigation. He didn't want to go balling the jack right into Mr. Ferris' lap. He didn't want to meet anyone now — just Dorry, and to hell with the rest. He went on in through the rear door and it squeaked like a wagon at the end of summer.

The old man was on his bed, not in it. He was in his long-johns and he still wore his trousers, one worn and greasy suspender up, the other looped down around his elbow. His bare right foot was hanging off the bed nearly touching the floor. He was asleep on his back, his mouth open, and everytime he breathed the phlegm in his throat rattled like a page being torn out of a magazine.

There was an old wheel lock muzzle-blaster hanging over the fire board on the limestone fireplace, but that had belonged to granddaddy Pol and anyone who was fool enough to try it was risking a blown-off hand. The Harks had used it only as a decoration for as far back as Shad could remember. He went to the large woodbox against the south wall and raised the lid.

The dusty rifle was in there, and the lid slipped his fingers and went down with a *plam!* On the bed the old man said. "Whuah?" and stirred himself a little, his right hand wagging in the air alongside the bedboard as though he were trying to row himself away from the disturbance. "Whaas' at?"

Shad ignored him. He hefted the rifle. It was an old stock-scuffed Springfield, rust-splotchy along the barrel. He worked the bolt back and forth, finding it stiff.

The old man managed to get his elbows cocked behind him and he propped his head and shoulders up on his spindly arms. He looked at Shad, a bleary-eyed, whiskery-faced stupid look.

"Thet — thet you — Shaddy?"

"Naw, it's Estee, come to see ain't they nothing else handy around here she can tote off to that brood of hern."

The old man started wobble-necking his head to and fro. He'd had a rough night; he hardly even felt like arguing with Shad. He'd planned on starting his south ploughing that morning, but that no-account Estee had come down the road last night, and then he'd dug out his jug of corn and — and my-my, wasn't it something the way women and corn tore a man up? He reckoned he wouldn't do much ploughing that day — maybe tomorrow.

"Now, Shaddy, now — now it don't do to come at me thataway. I plain ain't myself this morning — ain't hit morning? Uh — I thought hit seemed right bright. I got me a head — got me a head like —"

"Like a kid's piggy bank with no sense in it."

" — like a great big old drum, and the hull world a-coming at me and a-lining up taking turn a-banging hit, and some of 'em not waiting they turn, and a-clanging me with sticks and clubs and cypress trunks and — Lordy me-oh my, Shaddy, I just *do* hurt." His elbow props slid out at right angles to his stovepipe body and his head sank down into the striped pillow that had never been inside a case and was grey and shiny from wear.

"I don't see no great difference there than any other morning in your life," Shad said. "Except that they usually beat you with pink cottonmouths and twenty-legged spiders." He went over to the cluttered hutch and rummaged through the drawers for some ammunition.

"Sha — Shaddy — wha' you after there?"

"Your rifle. I done lost my carbine."

The old man thought about it, blinking up at the rafters.

"My rifle?" and finally he got it. "Well — well, don' go take hit, Shad. I mebbe need hit."

Yeah, and Shad knew why. "Pa," he said, "if you ain't more careful about selling things, that Estee goan end up owning the hull shanty."

A hesitant slyness stole over the old man. "Well, if'n I had me some dollars I wouldn't have to go and sell things." He closed his eyes and looked like he was prepared to pass on to another world at any moment. "I could buy me some food and things what I need — if I had me another one of them ten dollars — Shaddy."

Shad said nothing. He was wondering if he should tell him he was leaving for good. He could just hear what the old man would say —

Shad smiled. The old man should have been a preacher, he could sure rip hell-fire into a fella. But his amusement palled, and he suddenly sensed an irrevocable loss. Standing in the centre of the shadowy room, where millions of dust specks danced in the blocky shafts of sunlight that rammed through the windows and open door, a realization came to him like the spectacle of a foundering ship. He watched it sink with a sort of detached fascination until it drifted to the bottom, and suddenly it had meaning for him.

This's the last time I'm going to see the old man, ever. He went quietly to the bed. "Pa — Pa, I'm saying goodbye now."

But the old man had drifted off again, and Shad had spoken low. I could give him a prod. I could speak up and wake him.

He stared at the rumpled old man who had gone halves in giving him life, at the dirty, foolish, hung-over old man on the filthy bed. Maybe it was better this way, unsaid. Maybe this was the only way.

Shad hefted the Springfield and walked on out the back door, across the yard and left the shanty where he had lived for twenty years, left the corn-sodden old man asleep on the foul bed that a cat wouldn't litter on.

The night came in sections. It came creeping across the fields and under the trees, stretching the shadows farther out until they joined and lost all shape and meaning, and then everything was shadow all around; and the trees and the bushes and the weed lost their colour and turned to black and grey; and the moon never stood a chance, because with the night came the swamp mist; and in the woods and in the swamp the little creatures fretted and twitched and sniffed, because now their scent would be damp, active, and everywhere danger waited.

And that's how it was with Shad.

He left the skiff when he decided it was eight o'clock. He took his time, staying clear of the fields and meadows and the road; picked up a path that led to the bridge creek and found some steppingstones to cross over. Then he entered a shadow-pool grove of sycamores. He stopped suddenly and looked back, listening. Something that had crunched the dead leaves behind him stopped also.

He stepped into the shadow of a tree. It couldn't be Sam because Sam didn't make noise. Might be Jort Camp though. He looked up at the black leafy terraces overhead. The swamp mist was crawling off like a sick man, thinning out, and the moon was trying to show. Well, that would help some. He didn't hanker to be rushed when he couldn't see who or what was doing the rushing.

He walked along the shadow of the sycamore to the next tree and put his back to it. The who-or-what was making a move again. He heard it first, crunching softly on dead leaves, then saw it. Ten yards off a man's head raised above the shrub. It gave Shad the absurd sensation that he was a little boy again alone a night in the woods.

"I see you there, Shad Hark," the man called. "I see you agin that tree."

"All right," Shad said. "You win the gold paper ring off the cigar." He straightened up and stepped into the lane. "Why you tagging after me, Tom?"

Tom Fort left the shrubbery and started toward Shad, but slowly, as though approaching a pitfall.

"Ben looking fer you since late last night," he said.

"That so? Ain't I the popular one lately."

"No call to git sassyfied, Shad. I'm fixing to do you a hurt."

"Why's that?"

"Because Dorry Mears is *my* girl."

Oh, tired Christmas. Here was something he hadn't counted on.

"Well, who ever said she weren't?"

"Dorry did, last night."

"Well, Tom, I reckon that's her nevermind."

"I don't give a damn-fer-Friday hoot what she says," Tom snapped. " I'm telling you *she's my girl!*"

Shad was becoming annoyed. "All right. Go to hell ahead and call her your girl. Don't mean beans to me. Go write you out a big sign saying 'Dorry's my girl' and wear it on your backside. I ain't stopping you none."

"You kin cold toot that again. I ain't fixing to take no back seat fer nobody."

"Thataboy, Tom."

Tom Fort shuffled closer. He held his left hand slightly in front of his waist, fingers spread, palm down. The right arm was back against his body, obscure in shadow. Uh-uh, Shad thought. He's either going to pop with a knife er a six-gun.

"Go on," Tom said, "laugh. I'm fixing to cut you up good."

Shad held up a hand, flat. "Now, Tom— Tom, you don't want no fuss with me."

"Can't whup you with my fists, so I brung me a friend along."

The moon broke through the mist and the clean blade of a long hunting knife suddenly winked at Shad.

"Now. Tom — I don't want no trouble with you."

"Think you own the goddam world, don't you?" Tom Fort hissed and he crouched, his left hand far out now for balance, knife-hand in at the waist. "Think because you found all that money you kin tramp high and handsome on who you please. Think you kin buy a fella's girl away from him."

Shad edged to the left, trying to work the moon around into Tom's face, where he could see his eyes, and know when it was coming. This is just what I need. he thought, Kabar holes in me. "Now, Tom — Tom, listen at me —"

"Well, I'm goan set your clock, Shad Hark. I'm goan cut you up so you'll *need* them eighty-thousand dollars afore any girl'll look at you twice without gagging."

He means it. The little son-o-bitch pure-out means it.

"Tom — will you shet up here a minute? Will you let me

open my mouth? Tom, if you stick me with that air Kabar, *ten* times eighty-thousand dollars ain't goan do me no good. And if you kin just stop acting as green as tobacco in a field, mebbe we can come at a deal here."

Tom Fort hesitated. "Huh? What deal?"

"The deal on eighty-thousand dollars. You knife-stick me and that money is gone to the world fer good."

"Well, I don't give a damn. I want my girl. That air money ain't doing me no good nohow."

Shad nodded. "Ner me neither, once I'm dead. That's why I'm saying we got us a deal here."

Tom straightened up a little. "You mean you willing to cut me in on hit? You meaning that, Shad?"

Shad put a hand to the back of his neck and gave it a rub.

"Well, now hold on here a minute. We got to look at it proper. I need help gitting that money outn the swamp and outn the county, and if you do what I say, we'll split hit plumb down the middle. Forty-thousand dollars, Tom. Forty-thousand dollars."

"Yeah —" Tom said. *"Yeah."*

"Course there's one thing we got to come at first."

"How's that?"

"Dorry's *my* girl."

Tom didn't like the taste of that. "Well, now hold on here, Shad. I cain't have me none of that. I love Dorry Mears. I ben fixing on marrying up with her."

Shad came in closer, wagging his hands impatiently, "Marrying Dorry!" He nearly wailed. "Tom, Tom, I'm fixing hit so's you kin marry a movie star if'n you see fit. Forty-thousand dollars, Tom. Not beans er cow pies. *Forty-thousand dollars.*"

Tom blinked and stalled. "Yeah —" he whispered. "Yeah. Forty-thousand dollars. Yeah. A man could — a man — Look a-here, Shad, you really do got that money, huh? Hit ain't just village talk? You really went and found that air Money Plane? You got the money hid away? Is hit hard to come at, Shad? I mean, we ain't got to tramp way out in that old swamp fer hit, do we?"

A cold realization came to Shad. This was the price of love. This was the boy who wouldn't sell the girl he loved — not unless the price was right. The little bastard. He was

103

no better than Jort Camp or Sam Parks.

"No," he said, "we ain't got us nowhere to tramp to."

And then he swept his left arm swordwise, catching Tom's knife-wrist with the edge of his hand, and he stepped in fast and brought his right swinging into Tom's stomach. The boy doubled up around the sunken fist, his head leaning into Shad, and Shad shoulder-butted him on the point of his chin, snapping him straight, and then landed his left square into Tom's middle again.

He rolled sideways, grabbed Tom's wrist, raised his knee and snapped the wrist over it. The knife plopped in the weeds. He stooped, grabbed it, and sprang away as Tom aimed a kick at him.

He took the knife by the handle and fired it out into the night and turned as Tom rushed him; swung himself clear with a left hook to Tom's ear, got his balance, and then went in at him again.

They closed with a grunt, heads hunched and necks fumbling, and slammed into an oak trunk. Shad saw Tom's eyes, bugged and wild, mad with hate.

"They ain't no money, hear?" he hissed, "I never found no Money Plane. You sold out fer nothing."

Tom didn't answer, He brought up his knee. Shad expected that and he rolled, taking it on the hip. Then it was his turn and he kneed fast and sharp, but he was turned off center.

They lurched apart, panting, watching each other circling in the moonlight. Tom touched down with his fingers, fumbling blindly through the weed for a root, a stick, anything — Shad stepped in and Tom spun off balance and went down onto his back with a slam.

He had the upper hand now; it was all his way. He was straddling Tom, whacking away Tom's hands with his left and slugging him with his right.

"*That's* because you love her so much, Tom — *That's* because you'd sell your goddam ma fer a dollar and a new Barlow — *That's* because you need a lesson you won't soon forgit in foxiness — There never was no money, Tom. I don't have nothin'."

It was over. Tom was out of it, way out of it. Shad lurched to his feet, gasping, nursing his aching right hand, hugging it to his middle with his left folded motherly about it. He stumbled around a bit, aimlessly, looking for his hat. He felt sick in the stomach, which was the after effect of the fight. The other sickness was more general and was only vaguely concerned with fighting. It had to do with money.

"You're rather good at that sort of thing."

The quiet voice startled him silly. His head jerked up, turning everywhere, and froze when he saw the man standing near him in the shadows.

"You're Shad Hark, aren't you? I've been looking for you."

Chapter Fifteen

Mr. Ferris moved and a spoke of shadow swung across his upper face, leaving his lips and chin corpse white, as though a spectre in the moonlight, when his mouth began to speak.

"I was coming along the creek path when I heard the rumpus. What was it all about?"

Stall, Shad thought desperately. Stall him. I shore God ain't in no frame of mind to play dodge-the-question with him. Mebbe I just better hit him and clear out. But Mr. Ferris didn't inspire physical fear, not as Jort Camp could and did; it was something stronger, more frightening — a kind of superstitious awe.

"Nothing much, I reckon," Shad said. "At least not to me. I guess old Tom hates me worse'n a possum hates a tree dog, though. Thinks I stole his girl."

Mr. Ferris said, "Oh?" and came farther into the moonlight. "What girl is that?"

"Just a girl."

"I see." Mr. Ferris put his hand casually in his jacket pocket and produced a pack of cigarettes. "Care for a cigarette?"

"No thanks."

Mr. Ferris looked down at the cigarette he was tapping on his thumbnail. "I've been looking for you," he said, "to ask about that airplane — the Money Plane."

Shad's heart had taken a lurch when Mr. Ferris had reached into his pocket. After all, the man was some kind of policeman, wasn't he?

"Mr. Ferris," he said too quickly, "you driving your ducks to a mighty poor puddle if you think I kin tell you anything about that air Money Plane."

Mr. Ferris' smile went a little deeper.

"Shad, there really isn't any sense in your trying to maintain this fiction with me. You see, I know that —"

"Mr. Ferris, excuse me, but I cain't talk about hit now. I just ain't myself. I think I done a terrible thing just now. I think I kilt Tom." He hadn't and he knew it.

Mr. Ferris looked up. "Killed him?"

Shad nodded, putting his hands together as though his nerves were ready to fly apart. "Yes sir. I think I done busted his neck. I didn't mean to. I was just fighting him back, was all. But when I left off his neck felt all out of whack." Mr. Ferris stared at him.

Shad looked at the prone figure of Tom Fort. "Mr. Ferris, please sir, you look, will you? I just cain't — cain't bring myself—" His head went down and he hugged his hands again.

There was nothing expressive about Mr. Ferris except his eyes. He stepped easily through the shadows toward the sprawled Tom.

"Are you trying to put something over on me, Shad?" he suggested quietly. "I'm quite certain that other than having a face like a raw hamburger, there's nothing the matter with your friend."

Shad waited until he saw Mr. Ferris' back, then he turned, took one big stride into the bush, ducked down and was long gone on his way. Behind him he heard Ferris call, "Shad! Don't be a fool!"

He didn't like doing it that way; it wasn't in his nature. But he couldn't help it. There was something hypnotic about Mr. Ferris' eyes that beat him every time.

The night and the woods hung still around him now. He trotted, saving his wind, short-cutting to the Colt place. A bat went wing-clicking on ahead and lost itself in the black leaves of the upper branches. Shad could just see Mr. Ferris talking to Joel Sutt—

I'm afraid we can't waste any more time playing around with that Shad Hark. Don't you have a sheriff or a marshal in jurisdiction over this section of country?

Well now, they's Pat Folley; he's over to Tanner. We kin phone him up, Mr. Ferris. Well, I think we'd better do that then. So you figure to put the law on Shad, eh Mr. Ferris? Yes. I don't know what else I can do. I really don't —

Shad stepped up his pace. Yeah, that's how it was going to work. Well, it didn't matter. He was going to make tracks anyhow. He didn't want any lard-head, pistol-toting law after him. And that Pat Folley, he'd as soon shoot you as smile; he'd done it to moonshiners before.

Dorry was waiting under the sagging porch roof of the old Colt shanty, and she'd been waiting for some time and she let him know about it.

"Why you do me thisaway? Standing me up like I was any old body. I ben waiting here and wait —"

"Shet up, cain't you?" he snapped. "I ben busy with your boy friend. He went to stick a knife in me."

"Who? What boy friend? My goodness, Shad Hark, you don't go to tell a girl anything. What—"

But he didn't want to talk about it. She was round and soft in the moonlight glowing nearly. "Just Tom," he said. "It was nothing. Come here, will you?" He pulled her to him, arching her spine and kissing her hard, while his right hand slid down the curve of her back.

She wriggled away from him, all elbows and shoulders, and tossed her hair angrily. "You behave yourself, Shad! Kissing me like that, and me all over lipstick and no mirror er light to see how my mouth looks afore I go home."

He grinned at her. "You ain't going home. Not no more."

She looked at him, wide-eyed. "What you mean?"

"Dorry, you love me?"

"Course I love you. Think I'd let you do the things you do to me if'n I didn't? What you mean I ain't going home no more?"

"We got to clear out a here, Dorry. If I hang around much longer I don't know who'll git to me first, Jort Camp, Mr. Ferris, er mebbe the hull damn village will come at me. Seems like ever'body wants to know where at's that money. So you'n me is leaving fer the swamp tonight."

For a moment she couldn't say anything. She just looked at him as if discovering he was crazy. *"Me?"* she wanted to know. "Go in that old swamnp? Why, Shadrack Hark, I wouldn't be caught dead in that spooky old place."

Shad nodded impatiently. "I know it ain't nice, but we don't have a choice. I cain't afford to come back here again after I git that money, just to pick you up —"

"Just to pick up me? Well, I like that, I *don't* think so. Let me tell you, Shad Hark —"

"All right, all right," he wagged his hands at her. "I didn't mean hit just like that. What I mean is I'll be loaded down with all them bills and how kin I come sashaying through the woods here to find you like that? But if you come with me now, we won't have to come back here a-tall. We'll just kindly go on our way with that —"

"No." And she started shaking her head, not looking at him. "I ain't going in that old swamp fer love er money."

"Oh God," he said. "Yeah, but look here, Dorry —"

"No." And the head-shake.

Shad shut up and looked at her. He had a pretty fair idea just how much good it was going to do him to go on arguing with her.

"Uh-huh," he said. "And suppose then I decide not to come back fer you after I git that money?"

She slowly rolled up her eyes, giving him the look that went nearly everywhere except straight on, and her smile was a smirk that could mean a lot of things but none of them decent, and her voice was pure honey.

"Oh, you'll be coming back. That's one thing I ain't in any stew over."

Yeah. And how far would he get arguing that? He didn't even try. He grinned and reached for her again. "Dorry — Dorry —"

"Shad, this ain't the time ner — aw *Shad* — aw Shad *honey* — Now just hold on, Shad Hark! Not down there in all that dirt and ruck. My goodness!"

Those boys. She'd seen timber wolves that weren't near so crazy. But it was going to be nice, real nice, like nothing else she'd ever had. First off she was going to get one of those Natalie Renke silk outfits in the leopard print, because the ad in the magazine said they captured a primitive mystery in exotic design; and she might just have her hair tinted auburn like the girl in the ad too, and shoes with the open toes and made of—

"Goddam, Dorry," he complained. "You act like you wasn't even there."

She moved toward him. She put her arms around his neck again.

"I was just thinking how it was going to be, Shad. That's all."

"How what's going to be?"

"You and me and our life together."

Yeah — if he could live through it.

"Well," he said, "I best git shagging. I got my skiff hid out and I got to leave while hit's dark."

The thought of all that money suddenly so close to her, almost within reach, was overwhelming. "You be back tomorry, Shad?"

"God no, you think I got it hid on some hummock in the lake? Tonight I'm just goan take me to the head of the lake and then git some sleep. Tomorrow morning I'll go on in there; but I'll be lucky if I git back by the next morning. And then I got me to wait around in the bush until it gits dark afore I kin come fer you."

For a moment she was almost sorry she hadn't said she'd go with him. She would see the money two days before. My goodness — "Well, the sooner you git started the sooner you git back."

"Yeah." He looked at her in shadow, feeling the hint of something lost. "Look here, Dorry, want you should do me a favour." He dug in his jeans and brought out his roll of tens. Dorry stirred closer.

"I ain't goan see my old man no more — so you take one of these tens and give hit to him, will you? Tell him hit's from me, and tell him I'll send him more later on."

She took the ten, its tactile crispness sending a thrill of excitement through her, and watched him put the others back in his jeans. She really didn't see any reason why he shouldn't leave those with her as well. They weren't going to do him any good out in that old swamp, were they?

"All right, Shad. I'll tell him."

He looked at her and compulsively ran his hand over the

smooth melon bulge of her left breast, where it threatened to spill over the rim of her blouse.

She pushed his hand down impatiently and said, "Now, Shad, don't you go to start that again. My goodness, we'll never git that old money if you keep fooling your time away."

He looked at her. "All right, sugar doll, but Sally Brown never treated me thataway."

Instantly she was jealous. "Who's she? Who's Sally Brown?"

"Just a mulatto gal I knowt once."

"Well, Shadrack Hark! The idee of comparing me with some dirty little —"

Shad laughed. "Hit's just a joke, Dorry. Honest Injun, that's all. She's just the girl in the old song."

"Well —"

"You goan kiss me goodbye?"

"Well, I suppose." But she wasn't really mollified, and he knew it when he kissed her. Her mouth was nothing. Some day soon, he thought, he would have to swing her into line. She had a disposition like a bobcat dipped in boiling water. "Well —" he said.

"You git back soon's you kin," she said. " I'll be waiting to home."

"See you," he said, and he started for the woods.

"You be careful, hear? You take care, Shad," she called. And then — "Shad, you got something to tote that money in?"

The stillness of the night was like nothing around Dorry. She was unconscious of it. She strolled languidly through the pale phantoms that the moonlight threw on the road, head down and humming softly thinking of herself at a dance; the fiddler's fingers adroitly highstepping over the violin's neck, the bow dipping and rising and swooping, making the box sing, alive; the caller all Adam's apple and mouth and red silk shirt, beating his right foot on the platform, doing a vertical sashay with his right hand, his left in his pocket jingling change — I wish I were in the Dutchman's Hall! Lowlands, lowlands, hurrah, my boys! All the girls whirling by, skirts a-swirl; herself in her new dress, light of leg and tappy toe, cakewalking like a queen.

Away in the distance the palmettos were ebony silhouettes, and closer in a hooty owl challenged her but didn't really seem to care, and she didn't even realize he'd asked. Through a stand of oak saplings she could see the sombre black shack where old man Hark lived in drunken befuddlement, and her hand made a small fist around the crumpled ten-dollar bill.

Now it was just plain foolishness, she rationalized, to go and give good money to that disgusting old man who was never sober enough to remember to button his own pants. My goodness, if a girl didn't watch her pennies she'd end up in rags and barefoot like any poor white, and where was the sense in that she'd like to know. After all, something might happen to Shad in the swamp — or maybe someone else had found his money — or maybe someone would take it away from him. And ten dollars was ten dollars, and right now it was a bird-in-hand.

Her lacquered fingernails dug into her palm, and the bill was as captured as a coon in a drop-trap and had as much chance of getting away.

She went on down the road, humming the play-party tune, secure in the self-righteousness of personal conviction.

Two shadows separated themselves from the woods and stepped, dark and ominous, into the road before her. Dorry stopped with a jolt and her heart went *whunk* in her throat.

"Well, look a-here what we come at, Sam," Jort Camp said.

"Yeah," Sam murmured. "Yeah." And he began edging to the left, gradual and smooth and inhuman in movement.

She started to turn back, and with a flicker of motion he had her by the left arm and his fingers were like damp narrow bones in her bare flesh. She caught her breath and raised her fist to hit him, and then Jort had that arm and she saw his teeth white in the moon and she was being lifted from the road, and before she really knew what it was all about the black shadows of the woods had closed over her and she was standing with her back to a tree and Jort Camp and Sam Parks had her fenced in.

"What's wrong, Miss Dorry?" Jort asked. "We didn't go to scare you none, did we?"

Sam was fidgeting, dry-washing his hands, shift-footing himself like a horse in a stall, husking air through his mouth. "No — no, we don't want to scare you none," he whispered, and he tentatively reached for her arm to sooth her.

She jerked back as though he'd offered her a lizard.

"What you want with me, Jort Camp? I got nothing fer you."

"Oh, now that's where you're wrong, Miss Dorry. Be dog if you ain't. I got me a fat type idee you know something *I* want to know: and I'm God sure you got plenty that old Sam here wants. How about that, Sam?"

Sam giggled as though he couldn't help it. She was all dark in the shadow and reminded him of an unbelievably beautiful coloured gal, and her dress was all crinkly sounding when she moved.

"You leave me alone, Jort Camp. I'll — I'll sic my boy friend on you!"

Jort seemed interested. He straight-arm leaned himself against the tree, bringing his big face within six inches of her mouth.

"Who's that, Miss Dorry? Huh? Old Tom are you talking about?"

She didn't say anything to that.

Jort shook his head in a reflective manner. "No. Laugh at myself fer thinking so. Hit would be Shad Hark, now wouldn't it be, Miss Dorry? Yeah, I reckon it would be old Shad. Sam, don't you reckon it would be Shad?"

Sam's eyes were busy. He mumbled, "Yeah — yeah," absently.

"Tell you how it be with Sam and me, Miss Dorry," Jort offered. "We got us a fat old problem. We don heered about all that money Shad got hisself and we was thinking mebbe you could tell us where he's got it hid at."

"I don't know nothing about that money. I don't know nothing about Shad neither. And I'm goan tell my pa you holding me here, Jort Camp, and he'll cold come at you with his shotgun."

"Yeah, yeah, we'll worry about that later. Let's talk about Shad right now. You know — the fella you shack up with down to the shantyboat."

"You hush your dirty mouth, Jort Camp!" The tears were

starting to come now.

"What you hiding there behind your back?" Jort asked. "What you got in your hand back there — a play-pretty?"

She forgot about crying. "That's my nevermind."

"Let's have us a look." He caught her wrist and twisted her arm out of the shadow. She winced and said, "Don't—"

"Hayday," Jort whispered. "Looky here, Sam. A ten dollar she got here. Now I wonder where that come from?" He glanced at Sam. "By juckies, Sam. Will you kindly remember we ain't here to play peek-a-boo! Don't you see what this means? Shad must a just give this to her — er — yeah — er she knows where at he keeps hit hid."

"Well, where's that?"

"Dunno. She might a ben coming from the old Colt place. Yeah. How about that, Miss Dorry? That would be a good place fer Shad to hide his money, wouldn't it?"

She shook her head, panicky now, trying to wiggle her arm free from Jort's bear paw. "I don't know about no money! He ain't got none. I got that from my ma!"

Sam clawed the top of her blouse. "You tell us, you little devil! You tell us right out where he got that money hid!"

She jerked violently to one side, the blouse tearing, her left breast bobbling against Sam's hand. "You — you dirty little —" And she screamed, twisting and striking at him. "Shad!"

Jort grabbed for her hair, but missed as she ducked down pulling herself free. "Shad!" Sam's lips snapped wide from his clenched teeth and he swung at her backhand, clipping her hard across the mouth. Her head whipped away from the blow, slamming into the tree trunk, going *thonk!* against a knot, and —

The stars were suddenly glazed and brilliant like splintered ice and they were spilling into her eyes, and the fiddler's fingers were cakewalking furiously over the violin's neck, and the bow was leaping and squeaking and all the bright dresses were flashing by and twirling away with the stars and her dress was torn and that's the last thought she had.

Sam stood agape, watching her tilt slowly and stiffly away from the tree, leaning right at him, her eyes wide open and staring at his, filled with a glassy awe. He leaped aside with a gasp as she toppled past him. And then she was down, all of her and all at once.

She lay in a great opaque swath of moonlight.

"Sam, *Sam*," Jort whispered.

Sam's head jerked. He looked at Jort.

"Jort — Jorty, is — is she — she ain't —"

"Shet up," Jort squatted down and looked at the pale, still girl. "Dead as a mule-kicked tad," he muttered.

Sam was drying his hands at his sides, wagging them up and down witlessly. "No — no — *no*, Jorty! All I done was to try to stop her squawking. I didn't hardly — I only —"

Jort got up and came at him fast, grabbing one pipe-stem arm to give it a shake. "Stop that ruckus! We ain't got time fer you to have a case a hop-about fits. She's cold dead and that's that."

Sam went limp, dropped to his knees by the dead girl, his left arm still cocked grotesquely in Jort's hand. "Oh, God, oh my, Jorty — I didn't mean to do her. I didn't, Jorty. She was so young and soft and —"

Jort gave the scrawny arm another shake. "Will you stop yipping about her? We got us bigger fish to fry."

"What'll they do to me, Jorty? What're they goan do to me?"

"Neck-swing you, if you keep a-going like a chicken with a gator egg up her box. Now git away from that, Sam. *Sam* — you hear me? We got things to do."

Sam looked up and caught Jort's pants leg with his free hand. "Jorty — you goan help me, Jorty? You goan stand by me?"

"Well, I ain't got no choice, and me one of them what you call 'ems —'complice. Now here's what we're a-doing Sam. I'm going to pick her up and tote her, while swing on ahead and see do the woods be clear. We'll tote her down to my skiff."

Sam's head was bobbing like a marionette. "Yeah, yeah. And then what do us do, Jorty? And then what?"

"Why then we haul-tail out'n the swamp."

Sam felt a shiver tremble through him. He hated the swamp at anytime; but he nodded. "Yeah — and weight her down in a slough."

Jort looked disgusted. "No, we don't do no such fool

thing. You think I want the first butt-nosed gator that comes along to haul her back up again? No, we takes her way out to a sink-hole I know of. Hit's big and hit's just as soft as fresh cow pie with quicksand. And what goes in there don't *never* come up again."

Sam looked down at the dead girl. He didn't hanker any going out into that old swamp at night, but if it would save him from being neck-tied with hemp, he'd cold go at it like he'd been born there. Already he was feeling better. The claw crazy bobcat that was inside his chest was starting to relax a little. Everything would come out clean as long as Jort handled it.

Jort was staring at Sam, and all of a sudden he started to grin.

"You gaddam wood-colted little idjut!" he whispered. And then he began to laugh, and Sam went panicky, hissing, "What? What's wrong with you? What you meaning?"

He swung Sam up and around, and Sam felt as helpless as a checker piece being moved to a new position on the board. Jort gave him a flat-of-the-hand prod in the back. "Git to snooping," he ordered.

Sam went off like a deaf mute lost in a fog, his equilibrium running down a hill that wasn't there. He squinted at the darkness as though he didn't recognize his surroundings, but all he was really seeing was that new dress — pale white in the moonlight, pushed up and crumpled.

Genesis

In the Silurian ending was the swamp.

The sea made it and it was everywhere. The earth buckled, mountains reached up, land as soggy and porous as wet sponges spread out, and the sea drained back to its ocean basin and never returned. The weeds and plants, abandoned in this abrupt manner, cast about desperately for substance, and settled for the next best, the in-between of land and sea, the marsh; and the world was warm and damp and green, and the swamp stretched from Greenland to Antarctica.

One period followed another and each in turn brought something new—the arthropods, the amphibians, and the plants learned how to develop seeds and breed them on the wind, and this reproduction created land food. The Permian days came in with a slam, with the Appalachians and the Urals, and inland waters receded; ferns, rushes and plants died and covered the earth in huge rotting clumps, swamps drew in on themselves and glaciers crawled across the land, and everywhere the swamps were doomed; but no yet, not for a few million more years.

The Indians came and felt the soggy earth and it trembled, and they were superstitious and gave it a name, and when they went away they left a legend; and the white men followed and found the grave mounds, found the legends and the superstitions, and saw where it was written that the Great Spirit had sent his son down to earth to teach the red men right from wrong. And they said, "Why, look a-here — them Injuns had them a Jesus." But they didn't really believe it, because God made the swamp and *He* wasn't an Indian, and went away scoffing and spread some superstitions themselves.

And the swamp continued to rot and to wait for the end, and everything was as it had been in the beginning.

PART II

Chapter Sixteen

S had left the lake in the dark brittle hours before dawn and stobbed his way upriver, working close along the high silt banks, and when the sun winked over the far away pines and cypresses it found him approaching the true swamp.

The river narrowed, the banks fell away into a greyish black morass, and the tupelo and scrub oak were replaced by titi and laurels. The cypresses towered up from their swollen boles that sat on wet, spindly legs and fluttered their grey mossbeards. They stood rank-and-file as far as the eye could see, and everywhere cast their green reflection across the face of the mirror-tarnished slough. The poisonous breath of the swamp waited like an invisible barrier — as sharp and commanding as a wet hog pen on a rainy day.

He worked the skiff up an inlet, heading for Breakneck, poling quietly with a touch of caution, like a cross-eyed man trying to find his way in a delicate house of mirrors, uneasy about disturbing the sleeping giant. But it wasn't really sleeping. It was more, he decided, like a mute monster gaping at him, absently wondering why he was foolish enough to deliberately enter its trap.

He entered a long narrow, dead-still lake and drifted for a bit, letting the pole drag. The sad cypresses reached such extraordinary heights, and the jungled vegetation entwined with such fierce and ardent vitality that the sun could only find the swamp floor in white shafts. It lay like great slabs of light among the shadows.

This was Breakneck, and it always reminded Shad of a great deserted cathedral.

Evil he'd heard the swamp called, by those who had been in it and those who had not, and they were right. But it had always struck him that it was a purely beautiful form of evil.

At the north end of the lake was a tongue of land, giving the place its name, and beyond, a network of tributaries formed. The slough nearest the west bank was the one he wanted — the water course that would lead him back to the Money Plane. To save time he shipped the pole, sat on the thwart and used his paddle, and began cutting across the center of the lake.

A swallow-tail kite was tracing aerial patterns in the sky. It held a struggling lizard in its talons and was taking lunch on the wing. When it spotted Shad in the skiff it swooped down in an effortless dive out of pure curiosity and whanged past his head, totally oblivious to danger. Shad ignored the bird, other than to realize he was hungry himself. In the bow of the skiff he had put a blanket and a large tin box containing his knife, a box of kitchen matches, first-aid kit, and three or four cans of food. When he reached the Neck he would land and treat himself to a feed.

There were more of the stumpy bays now, and paintroot

and hurrah bushes, and the palmettos were thicker than the head of a new broom. The water shallowed, the bonnets and pickerelweed and never-wet leaves began clustering about the skiff, and he changed back from paddle to pole, stood up and balanced his body against the give of the boat and the heft of the stobpole. He worked his way around the Neck and entered a great secluded palm bog.

The towering battlements of vegetation seemed to roll up and over him like a great fiberous wave, and the mass of branches, leaves, creepers, festoons of moss threatened to squash anything as puny as man. He stobbed patiently through the maze, ducking and weaving as the trailing creepers came slowly at him. After he had his lunch he would pick up the trail he'd blazed and be on his way. He grinned as anticipation jacked up his spirits.

"Money Plane," he whispered, "I'm cold coming at you."

And right then someone called.

"Hi. Shad! You ben looking fer us?"

Shad nearly lost the stobpole. He turned, crouching, the skiff wobbling dangerously underfoot, as everything in him tightened into startled suspension. It was like watching the mainspring of a nightmare coming at him to see Jort Camp and Sam Parks pole Jort's big gator-grabbing skiff out of the greenery.

He was one of those men about whom lesser men like to boast as though by merely exhibiting their knowledge of him they have a claim on him, on his astonishing powers, though in secret reality they are scared to death of him, and probably hate him as well. But he was the type of man whom little, vicariously living men (like Sam) can create legends around. And Sam and his breed have done well by Jort.

You come into the county thinking you'll visit Sutt's Landing to see some real swamp folk, and right off one of Sam's breed will try to impress you with the legend of Jort Camp —

You ever heered of Jort Camp where you come from, stranger? Jort Camp? No, I can't say that I have. Is it an army post or a person? Is hit a — well, I should hope to hoppin God hit's the most stupyfyin person you'll ever meet! Oh? Well, who is he? Who is he? Who is he! Why he's the biggest, bestest, toughest, brawlin'est, gator grabbin, bobcat-beatin, cadaver-maker you ever see! That's who he is! And you say, "Oh," and though you don't really believe that he is the biggest of all these wonders, or necessarily the best, your subconscious automatically forms a picture of Jort Camp and you decide that you definitely don't care to meet such a person.

But the Sam Parks type of man clings to your elbow and continues to dangle the legendary Jort Camp before you. He tells you that Jort can pick up a whisky barrel an drink it like you'd drink a bottle of beer — a pint bottle, and that Jort can walk a ten-foot gator out of a moras with one hand tied behind his back and a rock in his right shoe, and that Jort once took on the four Keeley boys singlehanded, and three Keeleys having knives and Jort having nothing but an old length of tire chain, and WHANG! BANG! ZIP and CLANG! and Keeleys all ankles-over-appetite, and Jort a-standin, there not even breathless and the length of chain hangin' in his big fist, and him shouting, "Well good gawd aw-mighty, is that all the fightin' we goan have? I ain't even got my arm unlimbered!" And that what was even more important (nudge, nudge in the ribs) was that Jort had had every girl in the county over fourteen, and that the daddies over to Crow County best watch out because Jort was star-tin' to cast his eye in that direction, and — and say, stran-ger, I bet a purty you don't got no man like Jort Camp where you come from, now do yer?

And you say, "No — no; no one like that at all." And you head back to your car rationalizing that you don't really have the time to spend visiting Sutt's Landing, just to see some 'real swamp folk' in their natural habitat. And if your daughter gives you any guff about it you shout, "Get in the car and shut up!"

Jort knew his own legend (he should — he'd helped it with a story or two from time to time), but he didn't really believe in it any more than Shad did. He was a fun-loving, loud-mouthed bully boy. But he wasn't a fool. But still — where there was smoke—

He *was* big and tough, and he loved to fight, and he'd never yet met the man who could lick him. And when it came to drinking — well, look out, boys! I got me a hollow

119

leg to fill. And that fight with the Keeley boys wasn't just all talk either. It's true that only two of them had knives, and there wasn't really four Keeley's in the fight because Joe Keeley had been so drunk he'd passed out before anyone started swinging. But Jort was willing to bet that Shad would never come out of a fight like that top dog.

And girls now — well say, that had always been his speciality. Well — maybe some of 'em had had to be coaxed a bit, but they'd always said yes sooner or later. Yeah — let Shad sneer at the legend of Jort Camp if he dared. But let him try to build one half as big for himself. Just let him try.

Sam was sitting forward with a 12-gauge across his lap; Jort was standing aft working the pole. He was grinning like a fat boy over a surprise birthday cake.

"You didn't go forgit we-all was goan gator-grabbing together, did you, Shad?" Jort called. "We missed you at the shanty, so we come on out here on our lone. Pure luck running into you thisaway."

So that's how it was going to be, Shad thought. They were going to play cat and mouse with the Money Plane. But still it didn't make sense. They had known he was long gone from the shanty, and in order to get out here before him they must have left the night before. Why?

He glanced at the Springfield on the floorboards but decided against it. Sam was too jumpy a man to startle, and a 12-gauge could scatter an awful lot of space. The safest course would be to play along — seeing that Jort wanted it that way — and wait for a better break. He tucked a smile in his face.

"Jort," he said, "I'm God ashamed of myself. I pureout forgot about us going gator-grabbing. I left the Landing night afore last to come out here."

Jort's big skiff came alongside Shad's with a *thuuump*, and Sam reached a scrawny hand for Shad's gunwale. But Jort seemed right at home.

"What was your big rush, Shad?" he wondered, folding his huge hands over the butt of the stobpole and resting his chin on them. "Looking fer more skins?"

Shad nodded as though none of it meant a damn to him. "That — and looking fer Holly's body as usual."

"Oh yeah," Jort said quietly. "Pore old Holly." He looked

120

up and around at the green roof crowding over head. "Right easy place fer a man to lost hisself in," he observed. "I got to go nearly halves with Sam on my gators just to git him to come out here with me."

Sam, hearing his name, started.

Shad stared at him. "Something wrong, Sam?"

The little man flinched again. His head didn't come quite around as he said, "Huh! No — no they ain't nothing a-tall wrong."

Jort was offhand. "Sam don't cotton to this air swamp much. Git him out a the woods and he feels like a Georgia hick in a cee-ment city."

"Why you bring him?"

Jort's smile was wry. "Tell you, Shad. I'm some like Sam here, and not a bit like you. I don't take to being out here alone myself."

Shad nodded. "Hit's not so bad," he said. "If you know where you're going."

"Yeah." Jort said, looking at him. "That's what counts. Knowing where you're going."

Sam was restless. He wiped his hands along the sides of his pants, pulled at his upper lip, and hunched first one way on the thwart and then another. He swabbed the front of his buckteeth with his tongue; didn't look at anyone when he suddenly spoke.

"Well, we just goan set us here all the blame day?"

Jort looked at him, his eyes narrowing. "No," he said thoughtfully, "we're just waiting fer Shad to show us the way."

That was getting closer to the brass tacks, Shad thought. Too God close.

"What size gator you got in mind, Jort?" Shad asked innocently.

Jort stared at him fixedly for a moment longer, then started smiling. He was enjoying this. This was what he'd been saving for nearly fifteen years. He could feel the payoff of the premonition coming and he sensed that he would get more pleasure out of it than from the ultimate discovery of the Money Plane.

"Oh well, I'll tell you. Shad. I need me a big daddy. That's where the money is. But I don't want no old devil that's goan tear up the hull shop like a bear with a hurted paw. You know what I mean, Shad?"

"Yeah," Shad said.

He stared at the water reflectively, not thinking of Jort's gator. The thing he didn't want to do was to get too far removed from the vicinity of the Money Plane.

He looked up, looked across the slough to the palm bog, where all the known and the nameless little creeks meandered into Breakneck. He thought the one he had his eye on was the Money Plane creek. If he could only get closer he could be sure — could find his blaze mark. There was a patch of cypress breathers at the mouth of the creek that looked like a natural fish weir, and he thought he recognized the landmark. But there was nothing trickier than a landmark in a swamp.

He nodded at Jort. "You ready to ramble now?" he asked. "I know of one old daddy up Lost Yank way that's near ten foot. He's a loner and easy got at."

"He ain't likely rambunctious, be he Shad?" Jort wanted to know. "I ain't fixing to git myself gator-et, thank you kindly."

"Naw, he's wore-out. No vinegar left."

Jort grinned. "I don't look forward none to the day *we* peter out like that, eh Shad?"

Sam trembled suddenly, the tremor running through his entire body as though he were strung together by wire and under the automatic control of a master hand.

Shad looked at him. "What's wrong, Sam?" he asked. "Cold?"

Sam's head jerked as though Shad had struck him, and his voice leaped out fast and high like a wood duck taking off in startled flight. "No, I ain't cold. How in hell could I be cold out here?" He wiped at his face with the back of his wrist.

"Take hit easy, Sam," Jort said softly, and because of a certain quality in the big man's voice, Shad looked at him sharply.

Jort's great moon face swung back to Shad, frowning and smiling at the same time, and he tilted his head slightly, directed at Sam's back. That meaningful look of bewildered amusement was asking wordlessly if Shad didn't agree that

Sam was a caution.

Shad said nothing, but he didn't like it. There was a snag in the line somewhere, he thought. They've done something and Jort's afeered Sam'll kick over the bait can. He planted his stobpole deep, ready to shove off. But Jort said, "Why'nt you leave your skiff here, Shad? We kin all fit snug-like in mine."

Shad shook his head, not looking around. "Uh-uh. I like to keep hit handy." He shoved down on the pole, hard, sending the skiff abruptly into the slough.

Looking around a moment later he saw they were following close in his wake; Sam sitting forward with the 12-gauge, chewing his lower lip with his overbite, averting his eyes quickly when he saw Shad looking; Jort standing massive and sure in the rear, stobbing with one hand, the other tucked carelessly in his hip pocket.

Shad sent an underbrow look at the tangle of cypress knees that suggested a weir, and then turned the bow of his skiff into Lost Yank Creek.

"I tell you them Cajuns is crawly eaters. They eat snails, and snails is crawlies," Jort Camp claimed.

"Naw they ain't neither. A snail ain't a crawly," Sam said peevishly.

"Well, hit myself if they ain't! Shad, ain't a snail a God shore crawly?"

They were sitting in a canebrake that fronted Lost Yank Creek; only the creek had thinned out to a guzzle that a good spit with a little breeze behind it could span. They had stobbed up Lost Yank for two-three miles and had beached their skiffs in the early afternoon. Shad had picked up his knife and lunch and was starting for the Springfield when Jort had made the first move to show that the cat-and-mouse game was drawing to a fast close. He'd stepped hastily through the ankle-high water from his skiff to Shad's, beating him to the starboard gunwale by a fraction of a second.

"No need in us overloading ourselves, Shaddy," he'd said, and his grin had been affable enough but it hadn't reached his hard little eyes. "I ain't fixing to *shoot* me no gator, you know. Got to take 'em alive, else they ain't worth mud."

Shad had hesitated, watching Jort's eyes, wondering if this was really the moment both he and Jort had been waiting for. Then he'd glanced over his shoulder. And there was Sam standing on the bank by the bow of Jort's skiff, holding the 12-gauge in both hands, his trigger finger inside the guard, but not quite pointing the barrel at Shad. So Shad had scratched at the corner of his mouth and nodded. "All right. Suits me."

And he'd sloshed up to Sam and pushed on by him without a glance.

He'd led them to the gator's cave — a hole in the creek bank under a sycamore bole — but the old bull wasn't at home. Then they'd crept a little farther into the marsh to a shallow cypress pool where, Shad claimed, the gator liked to take the afternoon sun. But he wasn't there either, and so they'd crossed over the stream to hide and wait for him in the canebrake. And then Jort and Sam had started arguing about bugs.

"Ain't a snail a God shore crawly, Shad?"

"Well, I don't know." Shad gave it a little thought. "You cain't say they really crawl like bugs do, because they ain't got no legs — kind a squish and slide like a snake."

Jort pointed a commanding finger at Shad. "Well, but you say a snake *crawls*, don't you? You don't say a snake comes a-squishing, do you? Bet your butt you don't! Snails is pure-out crawlies, and anybody goes to eat 'em is a goddam crawly eater, like I said."

Sam said he didn't know about people being crawly eaters, but he knew too damn well that the crawlies were "people eating" him. He slapped at his face and missed a gnat, and then gave the back of his neck a slap.

Jort was pulling the makings from his pocket, and he grinned and said, "Perk up, Sam. Nothing's ever so bad hit cain't git a little bit worser." His eyes slid to Shad. "Take Shad here," he offered, "Bet when he first found all that money he reckoned he had him the hull world by the tail." Jort came to a dramatic pause like an act with perfect timing.

He shook a thin window of golden Durham flakes in a creased wheat-straw paper, leaving a slight depression in the middle, brought his thumbs up, rolling the inner edge

in and over the tobacco as forefingers flapped the outer
edge over and down. He ran his tongue along this edge,
crimped one end and tamped the other with a matchead.
He put the cigarette in his mouth and thumbnailed the
match aflame.

Shad didn't move.

"Bet hit seemed just thataway, huh Shad?" Jort
prompted.

Shad thought about the knife in the back of his belt. He'd
have to get Jort first. The 12-gauge was bad, but Jort was
worse. He looked around, his expression flat, sizing up
their positions. Jort was hunkered down a yard from his
right; Sam was squatting six feet away, half-facing him.
He'd have to make a full-armed sweep at Jort's chest with
the knife, and piledive Sam at the same time. "You talk like
a man with no sense, Jort," he said.

Jort stared back at him, the smile still lingering on his fat
face. "Shad," he said evenly, "you lying hard as you kin go.
You think fer a minute we don't know what you and Dorry
Mears was up to?"

Sam flinched. His eyes went all twittery, blinking rapidly
at Jort, at Shad, down at the shotgun in his lap.

"Ain't no sense you a-mean-eyeing Sam thataway, Shad.
Every'body knows about you'n Dorry." Jort folded his
hands behind his neck and gave his back a stretch.

"And," he added casually, "they ain't no sense that I kin
see in you gitting yourself busted up like kindling over hit. I
reckon they's enough fer three."

Shad looked at him, tensing his arms. "How's that?"

Sam's quick eyes caught the nearly imperceptible tighten-
ing in Shad's limbs and it was the last straw for his nervous
system. He went straight up in one movement like a jack-
in-box, stepped back a pace or two and swung the gun barrel around. He stared at Shad, a little bit of his pink tongue
slipping slowly under his overbite.

"That Sam," Jort said and chuckled. "He's hell fer
spooky, ain't he?" He studied his trembling friend for ten
seconds, as though he had nothing better to do. "Look at
him a-standing there, Shad. Straight enough to be used fer
a post, huh? Bet you could drive him like one too, and him
that skinny. Only he's got him that air scatter-gun and he

knows a thing er two about firing hit off. You folly me there, Shad?"

Shad pulled a grin into his cheeks. "Better not take that kind a bluff into a poker game, Jort. You'll kindly lose your money. If Sam kills me — ain't nobody goan find that old Money Plane."

Jort seemed to be appalled at the idea. "*Kill you,* Shad? My, my, what kind a fellas you take us fer? Ain't nobody said nothing about *killing* folks. But, Shad, you ever seen a fella try to run away with his legs all blown to Billy-be-damned by a scatter-gun?"

Suddenly Sam's skinny frame tightened into listening attention, then his head whipped around and he ducked behind the maiden cane.

"Something coming," he whispered.

Shad got his eyes off Jort and looked across the creek. The palmettos beyond the cypresses were rustling, and just before they burst apart the three men heard gator-grunting. The old bull waddled out of the palm bog and down to the sandy bank of his private pool.

He was all gator, ten foot of him, and the armour on his back was so dense he looked like a many-horned monster from a primordial age. He lumbered along with the peculiarly embarrassed gait of a gator out of water and fetched up alongside a long dead log that sloped from the bank into the centre of the pool. He raised his snout and the two excretory ducts under his throat discharged the God-awful musky fluid from his glands. Instantly the air all around the pool became tainted with a strong, sickening odour.

Shad looked at Jort "You still game?" he asked.

Jort blinked at him. "Huh?"

Sam cocked his head in alarm. "Hey, hey," he whispered rapidly. "We ain't got us no time fer gators now."

Jort glanced around at him as though annoyed by the distraction, then looked at Shad. "I don't reckon we'll be needing that air gator-money now," he said.

Shad nodded as though he'd found confirmation of his suspicions.

"I didn't reckon you'd go to tangle with him after you once seen him. Big, horny-looking old feller, ain't he?"

Jort's eyebrows puckered down at the bridge of his beefy

nose. He blinked at Shad's profile. "What you mean?" he snapped.

Shad turned a sardonic grin. "I always heered what a slam-bang gator-grabber you was; but I notice you never bring back but little five-six-seven foot fellas."

Jort wet his lips. He studied Shad's eyes for a moment "You saying I'm skeered of that big bastard?"

I've hooked him! He'd rather spook me with a show of muscle than find the Money Plane.

Aloud he said, "I don't see you busting your hide to go at him."

When Jort smiled thinly his face looked dangerous. "Yeah, you sly fox, and you know *why* I ain't going at him. Why do I need him when I got eighty-thousand goddam dollars waiting fer me?"

"What eighty-thousand dollars?" Shad asked.

Jort's face pushed in at him.

"Shad — you honest to God think I cain't make you tell me where that money is hid?"

If I've guessed him wrong, Shad thought grimly, he's goan pull me inside out like a coon goes at a gunny sack with corn at the bottom.

His left hand scraped together a damp clump of sand. It was the best he could think of. Maybe he could get it in Jort's eyes before Jort made contact with those gator-grabbing hands of his.

"I told you once," he said, "that if you ever decide to come at me — you best bring help."

Everything inside of him slipped into strained suspension. He watched Jort's eyes.

Jort stared at him, a flat, contemplative look. Then he grunted, started smiling, and pushed back on his haunches. He continued to watch Shad from his new position as he began unbuttoning his shirt.

I was right. He cain't help himself from showing off.

Sam couldn't believe his eyes. He pick-picked at Jort's sleeve. "Jort — Jorty, what you fixing to do?"

Jort smiled at Shad, almost fondly.

"Sam, you just tag along with the scatter-gun. Shad here's got hit in his brainbox I cain't grab me nothing but pint-size lizards." He flipped a huge hand at a coil of rope nearby in the weed.

"You fetch the rope, Shad."

Jort raised on his knees and looked over the cane. Across the way the gator had crawled out on the fallen log and sprawled himself on it for a siesta, his little stumpy legs hanging down on either side, his forepaws just touching the placid surface of the pool.

"I'll lead the way with the slipknot," Jort told Shad. "And you folly behind with the fag end. If I miss his snout, then I'll have to go at him bare hand. You coil the rope in and stand by, see?" Shad nodded.

Jort grinned and jerked a thumb toward Sam.

"I know you ain't planning no tricks while I'm busy gator-grabbing, because I know you ain't gone and forgot that chuckler about the feller trying to run with his legs blow all backtail-to."

Shad nodded, smiling. "I ain't forgitting."

"Let's go then."

They crossed up-creek and came slipping silently down through the palm bog to the pool. Jort was in the lead, carrying the business end of the rope. Shad tailed him with the rest of the line coiled in his right hand. Sam was some yards behind with the 12-gauge.

Jort stopped just where the palmettos screened the pool and straightened up, bringing his hands akimbo. Standing just behind him, Shad had to marvel at his massive bare back. It looked as big and hard and formidable as a moonshiner's still. The son-o-bitch was purely put together with horseshoe nails and the ends cinched over, he thought.

Jort and Shad eased through the palmettos, Jort passing the fronds to Shad so they wouldn't whip back; and then they went tippy-toe down the shore to the uprooted bole of the dead log. Jort looked around at Shad and raised an eyebrow. Shad nodded, meaning Go ahead — he's asleep.

Jort whispered, "Deep?" And Shad shook his head.

"Under three feet," he lied. Out in the center, he knew, the pool shelved to a good six. And it wasn't the first lie he'd told Jort. The gator was old but he wasn't worn out. Shad had seen him fight a young burly bull about a month before. What little was left of the young gator was now stinking up a bog about a quarter of a mile down-slough.

128

Jort took in breath, shook out the slipknot and started wading cautiously into the pool. Shad shifted after him.

A man can move only so far in water without making a noise a sleeping gator will hear, and Jort was doing pretty good at it. So Shad let his end of the rope drop—*spoop!*—

The gator snorfled, elevated his head and started to swing it around. Jort wasn't waiting for more. He lunged forward — foot-falling into a hidden sinkhole — toppled sideways against the log — said, "SON-O-BITCH !" an reared up and forward again.

The gator tried to do two things at once — tried to get his great body turned around on the log to see what was coming and tried to get his jaws open. His hindquarters slid off the far side of the log with a splash; his paws were scrabbling furiously against the wood. It was a mighty awkward way for a gator to enter the water.

Facing him across the log, Jort swung the loop at his snout, but the old bull whipped his head back and shoved his horny body to the right.

"I'll be damned !" Jort bellowed. He let the rope go and vaulted over the log after the gator.

Shad started reeling in the line, watching Jort and the gator thrashing through a welter of white and brown water. A Jort arm and leg, a gator paw and end of tail swung out of the water, flashed, and then it all went under again. Instantly Jort's head, soused and wild with water, shoved up and he shouted at Shad. *"The rope!* Goddam—" And he ducked under again and Shad saw the white-plated belly of the gator glint in the sun as it broke through the surface.

Sam was having a dancing fit on the bank.

"The rope, Shad! *Git in there with the rope!"*

Shad blinked. "Yeah —" he breathed. He heaved himself over the log and sank to his thighs in the churning water. And right then he was in the middle of the damn thing. Something cut his legs out from under him and he crashed, face and shoulder against the log and felt himself slipping down— and couldn't get footing anywhere.

His brain went all to pieces screaming, "Hell no! Don't let that big son-o-bitch" — and somehow he was on his feet again and a good yard away from the log, and that great armored tail lashed up, and he ducked, and the tail came down like a cannon shot, and then Jort's burly shoulder slammed against his hip, and one of the gator's paws clawed his denims, and that damn Sam yelling, "Jort! Jorty — hold'em, boy! Git in there with the rope, Shad! Ain't you never —"

When that gator wasn't trying to smash Jort and Shad to mush with his tail, or trying to clamp his jaws on one of them, he was trying to get to the deep water. And the only thing that was stopping him was Jort Camp. He got the bull around the chest, lifted him with an agonized gasp, and threw him over backwards and into the shallows. The gator flipped right side up while in midair, saw Shad slipping and falling in the water and slammed his jaws at him.

Jort went after the gator in a wild piledive, landed ful-bodied on its back and wrapped himself around and hung on. *"The rope! Goddam you, Shad ! Git his goddam snout with the rope!"*

The gator rolled, its tail spanking along the broken surface. Shad stepped back quickly, pawed water from his face, and looked down at the hopeless tangle of rope in his hands.

"Sam!" he shouted. "For God's sake *come help us!* I don't know what to do with hit —"

"God a jaybirds, Shad! His snout! *His snout,* boy!"

"Come in here and help me, you son-o-bitch! Don't just stand there like a goddam fool! I'm all end over rope!"

Sam made a helplessly frustrated gesture with his right hand, his face all a-squint and mouth-twitching, and came wading into the pool, holding the 12-gauge high.

"Git the loop shook out there — the loop —" Sam wagged his hand in the air. "Wait'll Jorty swings the snout up again — Jort! *Jorty! Look out, man!* You near to damn put my leg in his mouth!"

Shad step-sloshed backwards in the water hurriedly, getting himself a pace behind the frantically screeching Sam. He looked dow at the man-and-gator battle. Jort had a tiger by the tail —

Shad winced and rammed a flat hand blow into Sam's narrow back. The woods cold shot into an all arms and legs bellyflop, dragging a scream of terror after him. Shad turned and went high-stepping it for shore. When he looked back he saw pieces of Jort, gator and Sam all hurly-burly in the pool.

He ran all the way to where the skiffs were beached, heaved Jort's gator boat free of the mud and shoved it out into the creek, then got his own off the bank and piled over the bow. He stobbed out of the cane and pickerelweed, prodding Jort's skiff with the pole now and then to keep it ahead of him until he had it in mainstream. There a slug-gish current gave it a quarter-turn and started herding it down the creek.

Shad dropped on the thwart, breathing fast and thick, and grinned after the big skiff.

Something was coming God-awful fast through the pal-mettos and laurel bays. He looked back and saw a great chunk of glistening flesh ploughing the brush. For just a moment — because of the muscular bare chest, the swing-ing thigh-thick arms, the wild-on-end hair, and the eyes that should have belonged to someone in a madhouse — Shad thought he was seeing vividly Holly's last minutes in the swamp; and something, maybe only the sense of a cold loss, maybe the apprehension of premonition, touched him and he shivered.

Jort came through the last of the palmettos and planted himself spread-legged in the mud. He wiped at his face and stared out at Shad. Then both of them heard Sam's wild passage through the marsh. He was making more noise than a bull moose going to a cow.

Jort's head snapped around and he bellowed at Sam. "Go find that goddam scatter-gun!"

"But — but, Jorty, *it's underwater.*" "Good God, I *know* hit's underwater!* Git it!"

Jort looked back at Shad, then at his skiff that was drifting lackadaisically dowstream.

Shad grinned. "I wouldn't count much on using that shotgun, Jort," he called, "Them shells'll be swoll up like a dead doe's bladder."

Jort nodded. He was rubbing his right fist in his left palm.

"Reckon you're right Shad. Reckon you put it over'n me this time."

Shad had to laugh. "Say, Jort, did you git a chance to see old Sam when I shoved him right down the gator's mouth?

He looked about as happy as man being flung down a privy."

Jort chuckled his great naked belly jerking up and down. "That Sam," he said appreciatively.

Shad looked over his shoulder. "Reckon you'n Sam will have some foot rambling to do afore you come up with your skiff. Mind the cottonmouths now."

Jort nodded again. "I'll keep'em in mind."

"See you," Shad called.

Chapter Seventeen

"Yeah," Jort murmured. He watched Shad stob his skiff on round a bend and start north on the main artery of Lost Yank. Then he was gone and Jort looked down at his hands. "Yeah — I'll see you."

He didn't do anything for five minutes. He stood there in the warm mud and stared at the water until Sam came slogging back with the 12-gauge. Sam dropped right where he stopped. He felt like yesterday's newspaper left out in the rain. He gasped and moaned a little and looked around at the cane and palmettos.

"What we goan do now, Jorty?"

Jort blinked and looked down at him. "Do? We got us a lot a things to do. Got my skiff to go git first off."

Sam's alarm perked up. "Where is hit? Did that Shad go and —"

"Shet up. Hit won't go far. They's no end a log litter below here. Mebbe we might have to spend the night out here but that's all."

"Well, I ain't taking me back in no slough water again, Jorty," Sam said with conviction. "I tell you that right out." He stalled for a moment, his eyes slipping sideways to a hurrah blossom, but not really seeing it. "Did you see that gator's mouth, Jorty?" he whispered. "Did you see them stobpole teeth?"

Jort's pouchy hips jerked sardonically. "I shore God must a. Eight times I had my head down his throat. And that Shad said he was wore out. *Some* wore out."

"Yeah," Sam muttered. Then he trembled. "Why did you have to go to mention Dorry in front of Shad?"

"It don't matter. He don't know nothing about her."

"Well, I don't like talking about her is what. I keep hearing the noise that sinkhole made when we dropped —" His voice shut off and he trembled again.

Jort grunted and said, "Never mind about that now. If we cain't find that skiff, then we got to find us an islet. I ain't fixing to spend the night in no marsh."

Sam nodded and sighed. "Guess we just ain't never goan see that Money Plane now."

"You gone coo-coo?" Jort wanted to know. "We just made our last mistake when we went to stop Shad down at Breakneck. From now on we got us a plank and we're going to be God-busy nailing hit down. First off we're goan find my skiff; then we'll hustle back to Sutt's Landing and git us some more shotgun shells and pick up Shad's carbine from my place, and stock up the skiff with some eats."

Sam cocked his head curiously. "Why we doing all that, Jorty?"

Jort looked exasperated. "Why? Well, I'll tell you why. Because Shad is right now on his way to pick up his money, is why. And when he gits hit, he's going to come lam-tailing down to the Landing to git Dorry Mears — *he thinks.*

"Only you'n me is going to be waiting in Breakneck fer him, Sam. And this time they ain't going to be no hanky pankying er passing the time a day with Mr. Shadrack Hark. We goan blow holes in him, Sam. And we goan take care of him like we done with that girl. And then you'n me is goan take off to some *cee*-ment city with our cash and see how do other folk's live."

Sam's head nodded slowly, absently.

"Yeah," he murmured. "Yeah. That's what we goan do."

Jort put his fist in his palm and rubbed it. He looked around at the wild splendor of unrestrained and endless growth.

"Hell of a place, ain't it?" he commented matter-of-factly.

In the stillness of swamp hush Shad went up Lost Yank until he saw an opening on his starboard. The breach was between two pine islands and it was a water-lettuce prairie. He grunted with satisfaction. It was what he wanted — a cut-through to the Money Plane creek. He stobbed the skiff to the edge of the thick green carpet and started in. Within twenty feet he knew it wasn't going to work.

He shipped his pole and went over the side. The water and lettuce rushed up to his lower chest and stopped. He grabbed the painter and started hauling.

An hour later he was still hauling.

By six in the evening he had crossed three creeks, had climbed back into the skiff and explored each one of them for a mile down, looking for his markers. He hadn't found anything he could say he recognized. Each time he would return to the broad belt of water lettuce and start hauling the skiff east.

"Well," he said to himself, "I'll find it in a minute here."

But the sound of his voice was incongruous with the vast stillness and he looked up with a start. The sun was sitting on top of the trees like a red hot disk. He knew he wasn't going any farther that day.

He hauled the skiff, bow first, onto a pine island and made a fire on the beach with lightwood. He was Godawful hungry but his stomach had to wait until he'd gathered enough firewood to see him through the night. He wasn't about to go looking for wood in the dark. It was a warm, miasmic night and the cottonmouths would be out frog hunting.

He made a broad circle around the crown of the island, gathering lightwood, and then took a swing along the shore on his way back. It was there in the muck that he saw the water-filled depression that looked like a track.

It was—a timber wolf's track. He made a sharp little sound between his teeth and shook his head.

He hurried back to his camp. And after that he didn't make a move without first picking up the old Springfield.

The night folded in like a navy-blue blanket being drawn over the chin of a weary, golden-whiskered old man, and an osprey's shrill cry sent spine-tingling echoes against far-off cypresses. Shad finished his beans and counted his tailor-mades. Six left. He went *tsk* with his teeth and wished he'd brought his makings along. But he rolled up in his blanket and treated himself to a smoke anyhow. What the hell; tomorrow morning he'd find the Money Plane, and that evening he'd be a back at Sutt's Landing. Yeah.

He dropped fast into deep sleep and foundered there for a few hours, and then slowly started drifting upwards again and into the flickering imagery of dreams —

The swamp was smoking. A sort of ghastly whitish jelly had crept in covering everything like a sickening spread of grave clothes. It was like a disease, as if leprosy were secretly digesting the mud and water underneath. He hated to put his foot down in it, and yet had to, or else how could he go on. And he had to go on — but he didn't know why.

When his first foot went down it disappeared as though swallowed by mush, and it felt like that too, and he wanted to draw back but couldn't — could only go forward. He waded.

If there was a sky it was a dull lead grey, but it wasn't like a sky; it was the dome of an endless room. And then he realized he was lost in a nether land. There was no beginning, no end, only a profound sense of emptiness.

Yet there was no end to the swamp. As he waded he sensed the passing of the years, and when he looked down at his rifle — it was only a slender bar of scaling rust, the stock half-rotted away and busy with wood-worms. He tried to throw it down, but it wouldn't throw. Then he saw his rust-scaling hand. It had solidified to the gun.

He was in the very center of a great shallow-water prairie. The grey walls of the nether room were so far off it would take him eternity to reach them. And he asked, "Why am I here? What has brought me to this place?" Then a hummock rose out of the smoke like a monstrous black bear, and he waded out to it.

Something was sprawled spread-eagle on the black tattered crown of the hummock. He struggled up to it with great revulsion at every step and looked. It was the pulpy ash of a man's bones, except for the skull. The skull still wore its skin and hair in death. He looked at the dead face of his brother, and Holly stared back at him with stark blank eyes.

Shad sat straight up. He thought he'd screamed — but it was a wildcat sharing the island with him. He started to reach for the Springfield, and then noticed his fire was dwindling to embers. He heaped on more wood, got things going merrily again and felt a little better.

He curled up in the blanket again and thought about having another cigarette. But he decided to save it. Tomorrow this would all be over with, he thought. He closed his eyes and wondered what he was supposed to make of the dream he'd had of Holly. A warning?

In the morning the bull gators down the line began slaughtering the morning hush with a ferocious earth-trembling vigour. Shad kicked out of his blanket and stiffly stood up. He didn't do anything for a full minute but rub at the back of his neck, stirring up his circulation. His head felt as though it were riding sidesaddle to his body.

He ate some jerky and biscuit, found a little guzzle that wasn't too silty and had a drink, and then made some coffee and smoked a tailor-made with it. He was in the skiff and on his way before six-thirty.

The swamp was very gaudy, spread-out, dressed in vivid tatters of leaves, in a great hush of green and turquoise, where the cabbage palms mutely met the sky in a ragged line of enchanted silence.

Too silent. It gave him the willies, somehow.

He came to another cross creek and turned south to search the east bank for blazings, and after a mile of it, leaned on the pole and said, "Well, fer God sake. What the hell's going on here?"

But standing there mumbling wasn't getting any wood chopped. He stobbed back to the channel.

And it went on like that. Brooks, creeks, guzzles, leading into prairies, savannas, lakes, back to the channel —

And the goddam no-see-'ems zig-zagging about his head, in the corners of his eyes, up nostrils, zip into his mouth; and in the palm bogs there wasn't any air, only a thick heavy substitute of rank odour; and a gator in the water hissed at him instead of running when he jabbed him with the pole; and limpkins, bitterns, and ibises, and large-mouthed bass, gars, and fat pan fish, and monster cottonmouths, timber rattlers, and coachwhippers, and titi and paintbrushes and hurrah blossoms and catclaws and log litter — and by two in the afternoon he'd plumb had it.

He snatched the pole inboard and set it athwart, placed

his fists akimbo and glared at the swamp. "You goddam bitch, you!" he shouted. And the cry ran somewhere, maybe across the flat prairie on his starboard, and echoed faintly — *Bitchyou.*

Shad sat down and rubbed the back of his neck. He'd been stubbornly evading the truth for the past hour, but now the fight had gone out of him and he felt like an old hat someone had kicked to the side of the road. So faced up to it and said it right out.

"I've pure-out lost myself. That's what I've gone and done."

Then he sighed heavily, sat up and said, "Goddam," and reached for the pole. There was only one thing to do and that was to try to find his way back to Breakneck, pick up his markers and start all over again. And he hated the thought of it. Not only because of the time it was going to cost, but because he felt certain that Jort and Sam would be hanging around there waiting.

He didn't pay any attention to the gator at first. It was fifty feet off with just its eyes and tip of snout showing above the water, and one gator more-or-less didn't mean much to him. Besides, he was busy right then ramming the skiff over and through a dense bed of golden-heart. The gator's corrugated back broke the surface and it opened its jaws and hissed.

He noted that the gator had been in some kind of brawl. One of its starboard scuts was missing and he could see the gleaming stratum of reddish-black scar tissue. But he didn't think anything of it.

The gator sank hurriedly as the skiff cleared the lily bed and bow came at him. Shad gave a shove ahead and the bow went *tchuunk!*, upset his equilibrium and reared upward crazily.

Shad swung around, clutching the stobpole giddily, as the skiff settled with a *splamp!* He thought it was a submerged log, until he saw the gator scurrying away underwater. The slough was so-so clear and he could see the magnified back and the laterally-compressed tail hitching. Then the gator entered that realm of the creek where the sky mirrored itself on the surface. Shad couldn't see him after that.

What was wrong with that fool gator? He'd never seen one act that way before. "What's he think I got in here — a goddam dog?"

He eased the pole from the water, letting the skiff drift. He crouched and felt for the Springfield. If the big scut-busted bastard thought he was going to have a Shad dinner, then he had another think coming.

He came up, slipping off the safety. But the rifle was only half up when the gator made a mad rush through the reed for the deep water. Shad swung the gun into position, panning fast in the general direction of blurred moving colour, and jerked — *ca-blam!* and saw the reed whip and the water spurt silver, and knew it was a clean miss, and saw the gator's thick tail slash across the water.

The gun crash caromed off the slough, rolled into the sharp protests of the bitterns and squawk hurons and echoed somewhere in the south woods. After that there was the quick *flut-a-flutter* of many wings.

Shad looked around, but there wasn't much to see. The fool gator was probably long gone. He squatted on the floorboards, bolted a fresh cartridge home, snapped the safety and set the rifle down.

The skiff undulated as though a ground swell was moving under the flat bottom. Where's the current coming from? he wondered.

The skiff lifted sharply, canted to one side and began sliding off. Shad grabbed for the gunwales, starting to get up, then stalled. He was tipping over. Out of the corner of his eye he saw water breaking on the scutellated back of a gator, and there was that angry red stratum replacing the missing scut. The gator's humped back seemed to be coming right at him; then — last instant — he knew it wasn't so. He was going to it.

Gator reared — skiff skittered — starboard tilted high above Shad and all the swamp went with it, tumbling into a spinning green smear —

Silver and black shocked his eyes. He felt the solid impact of his weight slamming water — and everything was liquid. What he could see wasn't worth claiming. Straight ahead, an opaque olive, below, total blackness, above, a silvery sheen — the surface. He struck for it, broke it, felt cold air on his wet face, sucked a breath — half of it brackish water — and went kicking and flailing for shore.

He wasn't going in a given direction — *he was going*. He didn't know where the skiff was or where the nearest out-cropping of bank stood and he didn't give a damn. He knew a king-sized gator was right behind him and the panic was on.

He kept waiting for the sudden shocking snap of the gator-teeth in his legs, could actually feel it, could see himself being drawn down to the mushy decay on the black bottom, and the pressing scaly weight of the great gator over him, and the torrent of stagnant water pouring into his open, bubbling mouth — and he went wild.

His swinging left hand struck a spongy something, and then his chin bumped into it. He raised his head, brought his knees and feet under him and started crawling onto the soggy bank.

The ground, as far as it went, wasn't anything to boast of. It was marsh land, not an island. Semi-solid, and already it was trembling. Shad hesitated in a crouch, streaming water from clothes and body, smelling that damn musky odour. A matted hurrah and catclaw thicket fronted the bank, and it was tunnelled and a throaty rumbling was coming from behind it.

He looked back. The skiff was seventy feet away and drifting downstream (ironic — thinking of Jort — but not a damn bit funny), and the scut-busted gator was kicking around out there in the run, watching him with wide-awake eyes and snorfing and hissing, as though daring him to come back into the water.

The gator-ground was quivering rhythmically now, and it sounded as though a whole army of them were coming at him. He felt around the back of his belt for his knife and drew it in a hopelessly futile gesture of defiance. He started to go right, stalled, took a step or two left, got caught in indecision, and then began backing up, watching the thicket tunnels.

The first gator wasn't much — a clumsy female, and she veered off in a fright when she saw him crouching there. But the next one was a big granddaddy, and he came out on a direct line with Shad and his jaws unhinged, and Shad wasn't hanging around to see more. He legged it along the shore for the nearest water oak.

He put the knife blade in his teeth and hauled himself up into the branches. When he looked down he couldn't believe it. The ground was acrawl with gators. Down the bank they came with their peculiar stumpy-legged run and went *splam!* in the water. After a while their roars and grunts and hisses died down, and after a longer while the hurons and limpkins and what-all birds let off their squawking. The silence picked up again with a completeness that seemed smugly complacent.

There was the bogland—

He didn't know how long he'd been in it. He was convinced it was endless, and knew it to be timeless. A thousand years came and went and nothing changed. He'd long ago lost the creek — without quite realizing at the time what was happening. But it had been impossible to follow it along the shore for more than a mile. Too many gators, too many thickets — he'd kept turning off, and farther off, and he didn't know how far he'd slogged or where.

It was a step-over, climb-around, wading horror. Half-petrified logs, all sizes, all positions except straight up; broken old stumps like rotten teeth; ankle to knee-high stagnant water, the colour of old ale.

And sinkholes — he could never see them coming. And each time as he slip-shot down and the torpid, stinking water rushed up, his heart contracted with panic. And after a while he began to wonder how much of that a heart could take.

He waded.

It ended finally, as the sun ended. One moment it was there, and a moment later only the after glow blazed on the rim of the swamp, like a bright lamp standing on the grave of the sun. Then a pale grey twilight hung over the wilderness and Shad slogged through it wearily, watching the edge of the bog come at him with agonizing slowness. Beyond high land stood, with palmettos and pine trees and swamp oak — and food. Way, hay, he was hungry enough to eat a last year's poor-joe nest.

And then, right on the edge of the bog, he met a panther cat with the same idea in mind. Shad pulled his knife and crouched. The cat's head lowered and its hair started to bristle. Its eyes were beryl green and placed in its head on a down-slant to its nose, giving it a mean, sour look. Its lips lifted and it snarled.

Shad hesitated and then realized that the panther couldn't quite make up its mind. He decided to augment the cat's attitude by pulling back into the bog. He retraced his own track for a hundred-some feet.

The cat didn't like the water. There were easier and more familiar prey afoot. It padded off silently, glancing back from time to time to see that Shad was behaving himself. But they weren't always like that.

Taking it easy, Shad came out of the bog and started up the high ground. He went to where the first palmetto clump squatted and looked back at the darkening badlands.

"God," he whispered.

He didn't eat that night. It wasn't safe to hunt in the dark, and it was also hopeless. But he had a fire. He had three matches in his denims and he dried the heads by rolling them in his hair. He put his four tailor-mades on a flat rock and set it next to the fire. When he lifted the rock he found some slimy slugs stuck to the damp bottom. But he wasn't that hungry. He drank swamp water and had a cigarette, and then tried to go to sleep.

The night crawled by like a wounded snake. His sleep came piecemeal, and between the fits and starts fear expanded insomnia until finally he gave up the idea as useless. He threw fresh wood on the fire, lit another cigarette and listened to the whispering feet of nameless things beyond the palmettos.

"It's going to be bad," he murmured. "Going to be real bad."

He was up and moving with the sun, heading south.

In the runty bay bushes of another island he found the remains of a long dead wildcat. It was bones mostly, with a few patches of hair and hide and the claws. It was the claws that gave him the idea for fish lure. He tore a hunk of the hide loose and sat down with it on a log, then traced an outline on the hide with the point of his knife. When he was finished, the strip of hide he'd cut had the appearance of a lizard. He got the wildcat's claws and hooked them to his dabbler.

He cut himself a pole and attached the lure to it with some vine strings, and then went down to the first brook and started dancing the dabbler on the surface, pulling it in and out of the marsh bushes. Twice in over an hour he had a trout nibble, and then he had an honest to God strike; but the trout was five or six pounds and the catclaws weren't fishhooks. The fish got clean away and Shad gave up the idea with a mouthful of dirty words. He drank some swamp water and went on.

The sun dragged its feet across the sky like a poky fat boy in no hurry to get home, and Shad stumbled along under the heavy droop of foliage that seemed to hang motionless with the expectant air of a deadfall. He didn't know which he hated more — the bogland or the jungle. The air was punk and the sharp palmetto fronds were cutting him to mincemeat, and twice now rattlers had given him fair warning, and — and the Goda'mighty loneliness of the place.

He couldn't understand why God had to go and do this to him. I never kilt nobody, er took what weren't mine - well, nothing much ner important. You cain't call that eighty-thousand dollars stealing, because I went and found that. I never made fun a God, like some I know. Like Iris Culver fer one. Now He'd have a right to punish her, but Shad didn't see Him doing it. No; one-sided, that's what it was.

"Why me?" he suddenly shouted compulsively. "What You holding against me that makes You do me this way? What have I done?"

Instantly the swamp turned shrill. Squawk hurons cut loose as though they'd been picked alive, and limpkins began wailing their we-are-lost-children cry. And a startled, irritated grunting sounded in the palmettos.

Shad crouched, catching his breath. It wasn't gator-grunting this time, worse — wild hog. The leader came snorting through the fronds as mean as a walleyed bull with a rump full of buckshot. He was leggy and narrow, his back like a man's hand viewed edgewise. He spotted Shad and something went out of whack in his little piggy eyes.

He dropped his head and charged.

Shad forgot about God and went hell-for-leather out of there. He started for the tall timber, but too late — the hogs had cut him off. He veered sharply to the east.

They chased him right across a marsh and into the horror of the pin-downs. It was a vast thicket and he went dodging in and out of its bays, trying to find an easy way through. But there was no such thing. Shad said "Aw hell," and lunged into the jungle.

The Adam stalk of a pin-down grows out of water, pencil thin, nearly bare and red in colour, its branches bend down to the ground and take root wherever they touch, making natural hoop snares for feet, which in turn grow new stalks with branches that also bend down and take root, and the whole affair goes on like that endlessly— hoop after hoop after hoop. Shad had heard of men going insane when caught in the pin-downs.

He was ready to believe it. He went jumping, high-stepping, lunging and knife-hacking into the thicket, and within ten feet he was flat on his face in the slime and thought he'd twisted an ankle. He got up, panting like a blacksmith's bellows, and looked back. The wild hogs were snorting and head-ramming the edge of the thicket, trying to find an opening to get at him. Shad started picking his way farther into the pin-downs.

What made it bad was the God-awful hurrah bushes and the titi. They rose right over his head and so thick he couldn't see an inch through them, and they whipped at his eyes, ears and neck every move he made; and that meant he had to keep whacking at them with the knife, and to do it he must keep his eyes on what he was doing, and every time he looked up from the marshy ground the hoops would snare his feet, twist his ankles and send him tail-over appetite.

Then he saw a pine island a hundred yards away. It was like being offered a sky hook. He hacked toward the rise, gasping, sobbing, mumbling, "I kindly thank you, God. I shorely do."

When he staggered finally onto the solid ground of the island a lassitude came over him like a ton of damp, warm earth, and he had to rib himself up to keep going.

He was beat and hungry and lost and if he didn't come up with a trick soon the swamp would get him. He needed protection and food, and that meant a weapon of some sort, something more than the knife. He could make a bow and some arrows. When he was a kid they used to make them out of saplings. He got pretty good with one, too. He'd bowled over a plentiful of coons with arrows, so why not do it again? A coon dinner would go dandy right now.

An edge, that's all he asked for. Just give him a little bit of an edge and he'd take care of the rest.

Then he saw the shebang nestled forlornly in a stand of sycamores.

He gaped, not understanding it, then roused himself and went toward the trees, but cautiously and with uneasiness, as though approaching a sepulchre.

The shebang had been constructed from deadwood mostly, age-brittle branches and old ratty looking brown palmetto fronds. It was squatty and not much larger than a good sized doghouse, and he had to go on hands and knees to get through the little doorway.

There was nothing inside except dirt, a few nameless crawlies, and a litter of dead trash that must have been a weed bed once. The only other thing was an old stiffened deerskin pouch, with a leather thong to go over a man's shoulder. The flap had two letter burnt into it: H.H.

Shad sat down and rubbed at his cheeks with his fingertips. He'd swung full circle — right around to where his brother had ended four years before.

"Me'n Holly," he said quietly. "We both come out here to beat the pants offn this old slough — and look what we got fer our pains."

The lassitude was with him again as he left the lonely little wickiup. He walked a bit through the bays, and then looked up and around, wondering if Holly's body was somewhere nearby.

It was mid-afternoon when he stumbled upon the Indian mounds. That perked him up somewhat. He'd heard old-timers tell of how the Indians used to bury pottery, ornaments, tools, and weapons along with their dead. There just might be something in one of the mounds he could use to help along his survival.

He circled an enormous mound that from its extraordinary size suggested that its dead inhabitant had been ten-foot tall. He'd heard tales of Indians nearly that tall but he'd never believed it. He chose a likely spot and started digging with his knife.

The bones he unearthed went to powder in his fingers, and the weapons didn't stand up any better. He found some stone implements that he couldn't account for and didn't see how he could use, and so, doggedly, shifted on to the next mound.

He dug mechanically, loosening the dirt with the knife blade, pawing it aside with his left hand. Suddenly he snatched back his hand as though he'd touched something unwholesome. He'd uncovered a small part of a man's leg — but the leg was clothed in rotting denim.

Shad stood up, staring. All at once comprehension burst through the blank barrier that shock had created. It was George Tusca's body.

"Great God A'mighty!" he whispered. "This here's the mound I done buried poor George in two years ago!"

His head snapped around and for the first time he actually saw the nearby tupelo trees, saw the very tupelo that George Tusca had hanged himself from.

He knew where he was — he was out!

You go into that hurrah thicket there and down to the guzzle he'd named Tusca Creek, in honour of George's memory, and you follow the creek for two miles and it flows you right into Tarramand Lake, and you take Mink Creek for another mile and that brings you to the river. And way-hay, roll and go! You're heading for home!

Chapter Eighteen

Mr. Ferris was sitting on the edge of his bed in the Culvers' guest room. He was wearing a pair of khaki trousers and a corduroy jacket, both belonging to Larry Culver; and he was bending over, absorbed in lacing up a pair of Larry's boots. He looked up when he heard Iris Culver's heels click as far as the open door.

She was in a pink negligee so sheer it might have been made of gossamer. She was standing with one hand on the jamb, and after a glance at her bright, glassy eyes he decided she needed it for support. It was obvious that she'd been leaning heavily on the martinis.

"Why, Tarl," — drunk or not, you couldn't shake the smooth Vassar-intonation from her voice — "what are you up to?"

"I'm going into the swamp," he said. "With Jort Camp and Sam Parks."

"With — but why?"

Mr. Ferris finished with the right boot and switched to the left.

"I've just come from Sutt's. There was a great deal of talk about a girl called Dorry Mears who ran away with Shad Hark. Everyone seems to be of the opinion that they have gone off with the money."

He stood up and tested the feel of the right boot, took two heavy steps forward on it. He seemed satisfied. "This Camp person and his little friend were just returning from the swamp — from 'gator-grabbing' I believe they said. Camp said he saw Shad and the girl going downriver in a skiff."

Iris looked at him. "Then that's that," she said.

Mr. Ferris glanced at her. "No. I don't think it is."

He went to the dresser and began putting things in his pockets: comb, keys, wallet, cigarettes, matches, folded handkerchief.

"It seems that the genial Camp and his nervous shadow are going back into the swamp immediately — 'gator-grabbing' again, they say. I'm going with them."

"I don't understand, Tarl —"

"You don't need to. In my business I must know a great deal about the people I come in contact with. I know something about these two men. That is why it is imperative I go into the swamp with them."

Iris came into the room.

"What is it you know, Tarl?"

He smiled. "Don't press this insurance investigator, my dear. My information is my hole card."

She sensed that she was losing him; and he was her last

hope.

"Then you don't think it is too late to recover the money?"

"No. I don't think it's too late."

"You think Shad is still out there?"

"I'm certain of it."

Her eyes were too bright. They sparked as though the light had glanced from black spear points. "Tarl —" she breathed. "Tarl, I don't want him to come back."

"Iris —" his tone could be very official, "you must be very careful what you say. Someone might misinterpret —"

"He's a thief!" she hissed, and her breath was like warm gin on his face. "An outlaw. And he's dangerous, Tarl. You don't know —"

"Let's forget about Shad Hark now," he said coldly. "I'll manage that young man when the time comes." He made a move as if to go around her. "I really must be going now, Iris."

But she couldn't have it that way. She raised her white arms to his neck.

"But you'll come back to me? You'll promise to come back?"

He opened his mouth to promise, but she didn't let him speak. She ground her mouth on his.

"*Iris!*" The voice had the high bleat of shocked belief. It belonged to Larry Culver.

Mr. Ferris disengaged his mouth and looked up. All he could think at that moment was, this has never happened to me before. I must be growing very careless.

Iris turned a look on her husband as though he'd just asked her to come clean up the mess the dog had made in the living room. She was very annoyed with him.

"Don't stand there like a fool," she snapped at him. "Did you think this was the Victorian era?"

He was a slight man with the pasty pallor of a book lover, which he was not; and the horn-rimmed glasses he wore lent to his incredulous expression, a droll look rather than a studious one. He stood in the doorway with the hesitant stance of a man on the edge of an abyss.

"Iris — Tarleton —"

Mr. Ferris brought out his folded handkerchief and

rubbed the lipstick from his mouth. He glanced at his wrist-watch. Time to go.

"Iris — what *are* you doing? How long has this — this — Good Lord, Iris, don't just stand there with your — your gown open that way !"

Iris bunched her negligee together in the front. She swayed slightly on her high heels. "I want a cigarette," she said petulantly. "Tarl, I want a cigarette."

Mr. Ferris brought out his pack of cigarettes and offered her one. Then he struck a match for her. He deeply wished he might be dealing with someone a little more realistic than Larry Culver. He blew the match out and said, "I'm sorry, Larry. Really very sorry. I wish I had the time to try and explain — but I have business that can't wait." He looked at Iris, his expression politely void. "Goodbye, Iris."

He went through the doorway without looking at Larry Culver. Their bodies brushed and Mr. Ferris murmured "Pardon me." His guard was down pointedly because he didn't expect Larry to strike him. Larry didn't. It didn't even enter his mind.

Iris heard the screen door clatter and she said, "Gone." And then, "Over." Now there would be nothing more — loose pigs on the front lawn that wasn't really a lawn at all, only a pseudo-civilized extension of that filthy swamp; illiterate, barefooted swamp billies loafing along the edge of the lake, leering their imbecilic grins when they saw her; damp mould on everything, even on the people; they called it sweat. And Larry hiding in his ivory tower in hurt bewilderment trying to understand something that was as remote to his intelligence as Mars was to Earth. Over.

"Iris —" that terrible, incredulous whine. "Iris, don't you have anything to say to me? Aren't you — I mean — we can't just remain mute as though I hadn't seen what I *did* see."

She put the cigarette out in an ashtray on the dresser. She didn't look at him. "I don't want to talk about it." she said.

"*Not talk about it?*" He was aghast.

His insistent stupidity was too much for her. "You fool!" she cried. "Don't you understand you mean nothing to me? I'd as soon waste my time explaining my actions to that chair. I don't give a damn what you think, or if you think at all, which is doubtful."

He managed to shave some of the whine from his voice, replacing it with righteous disapproval. "Have you been sleeping with him?"

It was so like him to use that archaic expression. She almost laughed.

"Did you think *you* could satisfy a woman? Any woman? Do you think any woman could live with you and not go stark raving mad. Do you have any idea of what your love-making is like? It's like that watered-down slop you write!"

Instantly he found himself on the defensive, which, considering the circumstances, was incongruous. But he couldn't help it.

"Now wait a minute — now — wait a minute, Iris. You're not being fair. I may not be a Thomas Wolfe, but I —"

"May not be a Thomas Wolfe?" she cried. "Oh God!"

Suddenly she spoke with cold sarcasm. "Do you know what your work reminds me of? It's like the trash those hack writers used to pot-boil for the pulp adventure magazines back in the '20s and '30s. They always called their dashing Nordic heroes names like McCoy or McKay or McCloud or Quincannon — names which automatically had a connotation suggestive of rough, manly derring-do. Invariably they had sandy thatches of hair, frequently red, and always a scattering of freckles on the backs of their tanned square wrists. But best of all was the manner in which these literary giants would introduce those girl-killing, booze-drinking, saloon-brawling, quick-shooting, Scotch-Irish supermen. They would write, 'No plaster saint— *comma* — McKay.' "

"Now you're not being fair, Iris. You know I don't use that archaic kind of sentence structure."

But she kicked down his defence before he could even get its underpinning completed.

"A man that writes that sort of pap isn't really a man. Isn't really anything. And that's what I've been living with for eight years. A *nothing* man. That type of lame-brain should be put away in a glass cage and sheltered and protected and never be shown a newspaper. They shouldn't let you into bedrooms. It upsets your sensibilities, unhinges your nervous system."

She tottered toward him, the negligee flowing wide open again. Her eyes were wild.

"Shall I tell you the things I've seen, done? Would you like to hear?"

He stood in a dumb stupor, sick, listening to the things she'd seen, the things she'd done. And it evoked the imagery, having little or nothing to do with love.

He felt as if he'd been picked up by the heels and dipped headfirst into sewer slime and then cast limply on a mudbank like a carp just off the hook. And he stared at her with an awe of awakening, as though seeing her for the first time and seeing in her the definite end of something he had never really thought about.

He had always considered her rather frigid because of her lack of response. But he hadn't let it bother him because he was a low burner himself, and so had thought them perfectly matched.

He opened his mouth to speak. He had to speak — say something. But it wouldn't come. The words were rammed under gigantic air bubbles and the bubbles were hung up on something inside his chest.

Iris stared at him for a brittle moment, then marched determinedly toward the doorway — so determined that he had to move aside quickly to avoid being knocked down.

"No talent — *comma* — McCulver!" she sneered in his face.

She crossed the living room by rote, coming by instinct to the bar. Her hands trembled over the martini shaker. Then, abruptly, she set it down without pouring herself a drink. She stared at the bright, gleaming finish on the bar top.

That illiterate savage is going to win after all. He's going to beat all of us. I know it, feel it. Nature is perverse that way.

Then she closed her eyes, tight, and leaned against the bar, the pink flesh of her bare stomach folding softly about its edge.

"Oh, God *damn* Shad Hark!" she said fervently.

Larry Culver didn't know what to do. He stood in the guest room and gaped at the rug. Then he gaped at the bed — where it had happened. Or had it happened in his wife's room?

Suddenly he had to get out of the house.

He walked mechanically, through doors, down steps, across the yard, and entered his writing studio — the re-converted barn. The upstairs contained his desk and type-writer, his filing cabinet and reference books. One wall was plastered with a colourful array of magazine tearsheets — his printed stories from the pulp magazines.

He looked at the vivid illustrations, at the titles, at his name LARRY CULVER on each one of them. They were by way of a touchstone. *The Dark Dive, The Dark Tower, The Dark Voyage*— Funny, he'd never consciously noticed the redundancy of the adjective before. But it was an apt word for an adventure yarn.

He went to his desk and sat down. Then he opened the bottom drawer and brought out a .22 target pistol and set it beside his battered old Underwood. He had purchased the pistol five years ago, when a timber rattler came to visit his garden one day. But he could never find the snake again, and so he had never had occasion to fire the weapon. He looked at the gleaming metallic barrel.

He supposed, bleakly, that it was really the only thing left to do. The only kind of work he knew was hack writing. It was that or go hungry. And now his wife had torn it to shreds for him. He didn't see how it was possible to pick up the pieces.

His eye fell on the white sheet of typing paper that was captive in the Underwood's roller. What was it now? he wondered absently. Oh, yes, the scene when Reb comes aboard the yawl and Tab has just said, "Gosh sake, Reb. Why did you walk off with the marlinspike? I've been look-ing everywhere for it."

Yes — now what reply had he figured out for Reb (that good-natural clown) before he'd run out of pipe tobacco and had to go to the house for more? Oh, yeah — yeah. He remembered. But perhaps he'd better put it down before it slipped his mind. He squared himself in his chair facing the typewriter and typed, *"Marlinspike?" Reb cried. "I thought it was a blunt ice pick!—"*

After that — somehow — he just kept on writing.

Chapter Nineteen

The night was silver and black when Shad stumbled down the backwater bank and onto the gangplank of the shanty-boat. He was damp from having come downriver on logs, but he didn't mind it. Too beat to mind anything. Besides, the night was warm.

Inside, he found a match, got the lantern going, and then brought a can of beans and a spoon to the table. When he sat down it was as if he'd done something permanent, as though from now on he and the chair were one. His eating was automatic. He didn't think about it or even taste the cold beans. He was filling a void.

The can empty, he stood up and pulled off his clothes. Nothing — no, no goddam thing had ever looked better than his bunk. He climbed in groaning like an old man, drew up the blanket and closed his eyes. Immediately he felt like a submerged rock all wavering with undulating weed. Goan buy myself a God-awful big bed with me money, was the last thought he had.

At first the dream was only bothersome. It was Jort's face, all sweaty and unshaven and pig-eyed and rot-toothed, and the mouth kept asking the same question — You think fer a minute we don't know what you and Dorry Mears *was* up to? And why did it bother him? What was there about the sentence that didn't make sense? Every time he'd try to get hold of it in words, Jort would say it again — You think fer a minute we don't know what you and Dorry Mears *was* up to?

So finally he hit at the face, only to discover that it belonged to Tom Fort. And Tom was saying, What you done with my girl? I want her back. You give her back, hear? And then more faces and more mouths saying what had he done with her? And hands pawing at him, shoving him around, not letting him get his fists up where he could hit back. What you done with her? the mouths wanted to know. Where you got her? We want you should tell us where you got that old Money Plane. We want a share of her. You goan tell us? Or we got the stuffing to beat outn you?

And finally himself shouting back at the mouths. You

don't give a good damn about Dorry. You all the same. Money, that's all you care about. Money, ever' last one of you. And them clamouring. Yeah, yeah, the Money Plane. Where you got her? Money. We want that money. And then Edgar Toll's silly face too, slobbering— tongue wagging, hitting at him with a big stick. Kill un, he yelled. Kill un. And then all of them hitting him, and him not able to fight back, and Margy Mears in there too, saying what she had said to him the last time she had seen him, Take care of yourself, Shad — Shad —

"Shad — *Shad,* wake up now, hear?"

Normally he awoke as though it were judgement day, coming right up to startled attention. But today it was a long painful road back, a sort of sticky, misty passage out of warm darkness into vague, unfriendly light. And the path was flickering with half-formed images and nonsensical objects. One of them seemed to be Dorry — Dorry bending over him, saying something — wake up, he guessed.

He smiled hazily and put a hand out for her, pulled her down to his chest. Hello, sugar baby, he thought he said, and he cupped his free hand around her right breast. Funny — she'd lost weight, hadn't she?

Instantly the girl was all action and loud indignant protest, even slapped him.

"Shad Hark! You gone crazy? *Stop that* what you're doing?"

Shad got all of his eyes open then and looked at Margy. Her obsidian eyes sparked black fire. "If you weren't down I'd slap you good, and you so free with your hands." Then, surprisingly, she shut up and looked away.

"That's right," he said. "Never hit a man when he's down."

He looked around at the cabin. It was morning.

"What are you doing here, Margy?"

"Pa sent me down to see did you lock the shantyboat after you."

That didn't make too much sense to him. He propped up on one elbow and rubbed at his face. "How's that? What's hit his business?"

"Well, hit's his shantyboat, ain't it?" she demanded. "If you goan run off with his daughter, least he kin see is his

153

boat still all right." Then she dropped her indignation. "Shad — where's Dorry?"

Shad looked at her. For a moment he wasn't sure that he had successfully left the nightmare. "Home, ain't she? How in hell should I know where is she? What's your fool old man mean, me running off with his daughter?"

Margy put her hands akimbo and looked at him impatiently. "What do you mean what does *he* mean? Why, ever'body knows you'n Dorry ben gone fer days."

Dorry gone? He sat up. The first part of the dream was bothering him again. Jort — Jort Camp. He took hold of the blanket and looked at Margy. "Look out. I'm getting up."

She stepped back quickly. "Well, I'll thank you kindly to remember, Shad Hark, that I'm not a girl that can be —"

"Stop kicking up a fuss over nothing. I got my shorts on." He grinned. "And there ain't much to see nohow — or so some have told me."

"I'll just *bet* they have." But she turned her back.

He trotted out to the porch, doused a bucket of water over his head, then washed his face and rinsed his mouth. It tasted like an old tobacco pouch.

Margy was still facing the table when he went for his pants.

"It's safe. They's nothing fer you to bust your eyes over."

Her look was arctic. "Ain't that a relief," she said caustically.

He grinned at her. "Oh, I dunno, some gals might consider hit a disappointment." Then he hurriedly cut her off before she could snap back. "Look a-here, Margy," he said seriously. "I ain't run off with your sis. I ain't even seen her. I ben three days and nights tooling around out in that old swamp like a blind man in a cornfield."

The look in her eyes wasn't quite disbelief.

"You ain't lying, Shad?"

"God's truth, Margy. I was out there on my lone looking fer that Money Plane — but I didn't find hit. And that's the truth, too."

She couldn't understand it. "Jort Camp and Sam come back night afore last," she said. "They told my Pa and Joel Sutt and that Mr. Ferris that they ben put gator-grabbing. Said they seen you'n Dorry going downriver in your skiff.

Said they figured you was running off."

Shad couldn't believe what he heard. *"Seen me and Dorry running off down river?* Why that goddam Jort and Sam was out in the swamp with me the first day. They wanted that money but I slicked out on'em. They *knew* I didn't have Dorry with me!"

She didn't know why she had always wanted to trust Shad. It was something about him; maybe the way he acted, moved or looked. She remembered a day when she was twelve. She had met Shad and Tom Fort coming along the road. They'd stolen a watermelon from Uncle Peebie's place and were taking turns toting it. Tom had leered at her that way fifteen-year-old boys always did; had made an insulting remark. He'd thought it really funny, thought it funny when she'd blushed and started to turn off the road, half in shame, half in fear.

But Shad hadn't thought it funny at all. "Shut your god-dam mouth," he'd told Tom, and he'd meant it and right now, anyone could tell. "What's wrong with you?" Tom had wanted to know. "Ever-body knows how her sis —"
"She ain't her sis," Shad had pointed out. "She's just a kid." And then he'd nodded at her, as if saying It's all right. He don't mean it. And he'd given Tom a shove in the back.

She came a step, then another, toward him.

"Shad, you think something's happened to Dorry and Jort knows it?"

He rubbed at the back of his neck. "Dunno. Where's Jort and Sam at now?"

"They and that Ferris left fer the swamp again yesterday morning."

There was something wrong about it.

"Mr. Ferris went with'em?" He shook his head. "He ain't got the sense I thought he did."

"What's it mean, Shad?"

"Means they think I'm still in the swamp. They're either laying fer me at Breakneck, er they're scouting the north creeks fer that Money Plane. Well, all I kin say is that Mr. Ferris better hope they *don't* find it; because if they do — then he kin count his minutes on earth on one hand. That Jort —"

But Mr. Ferris' life expectancy wasn't his problem. He

snapped his fingers and went out on the porch for a gunny sack. Back in the cabin he started loading all his canned foods into the sack. Margy watched him with large, perplexed eyes.

"What are you goan do?"

He didn't look up. "I got time and blood invested in that Money Plane. Ain't nobody taking that away from me. I got to swipe me another skiff and git back into that swamp right fast."

She stared at his humped back. "What about Dorry, Shad?"

"What about her?"

"Well, she's ben missing fer days. Don't it mean nothing to you?"

He straightened up and turned to look at her, the half-filled sack hanging from his square fist. Neither of them said a word. He let the sack go with a clunk and came over to her.

"Margy," he said softly. "I guess you think me four kinds a bastard, don't you? But you cain't know how much that money means to me. You don't know what I ben through already trying to git hit.

"Right now old Jort'n Sam and that Mr. Ferris is out there tearing that swamp to pieces trying to find my money. And they got them a fair idea of the general direction in which hit's hid, too. It ain't but a matter of time afore old Sam with that goddam eagle eye of his spots my blaze marks, and then —"

He didn't like the way she just stood there, not saying anything, just looking up at him. A small girl, with enormous watchful eyes. He scowled and looked away.

"You kin think what you want," he muttered sourly. "I don't know what's happened to Dorry. And right now I ain't got the time to worry about her."

"You don't love her, Shad?"

He met her eye. "No," he said honestly. "I guess I never did. It was just that I — well —" So how do you explain to a girl like her that one look at her sister and something goes BLOWIE! in your brain.

Her gaze pulled down. She looked at the finger nails of her right hand. Shad did too, absently noticing that they

156

were clean.

"I know," she murmured. "I know how it is with Dorry and boys."

Shad nodded. He'd never before been embarrassed when talking sex with a girl, and he didn't quite know what was wrong here, and didn't have the time to give it more thought. "I got to go, Margy," he said. But he couldn't when she looked up at him, couldn't just walk out on that look in her eyes that he didn't understand.

"Shad — you won't be coming back this way again?"

"Not if I find that money I ain't. Cain't afford to."

He almost didn't catch what she said — it was so low and unexpected.

"Take me with you, Shad."

Now that it was in words, she was glad. Now she could finally admit it to herself. So she had loved him from that first night on her pa's porch, when they had swapped insults, maybe before that, maybe from the time she was twelve and he had stopped Tom's dirty mouth, maybe even before that.

He was tender with her — as she intuitively knew he would be — the only girl he had ever been tender with. He didn't even kiss her. Somehow a kiss would be the wrong contact at that moment, and he seemed to know it. He put his hands on her shoulders, lowering his head.

"You want to go with me — out there?"

She nodded.

"We mebbe won't git the money," he said.

"I don't think we will. I think there's too much against us. That ain't why I want to go."

No, it wasn't. He knew that, and so he said. "I'm sorry I said that about the money. You ain't like your sis."

"No. I ain't like her at all."

He'd be a fool to take her out there. It wasn't safe for one thing. And even if it was, even if he could outfox Jort and Sam and Mr. Ferris, even if he could find the Money Plane again, why would he want her tagging along? She was little and not much on build and a man could find a prettier girl by looking in almost any direction.

"If you go with me," he said slowly, "I might git you kilt."

Her head made an even, soft bob. "I know. But I got it to

157

do."

And then he kissed her, but not as he had ever kissed before. And it seemed to erase all the others — all the wet lips, and he wasn't sorry.

Funny, he thought, the way things work out.

The day was as brilliant as a washed window. Nature had scrubbed her house.

Margy sat on the middle thwart, facing forward; Shad was right behind her, standing with the stob. They had left the river an hour ago, and now were well on their way up Mink Creek heading for Tarramand Lake. It was round-about and they were going to have a haul-tail time of it in the water lettuce and palm bogs; but it was safer than going directly to Breakneck.

Getting a skiff hadn't been any problem at all. Margy had gone along to Sutt's Landing and rowed off in her pa's boat. No one had paid her any mind. Getting a rifle had been something else again. She had slipped up to her folks' place and had taken Bell's carbine and a box of ammo. Shad had said, "Fine," and hadn't thought anything more of it. Now the carbine was up in the bow and he might just as well heave it overboard for all the good it was going to do him.

The first gator they had seen was just as they were entering Mink Creek. He was a lazy, minding-his-own business type of bull, but he was big and Shad hadn't wanted to be caught napping.

"Hand me the carbine," he'd said. "Where you got the ammo?"

"Here," she'd replied, and had lifted a small canvas pouch.

"What you got in there?" he'd wondered.

"Nothing much. Just the box of bullets and some things."

"What things?"

"Just things."

Shad reached and picked the pouch from her hand.

There wasn't much; the ammo box, a carefully folded and freshly laundered nightie and Dorry's half-empty bottle of Sin's Dream.

Margy's head was down. He could see her cheeks were red.

158

He pulled his grin off and said, "Bet it smells mighty nice."

Then he had looked at the ammo. Then at the carbine. Then at the ammo again. .30 carbine. .30-06 ammo.

But it wasn't her fault. She didn't know anything about guns and calibres. So he didn't let on that she had made a mistake. The milk was spilt and what could you do about it?

A place like Breakneck had a stately solitude that gave it an imposing beauty; the lake was deep, the water clean, the fishing fair, and gators had never favoured it as a place to set up housekeeping.

Tarramand Lake had nothing to recommend it. It wasn't really a lake; it was just big and the swampers tagged that name on it as a reference. It was a prairie, so shallow a man could wade across most of it. Stobbing a skiff across was another matter. A bitch of one. When the pickerelweed and the water lettuce weren't holding you up, then it was the submerged log litters humping under the flat bottom and rearing the bow a foot out of the water, and if you didn't think so much of that, then there was the God-awful cypress knees rising here, there, every damn where like tank traps.

It was well into afternoon by the time they reached Tusca Creek, and after two hours there Shad threw in the towel for the day. He hid the skiff in maiden cane, picked up their belongings and led Margy through the hurrah thicket onto a pine island.

"You sit tight right here, honey," he ordered. "I'm going to scout around a little. They's a hut somewhere hereabout, and if'n I find hit we'll spend the night there."

She agreed and it was that simple. He went off feeling pretty good. She just up and left her life in his keeping. What he said was law. Yeah, it was a good feeling to have someone to care for, to protect. He looked back from the low lying palmettos. She was standing with the tall swamp pines rising behind her, and she waved.

It was the long, hushed hour of twilight when he returned. He was grinning with confidence and he told her about it as they walked.

"I found the hut first — just half-mile along here. Then I

159

scouted t'other side of the creek and found an old skinny looking waterway I think we kin git the skiff down. Should take us into Money Plane Creek. We'll have a crack at her first thing in the morning."

His euphoria took on a never-never aspect, and he looked up and around with wondering eyes. The swamp, the sameness of it, the way it was becoming a part of them because they were together, gave him an unrealistic feeling.

"Funny," he said compulsively. "Now that I don't see 'em — Jort and the others — it's like they don't exist fer me."

"Don't say that," Margy said sharply.

"What?"

She trembled. "When you took off an hour ago I went to feeling that *I* didn't exist — just because *you* couldn't see me. I never felt like that afore. It — it left me —"

He took her hand and squeezed it. What she had just imparted to him touched him as nothing else ever had. But the responsibility that went with it was frightening.

She was childlike about the hut. Like a little girl playing house in a pup tent. She whisked out the dirt floor with a palmetto frond, and brought in an armload of pine needles to lay a fresh bed, and then picked up the old deerskin pouch and showed it to him.

"You see this?"

"Yeah. Hit's Holly's."

"Holly? Oh — your brother's." She looked through the doorway at a far reaching bay studded savanna. "What you reckon become of him?"

"Dead. If he ain't then he must a turned wild."

"But he couldn't stay out here fer four years and him coo-coo!"

Shad scratched at his chin. "Dunno, Margy. I've heered of it happening afore. Old-timers tell of a Yankee boy went to got lost in here during the Civil War. Ever'body figured he was dead right off, but then one day in the '70s old Jim Dawes' granddaddy seen him wandering around out here. All naked he was and bearded, and his hide as tough as gator-skuts, but he still had that funny little mashed down cap them Yankees wore on his head.

"Story goes old Granddaddy Dawes give him a shout. Didn't do no good though. Yankee fella looks up all wild eyed and takes off into the titi. Granddaddy Dawes wasn't about to go after him, because he says that wild Yankee had a club with him the size of a sycamore trunk.

"Other people seen him from time to time too, least they'd say they did. I wouldn't know. Nobody never mentions him no more."

Margy shivered and gave a little laugh. "Mebbe them kind a people never die. Mebbe he's still in here — somewhere."

"Uh-huh. Mebbe. Mebbe him and Holly's teamed up."

Then they let the subject go; both aware that they were only stalling. He looked at her. After a moment she lowered her eyes.

"Margy —" he whispered.

She didn't look up. She held out her hand.

Outside and all around them it was a night of the first age. It was like the creation of the earth all over again. A gang of night-feeding ducks took off across the moon with a great batter of noise, and everything else continued its pattern.

In the morning he found one of his markers.

He was heading for home base now. He knew it. There was the big prairie with the log litter on the right, and there was where the land picked up again, the gator ground. It was the end of the rainbow.

"We're's almost there, Margy." He said it reverently.

She sat on the center thwart, facing him as he stobbed, watching him. She looked off to her left and shivered. Something that was too refined for the senses to understand touched her and her blood chilled, as though hostile shadow had fallen over her. But there was no shadow. Water, tules, silt, titi —

"Shad," she said. "If something should go wrong —" she turned back to him, "if mebbe somebody beat you to that money er —"

He held back on the pole, staring at her, his eyes narrow and warm. "What in hell's name you talking about?" he demanded. "Ain't nobody beating me to that money. That's *my* money."

She looked down at her moccasin-clad feet.

"Yes, I know. But things kin go wrong — sometimes."

161

"Not this time they ain't."

"I just don't want you feeling bad if they should, is all."

He started stobbing again, all starchy with determination and righteousness, watching the gator ground in the distance. Fool girl. There wasn't *nobody* going to take that money from him, noway. It was his. He'd gone balling through hell's gate to keep it and he'd do it again if he had to.

"When we git there," he said stiffly, "I'm leaving you in the skiff. That old slough ain't a safe place. It's a razor hole."

She didn't say anything.

He glanced down at her and frowned. He felt bad about shouting at her. She'd just been trying to help him; he knew that. But he just couldn't stand the idea of anyone else getting that money. He eased up on the pole, wondering if he should apologize. Poor little kid —

She was looking past him, downwake, and he didn't understand at first what was wrong when he saw her eyes go wide with alarm. It caught him off guard.

"Shad — pull in ashore."

"What?"

"They's somebody coming."

It hit him where he lived. Something inside of him leaped and he spun about, holding hard to the pole, and way down the prairie he saw Jort Camp's big skiff coming. He could make out Sam's scrawny figure crouching aft with the pole, and up forward was someone who had to be Mr. Ferris.

Shad hissed. "Ain't *I* never goin git 'em off my back?"

But it was no time for tears and he knew it. Blood, yes, but crying was for when you couldn't do nothing else. And he knew what had to be done now, and it was a wonder to him that he hadn't known it right from the first minute he'd found the Money Plane. He probably had known it deep down, but hadn't had the sense to recognize it. But it was going to be bad — without a gun it was going to be tail-busting bad.

He shot the skiff ahead, looking wildly around at the jungle. He had to get them well past the gator pond where the Money Plane was. There wasn't any chance of outrunning them and that meant he'd have to land. But the south bank was out — the Money Plane was there; and the north bank was clear to hell and gone across the prairie and Jort would cut him off in midwater if he tried that.

"What're you fixing to do, Shad?" Margy was gripping the gunwales, staring back at Jort's skiff with dread fascination.

"Shet up. Got to think." And he had to think about her too, not just himself now. God's grandpa but he'd been a fool to bring her into this. He'd known it was a mistake when he said yes. She couldn't outrun men like Jort and Sam, and she couldn't fight them.

Desperation made a punching bag of his nervous system. He was wild on the end of that pole now, nearly off-balancing himself twice for a header into the water. Got to land her, he thought. Got to ditch her and go at this business like I knew what I was doing. He'd rather have the swamp get her than Jort and Sam.

The prairie was skinning down to a slow, flowing waterway, and a bend in the southbank was coming toward them. He looked around and then up. A lone lop-eared cabbage palm soared high and mighty above the swamp. It couldn't be more than one hundred yards off.

"Margy," he said, "look up there. See that cabbage palm? In a minute now we're goan around a bend in the bank. Soon's we do I'm going to land you and take off up-slough. Want you to git in the jungle and make your way over to that palm. Want you to stay there till I come back fer you. You understand me, Margy? Stop shaking your fool head that way!"

"No," she said, and she was pleading. "No, Shad. No, I ain't goan leave you."

"You're goan do what I say! You're going over to that palm and you ain't goan budge till I come for you."

"No. Please, Shad. They'll kill you." She was crawling toward him now, reaching for his leg. "I want to be with you. If something happens to you, I got to be there too."

And he was a believer when he glanced at her face. But he couldn't have it that way. He scooted the skiff around the bend and down-dragged on the pole as a canopy of fronds swatted at them, turned the bow in and shoved it onto the mud. Then he squatted, grabbing her.

"Margy honey, you got to do what I tell you. Hit's the only way."

"No — Shad —" She was still trying to get at him, trying to get where she could wrap herself around him.

He slapped her hard with his hand, snapping her face away from him, grabbed her hair and pulled her back around. Her eyes were enormous, staring up at him.

"Goddam you, now you listen at me. I'm your man now and you got to do what I tell you. I got that right and if I don't got it then you ain't no woman fer me. You goan a-git in that jungle and keep out of sight and wait fer me by the cabbage palm."

She was dragging air through her mouth, her eyes wide and brown, both her hands clawed in his knees.

"Honey," he said, "you just gitting us both kilt this way. Give me the chance to save us."

She stared at him.

He nodded to her encouragingly. "Go on. Git out now. Git into the thicket." He gave her a little shove to get her started. "It's my job to protect us," he said. "You got to let me go at it best way I see fit. That's it — keep a-going."

She went like a sleepwalker, stepped out of the skiff and her feet sucked down in the mud. She looked back at him. "Shad —"

He straightened up and grinned at her.

"Hit's all right, honey. I'll be back fer you, hear? No matter what happens, I'll be back. Git on now."

He shoved off and looked back. The palmettos were just closing over her. And then he realized he had wanted to tell her he loved her. But it was too late.

Chapter Twenty

Everything was coming to a head; time was running out. The waterway was turning to morass and maiden cane; a pin-down thicket swung away from him along the north, and he wasn't having any more of that. And he still couldn't turn south — there was more than just the Money Plane to worry about now in that direction; there was also Margy.

He ran the skiff into the crackling tules until it butted heads with a breather and then, hunting knife in hand, he got out. The peaty earth sank under his feet, trembling, and ale brown water sped around his boot soles.

He started slogging toward a distant rising jungle, using the breathers and log litter to pave his way where he could. But the going was mean. He slipped and lurched and sloshed ahead and sank once — panic crawling down his back — in a sinkhole to his waist, and went on again, hacking at the cane and cotton grass with the knife.

A short-winged fool of a cooter bird came all duckfooted and lobate-toed along a half mud-submerged log and stopped short, beady eyes bright with curiosity. Shad shooed it off, climbed onto the log and looked back. He couldn't see any sign of his pursuers, couldn't hear them either. He jumped down and hacked on.

The marsh dust was balling in the air, covering him with a fine powder, turning to mud where his pants were wet, and the mosquitoes were growing pesky, and that sun was straight up and God-awful hot, but he didn't care. The jungle was looming now. He made some last cuts and plunged through the cane.

It looked like a long runaway island; cypress, titi, pine and palmetto all crowding each other for growing space. He spotted a deer run and started along it, the jungle closing in like a narrow green hallway. Two hundred yards into the bush he found a scrawny cypress with roots clutching the edge of the trail. A thick ten-foot dead log was leaning against it like a drunk on a porch post.

Shad studied the situation for a moment, snapping his fingers. Then decided all right. He went to work with his knife, cut loose a long rope of creeper vine, climbed up the cypress and tied one end of the creeper to a branch of the dead log. Right then he heard a distant shout.

"Sam! Look a-here! It's his skiff. Old Shad's gone to earth!"

Jort.

Shad grimaced and readjusted the dead log against the living tree. The blame thing was as heavy as petrified wood. He balanced it where he wanted it — just resting on the edge — and gave it a tentative prod. The log wobbled precariously. Good enough. He skinned down the cypress trailing the creeper after him, looked around and selected a root close to the ground yet with a three-inch clearance, and threaded the vine through it and drew it out onto the trail.

The run wasn't but two feet wide, and fronds were hanging over and touching down every which way, and that would make it just that much harder for Sam to notice the trigger. He stretched the free end of the vine across the path, under the fronds, and tied it to another root drawing it just tight enough to ease off the slack.

Then he cut a frond and hurriedly swept away his tracks around the area. That Sam could get by on less giveaway than that. Finished, he started stepping off new tracks, going toward the widow-maker; stepped over the trigger and went on his way.

It was a crude sort of deadfall, he knew, because he hadn't had time to lay out the job properly. But you just couldn't tell what you might catch when you cast your net — even if the net had holes.

Sam would be in the lead and he'd be coming with his nose to the trail like a vacuum cleaner, eyeing every blade of grass, every leaf and indentation in the ground, and maybe he'd blunder into the trigger before it could click in his brain just what it was. Yeah. That's the way he hoped it would work. With Sam out of the way he could lose Jort and Mr. Ferris. Lose 'em for good and all.

He didn't waste any time getting across the island. He was eager to see just what was waiting for him beyond. And when he did it was like a slap from the hand of God. Badlands.

First off it was a good-sized shallow prairie, studded with small hummocks; but swinging on around and beyond, and God only knew how far, was a thicket of pin-down, hurrah bushes and titi the likes of which he never dreamed could exist.

"The end of nowhere," he whispered in dull awe. "So

blame far out the hoot owls nest with water turkeys."

It was a trap all right, and it was ironic when he called to mind the one he'd just set for Sam. You pure-out reap what you sow. He'd known for an hour just what it was he had to do, but he'd stalled it off right down to the fag end of the inevitable. But I got to have something to go at 'em with. You cain't match an eight-inch knife against carbines and shotguns and expect to come off sassy and without more holes in you than God intended. Then he remembered the bow and arrows.

It wasn't much but it was going to have to do. He trotted back into the jungle, reaching here, there, any-damn-where for a suitable sapling. He found one. It had spring but not too much, and he started hacking it free.

That goddam Sam must a picked up my markers; and that means I'm as good as dead, and so is Mr. Ferris and probably Margy too — less I git them first. But if I kill Sam and Jort, I got Mr. Ferris to kill too, and there's no way around it and escape a murder charge.

A shout rang high and urgent, splitting his thoughts like an axe blow.

"Look out thar!"

And he heard the dull crash of the widow-maker.

A moment later Jort's voice bellowed all over the swamp. "Fer the love of God, Sam! You just about to got me log-mashed dead! You suppose to be keeping your goddam eyes open!"

And Sam's cry, all squeaky with after reaction, "Well, goddam-a-mighty! I done spotted hit, didn't I? You ain't deadfalled, is you?"

"No, but I'm just as well shoulder-brokt, is what I am!"

Shad couldn't hear the rest, and it didn't matter anyhow — he'd missed them, missed every damn one, and now they'd be on their guard.

He cut loose a stretch of grapevine and ran for the prairie. The panic was right with him now, hugging him like a wiry boy riding bareback the first time.

He went sloshing across the water, passing the smaller hummocks until he found one as long and fat as a fair-sized shanty and three-four foot high with thick green reed. He climbed up and in, lunging and worming and sprawling toward the center, hacking at the blame Moses reed. He went to work shaping his weapon, notching the bow nocks, skinning down the hunk of vine.

The world was a mean dog. Turn your back, step out of line, and it bit you good. The world didn't ask for you, didn't want you; and if your folks were stupid or careless enough to bring you into it, the world set out to do its best to get rid of you. If you were tough you might dodge disease, if you were lucky you might escape or live through accidents, but it made you pay for living.

And when you came into the world you had only one privilege and that was the right to howl. And even then if you howled too loud or too long someone or something would come along with a big stick and close your mouth. And it was like that even at the end. So you clench your teeth and you do your howling inside where only you can hear it.

If you have it, all right; you fight like a wildcat in a vice to hang onto hit. But if you ain't got it, and they ain't noway of gitting it, then you just as well go out in the swamp and drown yourself, or go put the lookout end of a 12-gauge in your mouth and tap off the trigger with your big toe.

And even if it was legal money they wouldn't let him keep it. They'd whack him with taxes. They'd clean him down to the change in his jeans and say thanks and look us up again if you ever get another fortune. So you learned to get in there and grab and hold what you got and keep your big damn mouth shut about it.

And now he was going to have to kill three men, or try to, and one of them would probably kill him. And in the vivid moment before it happened it would mean a great deal to him, but once it was over it wouldn't matter to anyone and the world would make another check mark on its slate and look around to see who it could mash next.

"God," he said. "God, God."

There was a crash of thicket somewhere nearby on the island, but when he looked around he found he was too deep in the tules to see anything. He could hear though.

"Well, I'll be double-damned! I never seen nothing like this here afore." Jort.

"Ner me neither." Sam.

"Must be the pure-out dead center of the hull shebang! Bet nobody ben here since way back when the devil weren't no more than knee high to a toad-frog."

And then the tone but not the words of Mr. Ferris speaking.

And Sam answering, "No sir. Ain't Shad ner nobody else fool enough to git him into that pin-down hell."

"Not draggin no gal with him, he ain't."

"Jort, I done tolt you he ain't got that little gal no more. The tracks cold show that."

"Mebbe so. But what I want to know is where's he at now?"

"I cain't have the answer to ever'thing, Jorty."

Shad started crawling from center out and worked into a mashed down place where some recent animal had made a nest. He could see through the tule-screen now, could see the three of them standing on the bank with the island behind them. He went back to work frantically. He cut three thirty-inch reeds; they were slender and with a fair heft to them, not all air inside. He sharpened the three piles and then began notching the string nocks at the other ends. For feathers he used soft, pubescent cottonweed leaves, running them through the nocks where he'd split the ends.

Something splashed and he looked up. They were moving into the water, Jort and Sam fanning out, Jort carrying a shotgun, Sam with a carbine, and Mr. Ferris staying back near the island with no weapon at all as far as Shad could tell.

"He's in one of these here tussocks, Jorty," Sam called.

"Well spread a little, cain't you? Stop riding my tail. He ain't armed you know, Sam, er he'd've bush-whacked us sooner."

"Well — yeah —"

There wasn't time to make more arrows. Shad humped over on his knees, pushed two of the arrows point first into the peat where they'd be handy, and set the third in the bow. He nocked it and tested the pull. Not much — maybe twenty pounds of pressure at best. But it would have to do. He looked out again.

Sam and Jort had passed the first two hummocks, coming his way slowly. Sam edged in toward center and there was about ten feet of water between them. They were panning their eyes over everything, tense and expectant, ready to spring in a split second, anywhere.

Shad bit his lip, hunched down further. If I could just git'em bunched up. I know I'd git me a hit then. If I kin just git Jort first off. Sam I kin handle. If that gator-grabbing devil will just keep on a-coming along the inside. Please God, let the devil come on the inside.

They cleared the third hummock, coming on, the dull black water gurgling around their knees, leaving just a wisp of a wake behind. Jort was still holding the inside and Sam was leading.

They were dead ahead now, coming right at his hummock. Shad looked and caught his breath. Jort had slowed, studying the tussock.

Is he going to go around the other end? If they flank me I'm through afore I start. No — wait — he ain't neither. That lard-butted lazy mother, he's fixing to keep on the same way. If it had ben Sam, he'd've flanked me. Come on, Jort damn you! You letting Sam git ahead.

He let his breath go and took in a fresh one. Sam was thirty-some feet abreast of him now, his head turned from Shad's position eyeing a smaller hummock on his right; and Jort was coming again, catching up. Shad swung the bow around and started the pull — but stalled. He hunkered, slacking the drawstring.

Cain't take him front on. He'll blow me to Sunday pie with that 12-gauge. All right. It's the back then. All right — I ain't fussy.

He closed his eyes for a moment, listening to Jort sloshing closer. His hands were trembling and his stomach was going out — Quit stalling. You've got it to do. Oh God, God. I don't want to die. And then he opened his eyes and looked and saw Jort wading by, flicker-bodied, through the reeds, and he wasn't twenty feet away.

Do it, you gutless fool!

He swung the bow, pulling back, came straight up on his knees and ran his eye along the arrow, his right hand drawing to his cheek.

"Look out!" Ferris, shouting.

Shad let it fly. The arrow went ss-wit! as Jort spun half-about in the water and it missed him by a foot and landed *thh-ok!* into Sam, catching him high in the left arm and just under the shoulder. Sam let out a sound that burst from unstrung nerves, staggered lopsided in the water, dropping his carbine, rearing his head away from his own shoulder as though expecting to see a cottonmouth sitting there, and then he screamed. And he went off like that, falling, lunging up, crashing through the water, still rearing away from the thing that was pinning his arm to his side. And the last Shad saw of him, he was heading for the pin down thicket.

Shad ducked and sent himself sprawling as Jort swung up his shotgun and went *CA-BALOWM!* at the hummock. The little balls of shot came burning into the reed like someone pegging a handful of gravel, and Shad felt his right leg take a piece or two.

He pushed away from the soggy earth, grabbing for another arrow, hearing Jort splashing up fast. Somehow, all thumbs it seemed, he got the arrow nocked and, kneeling on one knee, brought the bow around and pulled the arrow back to his cheek — the whole damn thing quivering so he knew he couldn't hit a barn if he was pegging arrows twenty at a crack. And then there was Jort showing, rising in sections — cap, head, chest, belt, the Moses reed parting, and he saw Shad and let out a sound that was heavy and fast and sounded like *Uh-huh!* only longer, and he started swinging the 12-gauge up, and right then Shad cut loose.

The arrow leaped at Jort, hit him so hard in the chest it whocked like a shot and pushed him back a step, fast. Then he took another as though trying to find his balance, and the 12-gauge *balowmed* off again, but in the air, and he dropped the gun, looked at that damn thing sticking straight out of him, started to take hold of it but hesitated, and all the time his knees buckling out further and him sinking down to the ground; and still he couldn't bring himself to take it in his hands.

"*God,*" Shad said. "*How it must hurt.*"

"By — by God — Shad —"

And then Jort went straight over, his hands flying out as if to stop the earth rushing up at him, at the butt of the arrow; but they might have been made of liquid because they acted that way when the earth struck them and the arms too. Everything folded and his body hit the ground, driving that damned stick right up through his chest, and he made a sharp *Uluuah!* sound, his head tilting into the muck, his torso raised slightly where twelve inches of that arrow was propping him, and Shad could see where the pile had poked though because it made a little tent in the back of his shirt but hadn't torn the material.

Shad dropped the bow and sank limply on his haunches. He stared at Jort Camp and then rubbed at his mouth with his wrist. His lips, tongue, throat, all were parch dry from breathing through his mouth so long. He didn't know when he'd last used his nostrils. Must have been two hours ago. He had to have water. Didn't matter what kind. Water, and right now. Didn't matter either about Mr. Ferris. To hell with Mr. Ferris. Water.

He crawled off through the reed, down to the edge of the hummock to the brackish water and went at it like an animal would. He drank it in great greedy sucking mouthfuls, and then sat back and held some in his mouth, letting it saturate, breathing hard through his nose. But it wouldn't work and he swallowed it and then panted through his mouth for a while, and then had another mouthful and sat there again holding it and looking back at the mashed reeds where Jort was.

He got up and tramped wearily back to Jort's corpse, went through the pockets looking for shotgun shells. All he found was a crumpled ten-dollar bill. Sam must have been carrying the shells. He stared at the bill and his eyes flickered as a wisp of distant suspicion passed them. Then he shrugged and returned to the water to wash his peppered leg.

Something was splashing toward him, but in no great hurry. He looked around and saw Mr. Ferris coming. The insurance man paused near the fringe of the hummock, looking at Jort Camp, then he came on with a slight shake of his head.

"This is a bad business, Shad."

Shad nodded soberly, thinking about killing Mr. Ferris but not making a chore of it. He'd never killed anyone before, never had to or wanted to; and here he'd killed Jort Camp and half-killed Sam. And now there was still Mr.

Ferris to worry about.

Mr. Ferris brought out a pack of cigarettes and offered one to Shad. They lighted up, and for a while neither of them spoke.

"Where is your girl friend?" Mr. Ferris asked finally. "What is her name — Margy?"

"I got her hid away."

"What about her sister?"

Shad looked up. "I don't know, Mr. Ferris. I ain't seen her in near a week." Then, remembering, he asked, "You happen to give Jort a ten-dollar bill fer anything?"

"No. Why? Anything to do with the girl?"

"Dunno." Shad felt numb, indifferent. He said, "You was in mighty bad company, Mr. Ferris. If you'd a found that Money Plane, Jort would've showed you the business end of that 12-gauge."

Mr. Ferris smiled. "Yes, I'd more or less counted on that."

"Well, wasn't it taking a hell of a chance?"

"Part of my work — taking chances."

God, he's got more guts than all the rest of us.

"In fact," Mr. Ferris was going on, "I believe that what happened here today constitutes saving my life — indirectly, of course. This killing is in the nature of self-defense, undoubtedly. And I'll certainly testify to that fact at a coroner's inquest."

"You mean you'll act as my witness?"

"Naturally. You did me a good turn, and now it's in my power to repay you."

"*If* I show you where that Money Plane is."

Mr. Ferris smiled. "That's why I'm here, Shad."

Ain't he a something? He don't seem to do much, just stands around and waits, and when the hull shebang's blow sky high he starts picking up the pieces.

"My original offer still holds," Mr. Ferris said. "Eight thousand dollars to the man who helps me recover that payroll. That's quite a bit of money, Shad — for a young man and his girl to start on."

Eight-thousand dollars. *Eighty-thousand dollars if I kill him.* But how can you kill an unarmed man who just stands there with his hand in his pocket, smiling at you, smoking, and talking kindly?

He stood up and tested his game leg.

"Does that hurt you?" Mr. Ferris asked solicitously.

"No. I'm used to hit." Then he grinned. "I still got some in my seater from when I was sixteen and old man Duffy caught me in the barn with his daughter."

Mr. Ferris smiled. "Chased you over the fence, eh? Like the proverbial shotgun farmer and the boy with the stolen watermelon."

"*Helped me* over the fence is nearer to hit"

And they both laughed; and then Mr. Ferris dropped his cigarette in the water.

"Well," he said, "Which way do we go — back the way we came?"

Chapter Twenty-One

S had decided to take Jort's skiff. It was a good craft, and now that Jort wouldn't be needing it there wasn't any sense in letting it rot in the bog. To Mr. Ferris' question, "Are you going to leave yours here?" he said, "Yeah. I'll pick it up another time."

Mr. Ferris nodded. "Well, perhaps it'll come in handy for that Parks person."

Shad looked up. "Sam? Sam's dead, Mr. Ferris."

"Dead?"

"Same as. If he ain't panther-clawed er gator-et er cottonmouth-bit, then the pin-downs will kill him."

"It's as dangerous as that?"

"Dangerous enough fer anybody," Shad said. "But it's real bad fer a fella like Sam. He'll go coo-coo inside an hour, and once you press your panic button *you're through*."

Mr. Ferris said nothing more. He climbed into the skiff and went forward. He was thinking how incongruously these people were made. Sam, Jort, and Shad would bend over backward to evade physical labour for wages — and yet would rush to this nightmarish land with open arms to pit their lives against gaining something for nothing.

They went on down-slough, slipping by the palmetto bend where Shad had set Margy ashore. But he didn't stop to go find her because he hadn't made up his mind about Mr. Ferris. He had to make up his mind right soon — yes or no. But if it was yes, what would he do it with? He'd left the bow and arrows behind deliberately because he never wanted to use them again on anything.

He skirted the skiff along the mudbank where the thicket of pink hurrah blossoms, white Cherokee, yellow jasmine and bloody ivy trumpets stood like a floral paper on one wall of a green room. He spotted the cross he'd blazed on a cypress trunk.

"This here's it," he said, and ran the skiff into the mud.

As Mr. Ferris climbed from the skiff Shad rummaged under the stern's seat and found what he thought he would — an old nick-bladed hatchet. Mr. Ferris stood in the mud, looked at the hatchet, then at Shad; but Shad had his eyes averted.

"We got to go easy," he warned. "This here's gator ground."

They went hands and knees through the thicket tunnel, Shad leading, Mr. Ferris close on his tail. Shad kept listening for gator-grunting but couldn't catch any. Even the musky gator odour was gone, as though vanquished by the poisonous scent of lush jungle flowers and the rot and decay of the bog.

The tunnel opened, the bank shelved down, and the pond stretched away to the far green wall, to the giant cypress all adrape with the brown tendrils of a bullace vine, and the suspended Money Plane. Shad straightened up, staring, unconscious of Mr. Ferris behind him.

Finding the pond and the Money Plane for the second time was like stumbling upon the materialization of a childhood dream — or nightmare. The enigmatic structure of the place brushed him with a peculiar uneasiness, and a sense of moral disturbance that he couldn't understand settled on him like in indescribable malaise. They stood side by side in the soft mud and stared.

There was nothing and there was everything, and all of it still. There was the torpid water, black except where the jungle reflected a dull green, and there was the water grass and the pickerelweed, and scattered on the surface the never-wet leaves and the bonnets.

A good-God flock of green-winged teal flicker-flacked overhead with their multitude of wings; and when the men suddenly looked up, the flock slammed the sky with a *whamp!* and veered into a new thunderous course.

The mood was dispelled. Mr. Ferris cleared his throat and said, "How do we get to it?"

Shad simply said, "Raft," and went into the thicket to chop up some lightwood logs. Mr. Ferris smoked a cigarette while Shad constructed the raft. It was a hurried, patchwork affair — five logs lashed with vine, a yard wide and two long.

"I ain't going at this proper," Shad said, "because I don't want to take the time. We'll have to ditch our boots and tail the bottom-end of us in the water."

"That's all right," Mr. Ferris said. He looked across the pond at the Money Plane. "As long as we get there and back." Then — "Are there alligators?"

Shad didn't look up. "Guess not. 'Pear to be all gone. Last time I was here they was a God-awful gator nest just down-slough." He stood up, raising the rickety raft, and said, "Let's go."

They left their boots standing four-at-attention on the bank and waded into the pond, prodding the raft ahead. Far off a poor-joe bird squawked at something, and closer in they heard a panther cough. Then there was nothing, only a water snake draped on a breather.

"We used to go rafting like this when I was a boy in Ohio." Mr. Ferris' voice had the quiet tone of camaraderie. "There was a river near our farm."

It startled Shad to hear that Mr. Ferris had once been a farm boy.

"That so? So did we when I was a tad." And right then he was quite certain that he wasn't going to kill the man.

The water slipped past their knees and they hunched themselves up on the raft, leaning forward on elbows, forearms and abdomens, and started scissor-kicking with their feet. The going slowed when they ploughed into the golden-heart bed, but there was no way around it. They pawed the lilies aside and kicked the raft on. Above them loomed the giant cypress and the rust-stained Money Plane.

They sloshed onto the bank, pulling the raft after them, and then, in mute agreement, paused to stare up at the wrecked airplane.

"You mind being around dead men, Mr. Ferris?" Shad asked. "I mean *old* dead men?"

Mr. Ferris looked at him.

"No," Shad said. "I reckon not. Well, let's git up and see how they ben keeping."

The scut-shot gator was hungry. He'd been prowling the waterway for hours but hadn't found anything to satisfy him. Now he entered the Money Plane pond. He looked around, saw nothing, and then submerged himself and tail-hitched over to the distant weed bed. He watched the translucent water, waiting to see what might come wandering downstream. His passage had stirred up a slimy colony of black leeches and they were wiggling around him worm-like. But he didn't pay them any mind. After a while he surfaced effortlessly. He looked just like a barely drifting log.

In the musty cabin of the Money Plane Shad and Mr. Ferris squatted where they could find room and looked at the mouldy bags of clothing that contained all that remained of the payroll agent known as Hartog and the pilot known as Willy.

"I like to think they was friends," Shad said. "Seeing that they had to go at hit together."

Mr. Ferris looked at him. "Where's the brief case?"

"Behint that bucket-type seater."

Mr. Ferris reached behind the seat and felt for the case. When he found it he drew it into the light and placed it before him on the floorboards, flat. He didn't do or say anything. He stared at the gutted surface and at the clump of green and black bills bulging up through the rent.

"Hit's all there," Shad said, looking hard at the brief case. "Except fer that hundred I took."

Ferris said nothing.

"Hit's a shore God heap of money, ain't it?"

There was a pause, and then Mr. Ferris murmured, "Yes — a heap of money." He seemed slightly mesmerized. When he spoke again his voice had a curiously disembodied flavour.

"Seeing it like this — face to face — brings one to realize

why men turn to schemes. Men like Jort Camp and Sam and —" He didn't finish it.

Shad nodded, looking at him. "How'd you come to get hooked up with Jort and Sam, Mr. Ferris? I'd a thought old Jort would try to avoid you like a fox going downwind of a hound."

A smile came and went in Mr. Ferris' face like a snap of the fingers. "No, no," he said. "I didn't have any trouble in convincing friend Camp that we should form a partnership. You see — I knew where the body was buried."

"How's that?"

"It's a city saying, it means I knew something about them that they wouldn't want published."

Shad's eyes narrowed. "What was that?"

Mr. Ferris looked at him. "It doesn't matter now, Shad. It was something I saw them doing in the woods that night you had your fight with the Fort boy."

It was bothering Shad again — Jort's face in the dream, the ten-dollar bill in Jort's denims. He tasted his lips.

"Did hit have anything to do with Dorry Mears?"

"It isn't important now," Mr. Ferris said flatly.

Shad stared at him. Mr. Ferris turned his head and stared back — and for the first time Shad saw more than just a pair of peculiarly penetrating eyes. It touched him like an ice pick at his throat, because he'd seen so much of it lately. Simply greed.

Mr. Ferris put his right hand inside his jacket and under his armpit. When he drew the hand out it held a snub-nosed .38, and he let Shad see the little round black hole in the end of the barrel. He smiled wistfully.

"You see, Shad, I wasn't quite unprepared to deal with Jort and Sam."

Shad couldn't make up his mind whether to watch Mr. Ferris' eyes or the goodbye end of the .38. He made a sound in his throat and got his tongue moving finally.

"You ain't got the idee I brung you here to kill you, do you?"

"It *had* crossed my mind, yes. I'm not going to be so foolish as to forget what happened to Camp and Parks today. You're a rather dangerous man, Shad."

"That was self-defence," Shad said. "You said so yourself. They was fixing on killing me."

Mr. Ferris nodded. "It follows that they would have to — in order to have all the money for themselves."

Shad got his eyes away from the .38 and looked at Mr. Ferris.

"Oh," he said. "I kindly begin to see. It ain't exactly that you're so afeered of me — but if I'm dead then there ain't nobody left kin tell whatever become of this money."

Mr. Ferris smiled. "That — I confess — has also crossed my mind. It seems to be the general opinion in this territory that you found this money and then proceeded to run off with that Mears girl. I feel that that's a nice comfortable way to leave the situation — the law hunting for two dead people, I mean."

"Then Dorry *is* dead?"

"The Mears girl? I have every reason to suspect so. But it doesn't really matter to you now, does it?"

"I reckon not," Shad thought of Margy waiting for him to come to her, waiting in the center of the swamp. No, Dorry didn't matter to him one way or another now. But Margy did.

"I guess you ben planning this here fer some time?" he stalled.

"Not so long — only four years. Though actually I seldom make long-range plans. The nature of things is too often perverse. Your former lady friend — Iris Culver and I had a little plan afoot; and oddly enough it nearly worked. Though I rather imagine that had you brought her this money, she would have walked out on both of us and not a word said."

Shad didn't give a Sunday damn about Iris Culver. He could feel his life petering out to the small end of the .38— Margy's life too. He looked up. "You going to bullet-hole me now, Mr. Ferris?"

"Yes, Shad. I'm afraid I must."

Shad grunted.

"I say if you go to kill me, you just as well turn the barrel around and trigger yourself a goodbye. Without me, you don't even got the chance Sam Park's got of gitting out a here. And Sam's got no more chance than an idiot trying to breed the razorback outn a strain of hogs before the third generation."

Mr. Ferris' smile returned slowly. "Don't try that on me, Shad. I've noticed your trickiness before."

"You aint' begun to see trickiness till you seen what this old swamp kin pull on a man. I ben coming out here since I was a tad, and twice I've gone and lost myself. And what about my brother Holly? He done got so lost he never has found hisself again. And he ain't the only one. You know how many men done died out in this swamp since you left here four years ago?"

He could see that he had Mr. Ferris going now. The eyes were the same except that the bright glare of greed had been replaced with intent concern.

"You know how I done lost myself last time? A great granddaddy gator kicked the skiff right out from under me, and me with a .30-06 bear gun. You know what a gator will think of that popgun of yourn, Mr. Ferris? He'll kindly think you're pegging acorns at him."

"All right, Shad," Mr. Ferris cut in coldly. "I'll admit that your suggested violence is ominous. But barring an alligator attack, I know my way out of here. All I have to do is go straight down this waterway to that large lake —"

"You know the name of that large lake, Mr. Ferris?" (Mr. Ferris didn't.) "Well, I don't mind giving you that much of a start. It's called Breakneck. You know why hit's called that? Because at the north end a tongue of land nearly cuts the neck in two. It's good to know these things, Mr. Ferris. A man needs every landmark he kin git in this end of creation. You know how many waterways lead out a Breakneck, Mr. Ferris? Eighteen that you kin see. But why worry about Breakneck — you ain't even out of this little old piddly lake where we got the skiff yet. Let's see — they must be — yeah, I kin think of eight waterways right offhand leading out a this lake. You know which is the right one, Mr. Ferris?"

He'd said it now, all that he had to say. It was time to shut up and let Mr. Ferris stew. So he finished with— "Now you set there and brood on it a bit, Mr. Ferris. And while you're about it, I'd kindly appreciate if you'd offer me one of your tailor-mades."

It was pure-out amazing the way that Mr. Ferris could

contain himself. There he was, still holding hard to that smile and dishing out cigarettes like they were the best of buddies.

"It's a pity, Shad, you were born poor white. I think you might have made something of yourself had you been given an even start."

"I manage to keep myself living — minute by minute."

"Yes, you do. And it looks like you've just talked yourself into a few more hours of it."

Borrowed time. I done got it. It's all I ask, God. Just give me a bit of an edge and I'll cold grab at the rest.

Minutes later they were wading into the pool, Shad going ahead clutching the torn side of the brief case to his body, prodding the raft before him; Mr. Ferris following a little to the left with the .38 trained on his back.

The water rose past Shad's knees and he placed the brief case on the raft and looked back at Mr. Ferris.

"What about my girl?"

Mr. Ferris shook his head.

"Better this way, don't you think?"

Shad stared at him, thinking. You cold little son-o-bitch. Then he nodded and started to lean half over the raft. Mr. Ferris waded up and carefully took a position with him. He held the gun at Shad's side. "No tricks now," he murmured.

Shad said nothing. They shoved off and began kicking and pawing their way through the golden-heart. A fat old soft-shelled turtle came tread-legging toward them and stopped abruptly to raise its reptilian head. It looked them over without expression and decided to sound. They were halfway across.

Shad saw what was trying its best to look like a log come drifting out of a tussock — just a few little woodish-looking knots poking above the surface and leaving an almost imperceptible wake. He glanced at Mr.Ferris.

"What's wrong?"

"Kink in my leg." He felt the .38 dig him slightly.

"Don't get gay, Shad."

Shad wet his lips and started kicking again. When he looked toward the tussock he saw that the 'log' had vanished. It was one of those far-out gators, he thought apprehensively. One that didn't give a damn for man or battle-ship. He felt like a man who steps deliberately in the path of a car, hoping to be sideswiped slightly and collect damages, but loses his nerve at the last moment and leaps back to the curb. He started to call a warning to Mr. Ferris — but stalled.

It's my only chance. It's a purely poor edge to hinge my life to, but the only one I'm apt to get.

He clamped his mouth, looked around at the water. Where was the damn thing now? What if it was coming up from the bottom to chomp his legs? Fear tingled in his buttocks, and automatically he started to haul more of him onto the raft. Right away his end tipped down with a gurgle of incoming water.

"What are you trying to do?"

Shad looked wildly at Mr. Ferris. He wanted to say it was the kink in his leg again, but he couldn't get the words started. That damn thing was coming for them, he could feel it — coming with that shopping bag it used for a mouth wide open.

"What is it? What's wrong?"

Shad couldn't hold out. He started to say gator, but it was too late. The scut-shot gator reared straight from the bottom and slammed the underside of the raft.

Shad flew up and backwards, the concussion-slam of the raft like a cannon ball in his chest, and — turquoise sky spinning into green-falling jungle — heard the *CA-PLAM!* of the .38, and then he struck the water, saw it crash in over his eyes all silvery, and then it was olive-green and he was turning in it, trying to find his equilibrium, vacuum packed and without air, and black bleary shapes were thrashing around him and something — maybe Mr. Ferris' foot — struck his left ear, ramming him farther down into the throbbing shadow, and he saw a torpedo-like form coming at him and knew it was the gator and there wasn't a thing he could do about it and —

Something in his left hand — the brief case. The oncomming shadow was bigger, taller, the jaws opening at right angles to the body. Shad tried to scream and swung the brief case around instinctively and into the teeth-studded mouth; felt it rip away from him as he went spinning in the gator's compressible displacement; and he was shouting, He didn't take my hand! God let me still have my hand! And a part of him tried—to send a message to the muscles of the hand to clinch or not to clinch, to confirm or deny; but his nervous system was all out of whack and nothing was getting through, and the rest of him was insane panic and it made him kick and thrash and got him up and out of there right now.

He hit the surface, lunging up to his armpits for air, and he grabbed at the sky without knowing it was silly, then he settled again, treading, turning wildly about, looking, and twenty feet off saw the great thrashing gator tail whip up and slam down *slamp!* at the pond, and just a rolling glint of the ivory-tiled belly, and incongruously — a small human hand widespread and clutching out of the welter of water. And then everything went under and Shad didn't give a damn because he was going all arms and legs for the bank.

He went crawling, water-wheezing and gasping up the bank and sagged into a soggy heap of shot nerves. He felt like an old shirt that had been manhandled on a scrub board by a husky washerwoman. Then, remembering with a start he looked down at his left wrist to see if his hand was still along. He started giggling, a low pitched, ghastly sound and couldn't seem to stop.

Chapter Twenty-Two

How long it had gone on he didn't know, but it seemed that all his life he had heard it — someone crying Shad — Shad — Shad over and over, and he couldn't understand it.

But it ended the giggle fit.

He sat up with his nerves vibrating like strummed guitar strings and saw Margy running along the bank; and it struck him suddenly that had she been her sister, Dorry, she would have stopped first to gawk at the Money Plane. But Margy never took her eyes off him, and for a second he thought she was going to run right over him. And then she was down in the mud and in his arms and clinging to him tightly.

He got her set back from him a bit so he could see her face, and he tried to be angry with her and said, "Thought I told you not to budge till I come?" But he was too happy because he was alive and she was alive and with him, and he pulled her back to him and hugged her again, keeping one hand in her hair and liking its tactile quality.

"I heered that shot," she said. "I thought — I just couldn't wait no longer —"

"All right. Calm down. Nothing's wrong now. That shot was just Mr. Ferris having his last say."

She straightened up on her knees and looked at him, and she'd never looked prettier to him, with her blouse all cat-clawed and her face mud-streaked and her hair wild and going every-which-way.

"What happened to him? Did you kill him?"

"No. He's down in the bottom of the slough gitting his self gator-drowned." And that gave him the trembles again because it might have been him. "I never seen such a gator. He was pure-out crazy."

She turned and looked at the water. The surface was placid and black except where the reflection smeared it green. She shivered.

"What about Jort and Sam Parks?"

"Dead. At least Jort be. Sam's gone off coo-coo in the pin-downs." He thought for a moment. "Margy, Mr. Ferris was a thief — just like the rest of us."

She didn't care about Mr. Ferris.

"You didn't find out nothing about Dorry, Shad?"

He looked at the water. He had a pretty good idea what had happened to Dorry. He reckoned that like Holly and Sam she was long gone without a trace. "No," he said. "She probably run off with some drummer. We'll probably hear some day."

Margy didn't pursue it, but she didn't believe it either. She held Shad's hand. It amazed him that she hadn't once asked about the money.

"That eighty-thousand dollars is down to the bottom of the slough," he told her.

She nodded. "Let it stay there."

He looked at her. "What?"

"Let it stay there. That's where hit belongs."

He couldn't believe her. "You done hit your head on a breather er something? *That money's ours.* Hit belongs to you and me, Margy."

She looked down at the mud without expression and shook her head.

"No, it ain't ours. It ain't nobody's. I don't want it."

"Well, I'll be bitched fer fair." He stood up and started taking down his pants.

"What you fixing to do?"

"That don't take no heap of guesses. Fixing to git me into that slough and find my money."

She got up and moved back from him. "No. No, Shad. Don't go to do it. I don't want you to. I don't want you gator-et."

He stripped the soggy pants from one leg. "Stop fretting. That old gator is long gone to his cave by now. Having Mr. Ferris fer Sunday dinner."

"Leave hit there, Shad. Please leave hit there. It's wicked money — blood money. It does nothing but evil. Look how many people it's hurt since it come into this swamp. If that gator don't git you, and if you bring it back up, you'll just be bringing up trouble again."

"You kin call it trouble if you want," he snapped. "But I call it eighty-thousand dollars."

She stared at him for a moment, and then said, "All right — mebbe you better. You goan need it to buy you a new girl with."

He was stooping for his knife but he paused.

"What in God's name you talking about now?" he demanded. "I got you. You're the only girl I want."

"Well, you ain't goan have me long. Because if you go in that slough — I won't be here when and if you come out again."

He straightened up and smiled. "Now, Margy. Now, honey —"

She stepped back quickly. "Don't you come at me, Shad. You ain't gitting around me thataway."

"All right, honey, all right. You just scared of that old gator gitting me, ain't that all?"

"That and other things. I ain't goan list'em fer you twice.

What makes you so blame blind, Shad? Cain't you understand I never did want that money? All I ever wanted was you. And reckon I wanted you right from that first night you come to our place to see Pa, and you all high-hat and cocky on the porch there and the way you went to smile at me and —"

Abruptly she started crying, making a soft, body jerking, offbeat sound of it. "I just plain love you. And you wanting to throw it all away, and not caring a hoot what becomes of us er —"

He went to her and held her trembling body against his damp one. He didn't say anything, just held her and looked over her head at the pond. No one he'd ever known had loved him, not for just himself. I always ben a loner, he thought I always ben looking in windows and wanting what none of my family never had.

And she would leave him, too. He knew it because she was that way. If I come out a that slough I'll be rich and I'll be alone. He held her out from him and looked at her.

"You want me — just like this? With thirty-some dollars to my jeans?"

Her eyes were all glassy with tears. "With er without the dollars," she said. "Er the jeans too."

Shad nodded. He felt like a split shopping bag; everything was dropping out. "All right, honey," he said. "Anything you say."

Then she was wrapped around him again, laughing and whispering and crying all at once, and none of it made sense because he couldn't concentrate on it. He couldn't get his eyes off the pond.

I ben through hell's furnace room fer that money. I ben gator-chased and buckshotted and fist-fighted and near drownt — and now I'm just cold putting my back to it and walking off. Just like it didn't matter a-tall.

"Let's go home, Shad."

He blinked at her. "Home?— Yeah — home. All right."

He picked up his pants and pulled them on. Margy started up the bank toward the thicket.

"Let's hurry, Shad," she called to him. "Let's go fast and git out a here."

"Yeah."

He started up the slope, his head low, watching his feet. He'd go back to his trapping and maybe he'd go in for Spanish moss gathering as a side line; might even try some gator-grabbing now that Jort was out of the business— little ones. And he supposed he would go on looking for Holly's body, and probably Sam's too. Yeah, he'd be coming out here again.

He paused near the edge of the thicket and looked around at the pond and the Money Plane, planting the image of the place firmly in his mind. It didn't do any good, he knew, to argue with a woman right when she'd made up her mind. Any fool knew you might as well go beat a dead horse. Yeah, but later—

"See you," he murmured.

He smiled at Margy and started after her.

About the Author

Robert Edmond Alter was the author of fourteen children's books and three adult novels, *Swamp Sister*, *Carny Kill* and *The Red Fathom*. His stories appeared in numerous magazines including *Adventure*, *Saturday Evening Post* and *Argosy*. He died in Los Angeles, where he lived, in 1966 at the age of forty.